ANNABEL'S EYES

John Macleod

Lois

ISBN: 978-1-7355213-2-9 (paperback)
ISBN: 978-1-7355213-3-6 (ebook)

This is a work of fiction. Some names of persons, places, or organization are real, as are
references to certain historic events, but the characters and the story are entirely made up.

ALSO BY JOHN MACLEOD

A Lawyer or a Priest
Snippets
Justice Hill

For Ann

CHAPTER ONE

The Crime (May 14, 2022)

Intelligent eyes looked out through streaks of blood. The man's face was kind, his hair gray and thinning with middle age and his once straight jaw gone spongy. His blood-spattered smile displayed the satisfaction and resignation of a man acquainted with happiness and pain. He had seen a lot from his perch on the easel. He had seen violence, a killing maybe.

The living room looked more like an abattoir than an artist's home. There was blood on the walls and floor, the sagging Salvation Army sofa, the overturned coffee table, and three of the five paintings, including the one on the easel. Sheriff Angelo Jones, a handsome young man of Italian descent, implored the bloody face to speak. *What happened here, old man? What did you see? Where are the bodies?*

"Sorry to drop this on you in your first week on the job, Angelo," said Chief Frank Betterman, a large, balding man whose quick eyes warned that it would be a mistake to judge him by his lumbering manner. "Woodstock just doesn't have the resources or experience to handle it. I'll give you my best deputy, Duane Foskey, to help out. Duane went to the house yesterday to check on Ivy, after people started to worry because they hadn't seen her for a few days, and this is what he found."

"Thanks, Chief. I'll look forward to working with Duane."

Disengaging from the man on the easel, Angelo surveyed the small living room. The sofa had been knocked askew, and the badly marred coffee table was missing a leg. There was no computer and no TV; the paintings and the scattered art magazines on the floor were evidently Ivy's entertainment. The only other furniture, if you could call it that, was an easel with a small table next to it and a wobbly wooden chair that lay on its side. On the table was a palette with mixed paints, now largely dried, a few brushes, and a couple of scrapers. *The tools of the trade,* Angelo thought as his eyes passed over them.

Each painting was three feet high and two-and-a-half feet wide. Each showed a man, impressionist in style but with distinct features. They were different men, different in hair color and age and weight and dress, but there was a similarity to them. Something about the eyes and the prominence of the cheekbones. *Who are these guys,* Angelo wondered, *and who were they to Ivy? Are they real people, or did she make them up? Are they different people, or are they all one guy she chose to portray in different ways?*

A fortyish man with a shaved head interrupted Angelo's thoughts. He was in blue jeans and a flannel shirt that hung loosely on a muscular frame. His penetrating eyes betrayed an intensity that defined him. "Sheriff Jones, I'm Duane Foskey. Chief Betterman asked me to work with you on this case."

"Nice to meet you, Duane," said Angelo, sizing him up and quickly assigning him to the all-business category. "What have you got?"

"We've done what we can for now, at least here at the house. Maybe the results of the analysis will say something different, but just looking at the blood and how fully it's dried, I'd guess everything went down the night before last. That would be Saturday. I'm trying to get the medical examiner out here to confirm that."

Angelo took out his 2022 calendar and wrote "crime committed?" across May 14.

"Seems like Ivy's been missing longer than that." Frank Betterman had wandered over and joined them. "She's loved in this town, Angelo. I sure hope this isn't her blood. Hard to imagine it isn't, though, since she lived here and never went out at night."

"I'm going to talk to the neighbors," said Duane, eager to get on with the investigation. "Maybe we'll get lucky and find someone who saw or heard something. I'll be back to you with whatever I learn."

"Thanks," Angelo said. He eyed the plastic evidence bag Duane was carrying. "What have you got there?"

"Something that could be important. It's one of those knives that artists use; I think they call them palette knives. We found it on the floor near the sofa. It has blood on it. Fingerprints too."

CHAPTER TWO

Ivy (2007-22)

Woodstock is a peaceful town of about five thousand people in Virginia's Shenandoah Valley. Situated near the seven bends of the Shenandoah River's North Fork, it lies between the Blue Ridge and the Appalachians. Roots run deep in the area, often tracing back to the German settlers who founded the town in 1752. The family farm still exists, but there are fewer of them. The people work hard and exhibit the refreshing patriotism of small-town America.

Ivy had been in Woodstock for fifteen years, well, ten anyway. She was a fixture, though no one knew exactly when she came or where she came from. She was suddenly just there, taking her daily walk around town, her "stu-tional" as she called it, wanting to say "constitutional" but not getting it quite right. She took the long way around from the small yellow cinder-block house she rented on Water Street, down near the dairy farm, because she loved the sights and smells of her adopted community.

Early each afternoon, at the halfway point of her walk, Ivy sat quietly for an hour on the bench outside the Woodstock Café. It was her favorite part of the day. She laid her single crutch beside her, then carefully went into her small backpack and took out a drawing pad and a set of colored pencils. She sat for a moment, thinking, and when she had decided what she wanted to draw, she acted quickly. Her movements were spare and sure, and her work was exceptional. When she finished a drawing, she held it at arm's length to give it a critical look. Then she carefully put it in her backpack and sat back for a short nap. Precisely one hour later, she rose to continue her walk, refreshed by her rest and ready for the last leg of her journey.

Everyone in town said hello to Ivy, and she said hello back, but the conversations generally ended there. She was friendly but guarded; her manner discouraged closeness. She seemed older than her forty-two years, yet she carried herself with elegance and beauty, even with the jagged scar below her left eye. And, of course, the lifeless leg she dragged behind as she negotiated her daily walk on her good leg and crutch. People wondered what had happened to her, but they didn't ask, and she didn't say. People were sad for her, for her difficult past and solitary present, but they accepted her wish to keep her life private.

Ivy only had two real friends in town. One was George Johnson, a kind man who owned the local art gallery. He had been buying Ivy's drawings for almost a decade. She visited him on the second Friday of each month, bringing her backpack with its accumulated inventory. George always bought what she had, usually twenty or twenty-five drawings, and paid her a hundred dollars for each. It wasn't just kindness; George had no difficulty selling Ivy's work and did well by being her benefactor.

The other was Sam Picken, a partner in the law firm of Picken & Lloyd. She and her husband, Chris Lloyd, had moved to Woodstock and started the firm ten years ago. They had built a successful practice and were the go-to firm for many of the town's businesses. Ivy was one of Sam's first clients. She had sought Sam out because she wanted a woman lawyer to handle her delicate problem. She also wanted the lower fees of a lawyer trying to build a practice. Sam made Ivy's problem go away in short order and never charged her a dime.

In addition to being Sam's law partner, Chris was the mayor of Woodstock. He took it seriously when the two people closest to Ivy expressed concern about her whereabouts within minutes of each other. Over coffee and a morning bun from Flour and Water, Sam was fretting about not having seen Ivy when George called. "Something's not right, Chris," George said without preamble. "Ivy missed our meeting Friday. First time she's ever missed a meeting. I've been stewing about it all weekend. You know everything that goes on around here. I figure you'd know if something's wrong, and if you don't, you'll damn sure find out."

Chris immediately called Chief Betterman, who sent Duane Foskey to Ivy's place. Duane was short and to the point when he called the chief back half an hour later: "Blood everywhere. No bodies. No Ivy."

CHAPTER THREE

Angelo (2017-22)

It had been a long day. Angelo got into sweats in his room at the Comfort Inn and poured himself a bourbon. Elijah Craig, of course—his favorite. He swirled the amber liquid in his glass and looked out at the county fairgrounds. *What the hell have I gotten myself into?*

It was Scott O'Hanlon's doing. Scott was the sheriff in Bath County and Angelo's former boss. Angelo was still green when a gruesome killing occurred at Justice Hill, a magnificent retreat near Hot Springs. Jason Worthy, a prominent lawyer from Washington, DC had lost his dignity to a box cutter and his leg to a chain saw. It was an unusually difficult case, and Angelo had solved it.

That had been in 2017, but Scott brought it up four years later as a launchpad for some advice he had for Angelo. "You and I both know you were lucky, Hotshot. I'll admit you worked hard, though, and luck has a way of following hard work. There's a special election coming up for the sheriff's job in Shenandoah County. Jim Beamer, the current sheriff, was a good man in his day, but he's had some health problems. Maybe some corruption problems too. I think you should run for the job. With your luck, you'd probably win."

"Are you trying to get rid of me, Scott?" Angelo had come to like the guy and couldn't believe he was once afraid of him. "What's in it for you?"

"I get to look for a new deputy sheriff. Maybe I'll find someone good this time."

Angelo took Scott's advice. He was ambitious in a reserved sort of way, a character trait rooted in an insecurity that stemmed from his family's being stripped of its Giovanetti identity in favor of the amorphous Jones at Ellis Island and his mother's pushing him to use his God-given talents to their fullest extent. She hadn't gotten him all the way there, but she had made substantial progress. Angelo didn't feel he had to be the best, but he did have a need to be in the conversation. At thirty-two years of age, after six years as Scott's deputy, he was ready for the next step.

He had a lot going for him. He had broken the biggest murder case in rural Virginia in decades. He had gotten an MBA at the University of Virginia, a nice credential even though he ended up pursuing a law enforcement career instead of investment banking. And he was handsome, the dreamy Italian kind of handsome with dark eyes and an easy smile. He won in a landslide.

Angelo had left Bath County and driven his forest-green F-150 pickup truck north on I-81 to start the new job only a week ago. His thoughts had drifted to his personal life as he put the truck in cruise control and settled into the mindlessness of the drive. He loved his large Italian family and couldn't wait to have a family of his own. He had to find the right woman first, though, and so far, that hadn't happened. His college sweetheart had broken up with him to date, and ultimately marry, someone else. He had no interest in the "nice Italian girls" his mother was constantly offering up—he loved her as a mother but didn't trust her as a matchmaker. There had been some sparks between him and Kate Strange, the attractive lawyer initially suspected as the killer in the Worthy case, but he couldn't pursue a relationship with someone he was investigating, and anyway, their lives and lifestyles were too different to produce a lasting fit. One benefit of his new job might be new opportunity. He hoped so.

Turning to the practical aspects of what lay before him, Angelo compiled a mental list of everything he had to do. Find a place to live and the sooner the better, because living out of a motel wasn't a long-term solution. Get his stuff moved—no big deal because he only had a one-bedroom apartment, but it had to be done. Meet the people in the sheriff's office and gain their confidence. That was critical and a first order of business. His biggest task, learning how to be a sheriff, would take some time, but he needed to show diligence and progress. He hoped people would be patient with him. Taking on a bloody crime a week into the job wasn't on his list of immediate tasks. Whatever the crime was—murder? kidnapping?—it was big. And there was no identifiable victim.

Angelo sat back in a chair and put his feet up on the coffee table. One sip of Elijah Craig and the world was a better place. He looked out at the fairgrounds and recalled the many county fairs he had been to as a boy growing up in rural Virginia, not far from Roanoke. He imagined the stands filled with people as the local community came together to enjoy fireworks or a tractor pull. Beyond the stands were the stalls, where the farmers and 4-H community would show their prize steers, hogs, and chickens. There was a set of low buildings to the right; he knew that was where there would be fierce competition for the largest pumpkin or the best blueberry pie.

The moment quickly passed. *This is OK,* Angelo thought, *but I didn't get elected to drink bourbon and think about the good old days.* Reluctantly, he picked up his notepad and began to formulate the questions he needed to answer if he was to figure out what went down in the small bloody house on Water Street. The first and overriding question was this: Where were the bodies?

CHAPTER FOUR

The Auction (2019)

"SOLD!"

Christy Guest, the chief auctioneer at Sotheby's in London, brought the gavel down hard. "Sold to the lady in the blue hat, paddle number 357, for 23.9 million pounds. Thank you, madam." Thunderous applause broke out as the suppressed energy in the room was released. Guest could hardly contain her excitement, adding, "That is a new record for an Ingersoll."

Guest hadn't needed to chum the waters to attract bidders to the fall 2019 auction. The interest was there, and it was deep. Included among the lots were works by Anish Kapoor, Ed Ruscha, Wayne Thiebaud, Sean Scully, and Pablo Ingersoll.

Ingersoll was not as well-known as the others, but he was an exceptional talent. His paintings of beautiful women evoked Modigliani playfully updated with a hint of Mel Ramos, and there was something unusually appealing and eerily lifelike about *Annabel's Eyes*. Guest found the work compelling; she had always loved it and was thrilled when the current owner, an estate in Sussex, chose Sotheby's to handle the sale. She had never doubted the painting would fetch a handsome price, but she had not expected this.

With flowing chestnut hair and a wry grin that was never expected but always welcome, Christy Guest projected the confidence of someone accustomed to commanding the room. She had twenty-one years of auction experience, the last fourteen with Sotheby's. She was indisputably one of the world's top fine arts auctioneers. She had prepared diligently for this auction, and her knowledge of the art and artists to be presented was exhaustive. So, too, was her knowledge of the major players who would be bidding. She had thought the battle for the Ingersoll would come down to Aziz Lazaar, a wealthy Moroccan who was amassing a formidable art collection at his Casablanca mansion, and Eddie Liu, an Oxford-educated private equity star who would bid by telephone from his Shanghai headquarters.

Guest surveyed the crowd as she took the stage. She saw Lazaar in his customary spot at the corner of the room and gave him a smile. She looked at Jenny on phone number two and got a nod affirming that Liu was on the line. *Good,* she thought. *Annabel's Eyes will be up in about twenty minutes, and the key players are in place. Should be a fun battle—and a profitable one for Sotheby's.*

The moment soon arrived. The art handlers removed the prior lot and placed the Ingersoll on the easel near Guest. It was a remarkable piece. At thirty-four inches high and twenty-eight inches wide, it could command a room without the risk that the scale would overwhelm the intensely human character of the woman in the painting. Annabel was shown from the waist up, reclining and playfully seductive with cocked head and slightly parted lips. Her fine features were delicately arranged on a soft mocha face. Her raven hair, gently tousled and adorned with a small red hibiscus, fell slightly over one shoulder. She was beautiful in every aspect, but it was her eyes that captured the observer, large eyes of impossible green, smiling eyes so alive they had to be real.

"She is amazing," Guest said, taking a long moment to admire the work. "Well then, let's begin the bidding at 2 million pounds." Eleven paddles shot up. Guest quickly and surely increased the bid, and the also-rans began to drop out. A rhythm quickly developed, separating the serious bidders from the less committed or less wealthy. Only four bidders remained as the price neared the high estimate.

At 8 million pounds, with the momentum strong and gaining, Guest knew something special was happening. "I have 8 million on phone number two, do I hear 8.5?" She looked at Lazaar, who quickly nodded. "The gentleman in the corner says 8.5. Can I have 9 million?" A pretentious art dealer from New York's Upper East Side raised his paddle.

"I'll bid 12 million pounds," said an unfamiliar voice, and all eyes turned to the attractive woman in the front row. "Well, we have a new bidder," observed Guest. "Things are getting interesting. Annabel is with the lady in the blue hat at 12 million, unless I hear 12.5." She turned to the art dealer and was quietly pleased when he looked down and shook his head. She glanced at Lazaar, who nodded. "Do I have 13 million from the gentleman on the telephone?" Jenny spoke softly into the mouthpiece and quickly raised a hand to signal Liu's acceptance.

And so it went, back and forth between Lazaar and Liu and the lady in the blue hat. The tension in the room was escalating. More than a hundred people were present, but the silence was absolute except for the bidding. Christy Guest appeared cool and calm despite the turmoil she felt from the excitement of the moment and the mystery of the new bidder. She had never seen the woman before. She didn't recognize her as part of the art crowd, and she knew the art crowd very well. Who could she possibly be?

Aziz Lazaar dropped out at 22 million. The lady in the blue hat was relentless, smiling and affirming without hesitation each time the bid came to her. On phone number two, the conversations between Jenny and Liu were getting longer. The contest was electric, and the room exploded when, finally, Liu passed at 24 million.

Over the deafening applause, Guest banged her gavel and shouted, "Sold to the lady in the blue hat, paddle number 357, for 23.9 million pounds. Thank you, madam." She paused, then added excitedly, "That is a new record for an Ingersoll."

Suddenly, there was a loud pop at the front of the room. The applause surrendered to confusion. Another loud pop, and people dived for cover. Then all was quiet.

The lady in the blue hat was standing, calmly facing the stage, with a pistol in her hand. She had put a bullet through each of Annabel's eyes.

CHAPTER FIVE

Laura (2019)

"Kindly remove your hat, madam, whilst we take your photograph," said Constable James White.

"Of course," said the blond woman, removing her blue hat and laying it beside her. She had been arrested and taken directly from Sotheby's to the West End Central Police Station in Savile Row.

"Would you state your name, please?"

"Laura Marcus."

"And what is your place of residence, Mrs. Marcus?"

"It's Ms. Marcus. I live in New York City, on Park Avenue near 79th Street. And in Southampton. That's also in New York."

"Why are you in London, Ms. Marcus? And where are you staying, if you please?"

"I came mainly to attend the auction at Sotheby's, but I also plan to do some shopping and enjoy the theater. I'm staying at the Lanesborough." She paused, then asked, "Am I being charged with a crime, Constable White?"

"Yes, madam. I'm afraid you are."

"And what is that crime?"

"We're still sorting that out, but I believe the elements will include destruction of property and endangering members of the public."

"Then I'll say no more until my barrister gets here. She's on her way now."

"Very well, Ms. Marcus. I will leave you until she arrives. Can I have some tea brought round for you?"

"Thank you. That would be lovely." As the constable left the room, Laura sat back and surveyed the stark surroundings. At forty-four years of age, she was still beautiful with ash-blond hair that fell to her shoulders in a slight wave, deep blue eyes, and a svelte figure. She ate well, didn't smoke, and took plenty of exercise. It was the Marcus family way: work hard, play hard, and take care of your body.

The interrogation room was small, grim, and unpleasant. *What else should I have expected?* Laura thought. *You can't just shoot up Sotheby's and take a stroll down New Bond Street. I'm glad I arranged for Jane to come. I hope she gets here soon.*

The door opened to admit Constable White and Laura's tea. "Your barrister is here," said the constable. "I'll bring her in."

Jane Parks burst in seconds later. A stoutish woman who looked to be in her early fifties, she had inquisitive eyes and wore her gray hair in a simple bob. She was dressed for business in a dark blue lawyer suit. She wore no jewelry, conveying the message that she was who she was, take it or leave it. She hurried to Laura, giving her a bear hug and kisses on both cheeks. "It's so good to see you," she said. "You look amazing. I must say I prefer you as a brunette, though."

Constable White noted the familiar greeting with interest. He knew very well that Jane Parks was one of the finest barristers in London. He had seen her in court—in fact he had once been cross-examined by her. She was all business, all very serious business. Her frivolous side was a surprise. "I see you two know each other," he mused.

"Oh yes," gushed Jane. "We were in law school together at Yale in the late 1990s, and we've been best friends ever since. But forget all that. Today she is Ms. Marcus, and she is my client. May I ask why you've arrested her, Constable White?"

"She attended the auction at Sotheby's and created quite a row. We were called by security, who told us she stood up in the middle of the auction and pulled out a gun. She shot a painting, of all things. She destroyed property and put the people attending the auction in danger. We have to charge her."

"I see," said Jane. "What was the painting she shot?"

"My notes say it was by a well-known painter named Pablo Ingersoll. It had just been sold at the auction for a record price."

"Do your notes show who the buyer was?"

"Why, it was Ms. Marcus herself. She was the high bidder."

"Did she disavow the purchase after she shot the painting?"

"No, apparently not."

"Is Sotheby's pressing charges against her?"

"No. They told us they had a word with her after the ruckus but before we arrived, and she confirmed the purchase."

"Let me understand this, Constable White. You are saying that my client damaged her own property, and no one is complaining, is that right?"

"Well, yes, I guess so. But this is highly irregular."

"It may be irregular, but that doesn't make it a crime. We shouldn't have to go to prison if we choose to alter, or even destroy, one of our own possessions. Don't you agree?"

"Well, if you put it that way, I suppose I do."

"I mean, if you go home this evening and take a hammer to your mobile because it's dropping too many calls, you can do that without fear of being arrested, can't you?"

"Yes, of course."

"And why is that?"

"Because it's mine. I'm free to use my property as I see fit, aren't I?"

"Exactly. All Ms. Marcus did was use her property as she saw fit. Now, was there anything else, or is my client free to go?"

"She fired a gun in a public building. She endangered the people at the auction as well as the Sotheby's employees."

"In what condition was she when you picked her up? Was she agitated or out of control? Did she seem deranged, or under the influence of alcohol or drugs?"

"No. In fact, she was very calm."

"Has she been at all disorderly whilst in your custody?"

"No, Ms. Parks. I must say she has been entirely pleasant and courteous."

"Did you conduct interviews at Sotheby's?"

"Yes, of course."

"And has anyone alleged that she was threatening, or pointed a gun at them?"

"No. The picture we have is that she was calm and rational throughout, that after shooting the painting, she stood in her place, put the gun on her chair, and waited for security to come to detain her."

"Well, it doesn't sound to me like she was very dangerous, and I should think a jury would see it the same way," said Jane.

"But she was dangerous. There were people all around. What if she had missed her target?"

"Have you determined what her target was, Constable?"

"It must have been the eyes of the woman in the painting. There was a bullet hole exactly through the center of each eye."

"So, apparently, she didn't miss her target. And let me share with you that there was no way she would have missed. Ms. Marcus served as a sniper, one of the American army's best, in the Iraq war. After leaving the military, she competed in the 25-meter pistol event for women at the 2004 Summer Olympics in Athens and won the silver medal. She wasn't satisfied, so she competed again, in the same event, in Beijing in 2008. She won the gold. I think a jury would be quite clear that if the painting was the target, as you have said, the painting alone was in danger. Wouldn't you agree, Constable White?"

"I take your point, but it was still highly irregular."

"Yes, it was. But not a crime. That leaves the question of what's to be done. I see two possibilities. One is that you proceed with your charges, and you and I can have another go-round in court. Or you can simply make the point that my client's conduct was 'highly irregular,' as you say, and give her a warning that she is expected to be on her best behavior whilst in London, and nothing less than that will be tolerated."

"The second choice seems the better one, Ms. Parks. Under the circumstances, I think your suggestion of a stern warning adequately addresses the Crown's concerns and provides an appropriate resolution."

"Thank you, Constable White. You have handled the matter very professionally. If there's nothing further, my client and I will be off."

They were in the street moments later. It was almost four in the afternoon, and Laura suggested they repair to Brown's Hotel for high tea.

"I have a better idea," said Jane. "Let's go to Duke's." They were soon seated at a nice table by the window, and a courtly Italian server who looked to be eighty brought them each one of the martinis for which Duke's is known around the world. They clinked their glasses, took a sip, and sighed with pleasure.

"You've been a very naughty girl," said Jane, reaching for a crisp. "Now tell me, what the hell happened between you and Pablo?"

CHAPTER SIX

Pablo (1969-91)

Pablo. An enigma. But a highly talented one. A genius.

His father, Dicky "the Doorknocker" Ingersoll, was an Englishman from Devon. He left home to see the world when he was eighteen and ended up selling farm equipment for John Deere in Dubuque. He was good at it; his eagerness to chase any and all business was how he got his nickname.

As a reward for leading the company in sales, Dicky spent a week at Punta Cana in 1969, all expenses paid. He fell in love with the bartender at La Brisa, a small, thatched beach bar at his hotel. Maria Elena Hernandez Garcia, a dark-eyed beauty from Veracruz, had come to the Dominican Republic a year earlier to make some money so she could go to college. Her dream was to be an *abogado*, a lawyer, but her family was poor. She was determined to pay her own way and was making good progress until Dicky came along and stole her heart.

Maria Elena never imagined she would be pregnant at nineteen and live in a small city in the American Midwest, but life takes unexpected turns. Her lawyer dream was on hold. She would have hated Dicky for that if she didn't love him so much. The pain was eased when their son was born, a scant ten months after she made Dicky his first pina colada. Dicky was over the moon. "Let's call him Paul," he said. "Paul Ingersoll."

"Just a minute, hombre," said Maria Elena. "You don't get to choose both names. You can choose the first name or the last name, but not both."

"Well," Dicky said, somewhat dismayed. "I guess that's fair. I'll choose the last name. The boy will be an Ingersoll."

"And he will be Pablo. Pablo Ingersoll." They were both pleased with the outcome of their negotiation.

Pablo was a handsome boy. He had his father's blond hair and his mother's dark eyes. He was quick in school and good at athletics. He loved his parents and honored their wishes, helping out with farm chores for a few hours each day and going to church on Sundays. His personality, an engaging amalgam of Maria Elena's generosity and Dicky's bullshit, made him the most popular boy in his class. But what truly set him apart was his ability to draw. Pablo was passionate about making pictures.

Maria Elena first noticed his talent when he was six. As she and Dicky talked at the table after dinner one night, Pablo quietly drew on his napkin. Maria Elena thought he was just doodling, but then she saw that he had drawn a picture. "May I have a look at that?" she asked.

"Sure," Pablo said, handing her the napkin.

Maria Elena couldn't believe her eyes. It was a picture of their preacher, Brother Miles McFluff, delivering a sermon. It was precise in every detail, including the clothes he had been wearing at last week's service. It showed him with an angry finger in the air and upraised eyebrows as he reached the height of his bombast.

"How did you do this?" she asked. "How did you remember what he looked like so well?"

"I don't know. I was watching him, the way he was getting so angry. I thought it was funny, and I just remembered."

With Maria Elena's encouragement, Pablo continued to make pictures. He spent most of his spare time drawing, and he loved it. He could draw anything, but he particularly liked drawing people's faces, recording their unique characteristics, their expressions. Then, when he was fifteen, it began to lose its appeal. Perhaps he needed better tools, or maybe professional guidance. A broader exposure to the art world would surely help. Whatever was missing, he knew he wasn't going to find it in Dubuque.

As he thought about it, Pablo realized he was feeling confined by Dubuque more generally. It was quiet, predictable. He saw his only future there as farming or being the local State Farm agent, and that wasn't a future he wanted. *Everything's the same, every single day. You get up early, go to work, have a sandwich and a Coke at Millie's, then go back to work. Dinner, TV, then to bed so you can get up early and do it again. Every day. Except Sunday, when you go to church and suffer McFluff's rantings about hell and damnation. There's no creativity. No ambition. No excitement.* Pablo had to get out of Dubuque.

He graduated from high school with honors. He wasn't excited about going to college—his parents believed college was a path to a profession or an advanced degree and not a place to study art, which they viewed as an enjoyable hobby. Besides, they wanted him to stay near home, and that meant college in Iowa or a neighboring state. He ultimately decided, with Dicky's encouragement, to join the army. That would give him broader exposure, a respectable job, and a chance to earn some money. It would also give him some distance from his parents and fulfill his strong sense of duty. It was a fortuitous decision.

He was assigned to an infantry unit stationed in Frankfurt. By chance, he was on temporary duty in West Berlin when the wall came down. He experienced the inexpressible joy of German reunification as he moved through the crowds that were dancing and singing as they dismantled the wall. With genuine interest and admiration, he studied the graffiti, some of it quite good, that had sprouted up on the remnants of the wall. It was different in form from the art he had made in Dubuque, and it gave him an undeniable rush, the same rush he had gotten from drawing. Suddenly he saw the path forward.

Pablo was energized by his renewed interest in making art. He realized it might go nowhere, that he would have to find something else to do, something more practical, if his pursuit of art didn't pay the bills and enable him to send some money home to his parents. Still, he had to give it a try. At worst, his talent for drawing was his ticket out of Dubuque. When he left the army in 1991, he went home to spend two weeks with his family. Then he headed for New York. He had a scholarship to the prestigious Pratt Institute.

CHAPTER SEVEN

Pablo and Sally (1991)

"That's the thing about Brooklyn." The woman with the freckles and frizzy hair was on her knees, collecting her things, muttering.

"What's the thing about Brooklyn?" asked Pablo, bending over to help her.

"People just don't care. They knock you over in their hurry to get somewhere and don't even stop to see if you're all right. I'd hate the place if it weren't so interesting. I'm Sally. Sally Sullivan."

"Pablo Ingersoll." He took a hard look at Sally as they stood. She was a little older than he, and her freckles and frizz decorated an oblong face that was getting too much sun and would soon be leathery. There was a lot going on in that face. It reminded Pablo of a Chuck Close painting: from two feet away, it was busy, complicated, indecipherable, but if you stepped back a short distance, it was beautiful. "Are you here at Pratt?"

"Yes. It's my first day of class. I'm a little nervous."

"Good luck. Want to get a beer later and compare notes about whether we learned anything?"

"Sure," Sally said and hurried down the hall.

Pablo grabbed what he needed from his locker and headed for his classroom. He took a seat near the back, not knowing what to expect but preserving his options for distraction if the lecture turned out to be boring. He sat up, startled, when Professor Sally Sullivan entered the room. Sure enough, from this distance she was beautiful. More than that, she was smart.

Sally took a long moment to put down her things and arrange some notes on the lectern, knowing every eye in the classroom was on her and all-important first impressions were being made. Finally, she looked up, smiling and scanning the expectant faces and enjoying the moment when her eyes met those of a stunned Pablo Ingersoll.

"Good morning," she said. "Drawing is easy. We're not here to learn how to draw. You already know that, or you wouldn't be here. We're here to talk about imagination."

Pablo was intrigued. This was an exciting start, more than he expected.

"There's a big difference between drawing and thinking," Sally went on. "Drawing is an instinct, a talent. If you have that talent, you can be a camera. You can be the best camera there is, but at the end of the day, you're just recording what you see. There's nothing wrong with that, but if you spend all your time copying what you see, sooner or later you'll get bored. And you'll be bored because you're not expressing *yourself*.

"That's where imagination comes in. You look at an object, and instead of copying what you see with your eyes, you create a new and different reality, an abstract reality. You do it with your mind. That's how you challenge yourself. Every reality you see can be a thousand different realities, and you are the master of those realities. Let me show you what I mean."

She pulled up the six prints in Roy Lichtenstein's famous Bull Profile series. "As you can see, the first print is a very realistic bull. It was drawn from a photograph. In stages, the bull becomes more abstract, so that by the sixth print you don't recognize it as a bull unless you've seen the series from the beginning. You can't see the bull; in fact, you may see what looks like a mess, but the bull is clearly there and very important to the artist. It is the reality he saw. As Lichtenstein explained, 'I didn't want to destroy the bull … because whatever else I was doing, it had to look like a bull. I mean, all the marks … are made for other reasons, but it can't look *un*like a bull, it would be inconsistent with the idea.'

"The abstract image is the reality *you* see. You see it with your imagination, your mind, your heart. It is what differentiates a thinking person from a camera. You are an interpreter of objective reality, a translator, a dreamer. You are a thinker, and the possibilities for your reality are boundless."

Pablo was inspired. He had never thought about art in those terms. This was just what he needed to free himself from the confinement he felt in Dubuque, to enlarge his world. He couldn't wait to meet up with Sally and hear more. Later, at the Brooklyn Public House, he clinked his Lagunitas against her black and tan. She smiled and coyly asked, "Well, did we learn anything today?"

"Yes. The thing about Brooklyn is that the woman you try to pick up in the hallway may be your teacher." They enjoyed a laugh. "Seriously, I worried because my drawing had gotten too easy, too mechanical, too limited. This afternoon, you opened my eyes to possibilities I never imagined. I'm eager to explore the other realities out there, *my* realities. In one lecture, you've taken my excitement about making art to a new level."

CHAPTER EIGHT

The Investigation (May 2022)

Angelo met with Duane the next morning. Despite the bourbon, he hadn't slept well. He was fidgeting about the case and trying to develop a plan. He kept wondering how Scott would proceed.

"We've got some lab results," Duane said. "The blood in the room isn't Ivy's."

"That's a relief," breathed Frank Betterman, who joined the meeting out of curiosity and an interest that was personal as well as professional. His smile quickly became a frown. "Except it makes Ivy our number one suspect. Hard to think of her that way."

"I know," said Angelo, "but we need to deal with facts, not emotions. She lived alone in that house. Until the facts say otherwise, she's got to be the number one suspect."

Angelo was keenly aware that Frank and Duane had many more years of law enforcement experience than he did. Frank had joined the Woodstock police department in 1983 after fixing appliances for five years and tiring of it. He was promoted to chief in 1995 and was widely appreciated in the community for keeping the town safe and clean. Major crime was a rarity in Woodstock, largely because Frank was alert to any signs of a growing presence of drugs or gangs and did a good job of keeping them under control. Duane was a major reason for his success; Frank had hired him in 2006 after he washed out of the Navy Seals school and decided he never wanted to see the ocean again.

With only six years in law enforcement, Angelo was uneasy about taking charge and reluctant to assert himself. But he was the sheriff, and that was his job. He thought about a poster his immigrant father had on the wall of his first bakery, before he built the largest bread-making facility in western Virginia. Superimposed on the drawing of a butterfly were the words, "You can fly, but that cocoon has to go." *I can do this,* Angelo said to himself. *I have to do this.* And for the first of many times in this investigation, he willed himself to step off the ledge.

"What can you tell us about the blood work, Duane? How can you rule out Ivy?" Angelo quietly waited for someone to snicker or snort, but no one did.

"We sent blood samples taken from the room for DNA testing," Duane said. "We'll know more when the results come back tomorrow. But we already know the blood was AB negative. Ivy's blood was O positive. Not her blood."

"How do we know Ivy's blood type?" Angelo asked.

"She had a bad fall a few years back," Frank interjected. "She hit her head and needed some stitches. Our local hospital made a record of her blood type."

"Everyone knew about her fall," Duane added. "I called the hospital to get the information. I wasn't sure they'd give it to me because of HIPPA and all that medical privacy stuff, but those laws have pretty broad exceptions for law enforcement. It turned out not to be a problem. This is a small town, and people try to help each other out.

"Anyway, the blood at the scene belongs to someone else, someone who's AB negative. That's not a common blood type. There are only three people in the local hospital database who are AB negative, and one of them is dead."

"Who are the other two?"

"They're both people who have lived in this community a long time. One is George Johnson, the art dealer. He can't be involved, though. He was a friend and supporter of Ivy's. Besides, I saw him on the street yesterday, and he looks to be in one piece. The other is a dairy farmer named Steve Loudermilk. He has a place out Route 42, near Conicville."

Frank jumped in. "A dairy farmer? Did he have any dealings with that dairy farm down near Ivy's house?"

"Good thought," Duane said. "I'll find out."

Angelo was pleased with the collaborative effort that was developing. He was also impressed with Duane, who was serious about his work and didn't waste time on things that didn't matter.

"One other thing," Frank said. "Do we have results on the fingerprints that were on the palette knife yet?" With an aside to Angelo, he said, "I apologize. I don't mean to be taking over your investigation." After twenty-seven years as chief, Frank was used to being in charge, and playing a supporting role didn't come easily to him. He chided himself for his overreach and vowed to do better.

"No worries," said Angelo. "This will work best if we all jump in without standing on ceremony." He nodded to Duane, signaling that he should answer Frank's question.

"There are two distinct sets of prints on the knife. Most prints are Ivy's, which isn't surprising since she used the palette knife in her work."

"That's a fair point, but it doesn't exonerate her," Angelo cautioned. "There's nothing that says she didn't also use the knife to stab her visitor. How about the other prints?"

"It's a clear set, but we have no matches. Apparently, the owner of the prints hasn't been a guest of the criminal justice system."

No one seemed to have anything else to offer. Frank looked at Angelo. "So where do we go from here?"

Angelo didn't have a clue. But something was eating at him, something he couldn't put his finger on. Beth Lasker, longtime deputy sheriff under Jim Beamer and now Angelo's number two, nailed it. She had been quiet so far, but now she flagged an important issue that needed to be pinned down.

"There's a bucketful of blood in that place, which is consistent with physical evidence suggesting that a real brawl happened there. Did *all* your blood samples show AB negative results, Duane? Is it possible one person did *all* the bleeding?"

"That's been bothering me, too, Beth," Angelo interjected. "It's critical that the sampling was broad enough to eliminate the possibility of a second blood type. Are we good on that score, Duane?"

"We are. We covered the waterfront. I had my people sample every-where—the walls, the sofa, the paintings—because I couldn't believe only one person was bleeding in a fight as violent as this must have been. The samples all came back AB negative. There was only one bleeder."

Beth was now fully engaged. "Which means one of the people in the fight had serious physical superiority, or a major element of surprise. Or both."

"Probably," Angelo thought out loud. "But there's another possibility, unlikely as it is. The blood came from both of them, and both were AB negative."

"Wait a minute, how do we know there were only two?" wondered Frank. "Maybe there were three. Two against one would be consistent with Beth's observation that one side had a distinct physical advantage and might explain why the fight was as one-sided as it apparently was. It might also explain the absence of any bodies. Two people could move the victim, let's call the bleeder that, much more easily than one."

"That seems plausible, but where does Ivy fit in?" asked Duane. "This was her house, and she hasn't been seen since, so presumably she was part of whatever happened. We know she wasn't the bleeder since she isn't AB nega-tive. That would make her one of the two who beat and stabbed the victim. Is that even conceivable?"

"Not from what I've heard about her," said Angelo. "It just doesn't make sense. None of this makes any sense." He looked at Duane and Beth. "Someone must have seen or heard something. This couldn't have been a quiet event, and a body was somehow taken out of the house. Go out and talk to people. Find out everything you can. Check out the dairy farmer with the AB negative blood. We need to rule him in or out. Let's meet again tomorrow morning at nine. We've got to stay on top of this."

CHAPTER NINE

Chris (May 2022)

When Angelo returned to his office, Mayor Chris Lloyd was waiting for him. "I'll just take a minute, Sheriff. I've been meaning to come by to congratulate you on your new job and welcome you to Woodstock. With the terrible news from Water Street, it couldn't wait any longer. Frank Betterman tells me you've jumped right in, and I want you to know that this town and I will support you in every way we can."

"Thank you, Mr. Mayor. I've been meaning to call on you, too, but settling in has been slightly more dramatic than I anticipated."

"It's Chris, please. By the way, I admired your work on the Worthy case down in Bath County. I almost feel I know you."

"How's that?"

"My wife, who's also my law partner, is Sam Picken. Her good friend Judge Jessie Macaulay presided over the case your office brought against Kate Strange for Worthy's murder. Sam followed the case closely, not only because of her friendship with Jessie, but also because she's a former prosecutor and had a keen professional interest in the matter. She was in the courtroom during your testimony. She didn't think you seemed convinced about the defendant's guilt."

"I wasn't. We were under a lot of pressure from the governor's office to act, and there was a strong circumstantial case against Ms. Strange, but I had gotten to know her from interviewing her, and it just didn't feel right. I was relieved and my belief in her innocence was vindicated when the killer turned out to be someone else."

"Yes, that was my second point of contact with you from the Worthy case. The person you identified as the real killer was a client of mine when I practiced law in Charleston before coming to Woodstock. I had served in Iraq with her husband."

There was a silence as both men reflected. Then Chris said, "I have a personal reason for wanting to know what's going on here, Angelo. Everyone in Woodstock cares about Ivy, but Sam is one of her few true friends. Sam is very worried about her."

"I'll do everything I can. As I'm sure you can understand, part of that will be interviewing you and Sam in the next day or two."

"We'll make ourselves available whenever it's convenient for you. I'm glad you're here, and good luck with the case."

They shook hands, and Angelo watched Chris walk down the hall with a noticeable limp. He assumed, correctly, that it was a souvenir from his time in Iraq. He silently thanked Chris for his service, then turned his full attention to the case.

One of the things Angelo had learned from Scott O'Hanlon is that you're better at what you do if you take time to think. Scott used to say, "You'll never find what you're looking for if you don't figure out where to look." It was ironic coming from Scott, who wouldn't easily be confused with a big thinker. He was Irish, after all. You look to the Irish for passion and emotion and blarney, not wisdom. Reflecting on Scott's words, Angelo chuckled quietly and thought, *The dumbass Irishman nailed it, so maybe there's hope for an Italian like me.*

Slowly, systematically, he began to think about the case. He wrote out the questions that needed answers if he was to solve it.

- Where were the bodies?
- By all accounts, Ivy didn't have any close friends. Or any enemies, for that matter. Yet someone went to her house. Who? Why?
- Since the blood wasn't Ivy's, she had to be a suspect. But given her

physical limitations, could she have defended herself? Could she have overcome and seriously injured her visitor?

- What if she didn't have to defend herself? What if she was expecting the visitor, had maybe even invited him (or her?) to come, and had lain in wait with her palette knife? What if she had used the element of surprise to offset her physical disadvantage, attacking the visitor when he or she arrived? Or what if the visitor, too, was physically impaired, and Ivy wasn't really disadvantaged?

- What if Ivy had an accomplice? That could explain how she managed to maim and maybe even kill her visitor. But who? Why? What would be in it for her accomplice?

- In any case, where were the bodies? It seemed unlikely that either Ivy or her injured visitor would have been able to move the other. That gave support to the accomplice theory.

- Why would a local dairy farmer who lived out of town come to Ivy's house and have a violent encounter with her? What could they possibly have had in common? That just didn't make any sense. Still, he had the rare blood type found at the scene, and it had to be run down.

- If the visitor wasn't a local, who could it have been? Ivy was a poor woman and a private person. Who would come to Woodstock to see her? What motive could that person, or Ivy, have had to harm the other? Sex or money were the usual suspects when it came to motive, but they didn't seem to fit here.

- If Ivy wasn't injured, where was she? Why was she hiding?

Angelo sat back and looked over his notes. He knew the list would be refined as the facts developed. Some questions would be eliminated, others added. This was at least a start. One thing was certain: there was a lot more to Ivy than met the eye, and he was going to have to find out what it was.

CHAPTER TEN

Pablo and Sally (1991-2001)

Pablo was on fire. He got his undergraduate degree in 1995 and stayed at Pratt for two more years to get his master's. Pushed and encouraged by Sally and others in the Pratt community, he worked hard and learned. No longer confined to what his eyes took in, his vision roamed the wide seas of his imagination. Excited by the possibilities, he experimented with various art movements: impressionism, abstract expressionism, cubism, even surrealism and minimalism. He studied the diverse styles and magnificent artwork of distinguished Pratt alumni like Ellsworth Kelly, Eva Hesse, Jacob Lawrence, and Robert Mapplethorpe. He admired them all, but he wanted to find his own way.

Getting to know the tools and materials available for making art was a critical part of the journey. His commitment to painting narrowed the process. He wasn't attracted to photography or sculpture, and he couldn't understand why anyone would make art with "found objects." He had tried printmaking, but it didn't give him the gratification of working brushstrokes onto a canvas. His desire to paint shortened the journey, but there were still choices to be made.

Growing up in Dubuque, his tools had been a pencil and a pad of paper. Now he could create art using brushes, scrapers, sponges, painting knives, erasers, masking tape, and brayers. He could paint with acrylics, oils, gouache, or watercolors. He experimented with the various tools to see which were most comfortable for him and, more importantly, which produced the look he wanted to create.

After rebelling against the limitations of drawing what he saw, Pablo was somewhat surprised and faintly amused to find that he preferred working in a traditional vein. He loved abstraction but took his greatest pleasure in making paintings that, despite their distinct "Pablo license," were recognizable. His primary tool was a flat brush, and he worked with acrylics and oils. Being water soluble, acrylics were easier and cleaner, but there was something compelling about the shine that only oil paints could produce.

He still had a penchant for drawing faces, and he knew why. *Humans are uniquely interesting. They live in their faces. Four of the five senses make their home there, each expressive in its own right. Faces show love and hate, anger and joy, confusion, serenity, happiness, sorrow. They tell us who we are, at every moment. They are endlessly fascinating.*

In truth, Pablo's penchant was for drawing a single face, that of Sally Sullivan. He had painted her a hundred times, as he had seen her with his eyes and in his mind. He had painted her young and old, happy and sad, slender and full. He had painted her with different hues, hairstyles, hats, and jewelry. He had painted her with myriad expressions, real and imagined. He had painted her beautiful and less beautiful. But he had never painted her ugly. Whatever the changes, the differences, the ups and the downs, it was always Sally. She was the point of it all. The painting couldn't be *un*like Sally.

Pablo and Sally were married in 2001, the day after his first solo show. He had been part of several group exhibitions, dating back to his final year at Pratt. He hadn't taken the art world by storm, but the reviews were positive and promising. Finally, the well-regarded Stockbridge Gallery in Soho decided to give him a one-person show. It was styled *A Distinctive New Talent: Twelve Paintings by Pablo Ingersoll*, and it was well-promoted. This was heady wine—Pablo was by turns proud, happy, nervous, and terrified as the weeks counted down to the opening.

When the day finally arrived, Pablo and Sally prepared with dirty martinis as they dressed in Sally's Brooklyn loft. Unlike many in the art world, who dress down to promote a nonconformist image, Sally and Pablo loved to dress up. Shopping at high-end stores was out of the question, but they knew that customers of those stores occasionally donated clothes that didn't fit or look quite right to "Dress for Success" programs, and they used their knowledge to ready themselves for the opening. As he pulled a twice-worn Zegna sport coat over a never-worn Eton shirt, Pablo smiled at Sally.

"I'm very excited. How do I look?"

"Like a Greek god. I'm so proud of you."

"You made this happen, Sally. I love being with you. We've talked about marriage for a long time, but we've never gotten around to making it happen. It never seemed important somehow, but it seems important now. Whatever happens tonight, let's go to the courthouse tomorrow. I want to spend my life with you. Then, for our honeymoon, let's take a trip, using the money we make from this show to pay for it. We can go to Paris or Florence, or if we don't sell anything, we can stay in New York. I hear there's good art here too."

"You're crazy, and I'm all in. Now let's go to Soho and see if we can sell something."

As with all art openings, the wine served by the gallery was mediocre and ran out way too soon. But the crowd was impressive, and most weren't there for the wine. The art critic from the *New York Times* attended, as did critics from art-specific publications. There were a few art students, some from Pratt, and a handful of artists who were friends of Pablo or Sally; these two categories of attendees *were* interested in the wine. And there were some serious collectors, not the big-timers but the ones who might take a risk on an unknown artist and could afford the work. Jennifer Stockbridge, the gallery owner, worked the crowd, sniffing out potential buyers and introducing them to a bemused and highly flattered Pablo Ingersoll. Jennifer well knew that buying art wasn't just about the quality of the art; it was about knowing the artist.

Pablo was on his best behavior. He couldn't believe Jennifer had priced his work in the $12,000 to $15,000 range, which he found embarrassingly aggressive. He tried his best to make potential buyers see that as a bargain, and he worked hard to show them a serious artist who had, aw shucks, grown up on a farm. He wanted them to admire what he had achieved, and to like him enough to put skin into his launch. His personality made him a natural and joined with the compelling nature of his work to vault him toward stardom. Eight of his paintings were sold at the opening, and two more were placed on hold. The *Times* critic gave him a rave. Pablo and Sally were going to Paris *and* Florence.

CHAPTER ELEVEN

The Investigation (May 2022)

The DNA results taken from the blood in Ivy's house came back the next day, as expected. They confirmed what the blood typing had shown: Ivy was not the bleeder. The presence of X and Y chromosomes in the blood disclosed that the bleeder was male.

Even in small towns like Woodstock, the world of criminal investigation was altered when DNA analysis was introduced in England in the mid-1980s. But while it was an unquestionable step forward, DNA profiling was not the panacea that popular TV shows like *CSI* made it seem. It never gave the investigators as much information as they wanted; it always left them with the hard, dirty work of collecting samples, running tests, talking to potential witnesses, aggregating relevant facts, thinking through what the disparate shreds of evidence might mean, and building a case from the ground up. DNA analysis was a welcome tool, but no silver bullet.

"Good to know the bleeder's gender," said Angelo, "but what else does the analysis tell us?"

"He had dark eyes, either black or brown," replied Duane. "DNA analysis is sufficient to assign eye color to one of three groupings—light, which is blue or gray, dark, which is black or brown, or hazel—with a ninety-seven percent confidence level. This guy's eyes were either black or brown."

"Well, that narrows it down to eighty or a hundred million people."

Angelo's frustration often manifested itself as sarcasm. DNA analysis always seemed to promise so much and deliver so little. "Is that all we get? Nothing about race or ethnicity?"

"Sorry, that's all you get."

"Not even hair color?"

"Only if it's red. This guy didn't have red hair."

"That's a relief," offered Beth. "It wouldn't do to have redheads at crime scenes. Think Howdy Doody, Lucille Ball—the image just doesn't fit. Besides, the bad guys would be too easy to catch if they had red hair."

"Are you saying the bleeder was the bad guy in this case?" asked Angelo.

"I guess I am. What are the chances that he wasn't? Why else would he have been in Ivy's house? I know, I came up with the accomplice theory, and this guy may have been the accomplice, but I'm putting the over-under on the bleeder being the bad guy at ninety-two percent."

"Is that woman's intuition?" taunted Duane.

"Experienced detective's educated guess is how I'd put it." The rivalry was evident in Beth's retort. So was the friendliness.

Angelo enjoyed the moment of camaraderie, but it wasn't getting them anywhere. "If you two can establish a brief truce, we have work to do. We know the bleeder was a dark-eyed male with AB negative blood. That's not much, but it's something. Duane, that dairy farmer has two of those three characteristics. When can you get out to check his eye color and, more importantly, see if he's carrying wounds from a recent fight?"

"First thing tomorrow morning. If he seems at all like a possibility, I'll ask him for a DNA sample that we can compare against the blood from Ivy's house."

They all knew it wasn't going to be the dairy farmer. That would be way too easy.

CHAPTER TWELVE

Paris (2006)

Because of their respective gallery commitments, it was 2006 before Pablo and Sally made their trip. Paris blew them away. They made the obligatory visit to the Louvre, but Pablo's primary art interest was the astounding collection of works by impressionists and post-impressionists at the Musée d'Orsay. He was captivated by the life and joy radiating from Renoir's *Bal du moulin de la Galette,* and he stood in awe for an hour absorbing the use of light in van Gogh's *Starry Night Over the Rhone.* He didn't agree with the common sentiment that Claude Monet was the greatest of the impressionists, but he quite liked *London Houses of Parliament* for its fog-shrouded vagueness.

Pablo's fascination with the human face drew him to three paintings that significantly affected his future work. One was van Gogh's self-portrait, in which the artist's head and face are expressionless while everything else—the backdrop wall, even van Gogh's clothing—displays energy. The power of the piece was its challenge to Pablo's notion, previously held as an article of faith, that the opposite should be true. Another standout was *The Absinthe Drinker* by Degas. The unremarkable body language and faraway facial expressions of the hungover couple seated in a bar, together but not quite together, perfectly capture a slice of the human experience. The final and most inspiring piece was Edouard Manet's *Olympia,* which portrays a reclining nude prostitute with a flower in her hair, staring brazenly at the viewer. Her undetailed face gives away nothing except a frankness, perhaps a smugness, a look that says, *Who are you to be staring at me?* The faces in the paintings are blank but haunting, each drawing the viewer in to imagine the untold part of the story.

Sally's favorite art venue in Paris was the Pompidou Centre. She was into abstraction, and she loved the Centre's fine collection of Kandinskys and Mondrians. Her favorite, though, was the monumental Miro triptych commonly referred to as the "three blues." She had been a Miro devotee ever since she saw his retrospective at the Guggenheim in New York in 1987. She fondly recalled a sequence in that show in which Miro progressed from realism to abstraction, as Lichtenstein did in his Bull Profile series; that sequence caused her to "get" abstraction and profoundly influenced her decision to pursue it as her life's work.

On their last night in Paris, Sally and Pablo walked hand in hand along the left bank of the Seine before settling into a quiet sidewalk cafe for a reflective drink. Over coquilles St.-Jacques and a crisp Chablis, they spoke of what they had seen during their visit and compared notes about the works they would take home if they were granted any five. They talked of what lay ahead in Florence—Michelangelo, particularly *David,* Botticelli, Titian, Brunelleschi's Dome, Ghiberti's doors—and were torn between wanting to get there and not wanting to leave Paris. It was magical; they wanted their lives to freeze right there, in that moment, at that café, eating scallops and drinking wine and being more at peace than they had ever been.

A hand on Pablo's shoulder broke the spell. "Mr. Ingersoll, isn't it? I saw your show at Jennifer Stockbridge's gallery a few years back and was quite taken with your work."

The woman was middle-aged, large-chested, and throaty. She was too well dressed for a left bank afternoon in Paris, and her highlighted dark brown hair looked freshly done. Despite speaking slowly, inspecting each word before releasing it, she quickly got down to business. Her accent was refined and distinctly British.

"I'm Ann Merriman. I have a small art consultancy in London. It's in Mayfair if you're familiar with London." Her hazel eyes seemed incapable of staying in one place. They took in Sally, then darted back to Pablo. Then quickly to Sally, then Pablo again.

"Pleased to meet you," said Pablo. "I'm glad you enjoyed the show."

"I did. You have a way with expressions, and your surfaces, your textures, are wonderful. I was charmed by your solitary subject, who if I'm not mistaken sits beside you now."

"This is my wife, Sally Sullivan. I guess the show gave away the secret that she's my favorite model."

"Are you willing to stray beyond your wife to paint other women?"

"I suppose so. Sally is where my art and my heart have taken me so far. Why do you ask?"

"I have a business proposition for you, one that could be quite profitable. Do you ever work on commission?"

Pablo was thoughtful. "I've never been asked, and I've never considered it. Off the top of my head, I don't see why I wouldn't accept a commission."

"Good. Then stop by my office in London on your way home from Florence," she said, handing him a business card. "It's in Curzon Street, not far from Berkeley Square. You can call my assistant for an appointment. We'll talk then." Ann Merriman stood, shook Pablo's hand, smiled at Sally, and bustled off toward the Boulevard Saint-Germain.

Pablo and Sally looked at each other quizzically. Pablo spoke first. "I wonder how she knew we were going to Florence."

"I wonder how she knew we were here."

"I wonder what this is all about."

Sally weighed the next bit before saying it. "I don't trust her."

CHAPTER THIRTEEN

Ann (2006)

Florence lived up to expectations, and all too soon, Pablo and Sally were at Ann Merriman's office in Curzon Street. They had serious misgivings about being there, but they hadn't been to London, and this was an opportunity for a visit on someone else's dime. The meeting with Ann was the least anticipated but most intriguing part of the stop in London.

The office occupied the first floor of a magnificent brownstone. They walked up four steps to a double door of solid English oak. Ann opened it before they could knock.

"Welcome," she said, "please come in. Would you like some tea?"

"We'd love some," Pablo replied. "Sally takes sugar, and just a little lemon for me, please. We weren't sure we had the right place. We were confident about the address, but there was no sign on the door."

Ann looked amused. "That's a minor inconvenience but not a real problem. Whenever I think about putting out a modest sign, I remind myself that I've built a solid business by being discreet."

Sally wondered what could be indiscreet about identifying your business. She opted for saying, as she looked around the comfortable library in which they were seated, "This is a lovely room. I'm quite surprised and flattered to see my face on the far wall."

"I was very impressed with Pablo's work, as I told you in Paris, and was fortunate to acquire that painting before his show opened at Stockbridge. Jennifer and I have known each other for years, and she gave me a preview. She was delighted that I wanted to buy a painting. These gallery owners love their little red dots—it stimulates sales to have some works already spoken for when a show opens."

A moment of silence followed. As tea was being poured, Pablo said, "We're pleased to be here, Ann, but the suspense is more than I can bear. Exactly why are we here, and what do you have in mind?"

"I want you to paint beautiful women, and I want to pay you for it."

"Hmmm, let me think for a moment. OK, that sounds good. What's the catch?"

"There is no catch, but there are terms. Once every two years, I will give you a photograph of a woman. It will be a different woman each time. You will make a painting of the woman in the style of a particular artist I will identify when I give you the photograph. I'm not looking for an exact likeness of the photograph—you can change the pose, the background, make any adjustments you want to make the painting your own—but when it's finished, the woman must be recognizable, and the work must appear to have been painted by the indicated artist. When you give me the painting, I will give you one hundred thousand dollars."

A gasp, as Pablo looked through wide eyes at a wider-eyed Sally. "That's very generous. You must know that's more than I received for all twelve of the paintings in the Stockbridge show."

"I think you have a special talent, and I want you to find my proposal worth your while. I will, of course, require you and Sally to sign a nondisclosure agreement regarding the arrangement."

Sally looked for the right words to express her concern. "I have no problem signing if this is something Pablo wants to do, so long as it's not illegal or unethical. My hesitation is that the arrangement, as you've described it, sounds like you're asking Pablo to make forgeries."

"Not at all," replied Ann. "Pablo will be making the paintings for me and me alone. Neither his name nor the name of the artist whose style he's using will be on the paintings. The women he paints will be women who are important to me for one reason or another. The artists I choose will be artists I admire, artists whose original works I could not afford. The paintings will be for me, and I intend to use them in connection with a project I have in mind that will seek to advance the stature of women; you have my word that I will not sell or attempt to sell them."

"That's helpful, and reassuring," Sally said. Pablo nodded his agreement.

"I'll give you some time to consider the proposition. Let me know when you're ready for me to return." Ann left the room, closing the door behind her.

The conversation between Sally and Pablo was brief. When Ann rejoined them, Pablo said, "I'd like to do this if you promise not to saddle me with any Renaissance artists or old masters. I'm afraid I couldn't do them justice, and I wouldn't enjoy the work. Also, I want to be clear that while I can try to channel the artists you name, and hope do a creditable job, I am not those artists and can never be what they have been."

"Fair enough. I appreciate your keeping my expectations in check. All I'm looking for is your best effort."

Thanks," said Pablo. "That gives me comfort, but I'm still a little uneasy. Can we go ahead with the first assignment and reserve for later the decision about renewing the arrangement?"

"Of course. I have the first photograph for you if you're ready to get started."

Things had gotten real in a hurry. "Let's do it." Pablo gulped. "What do you have?"

Ann smiled and handed him a photograph. "This is Lydia. I would like you to paint her as Jawlensky would have."

CHAPTER FOURTEEN

Ivy (May 12-14, 2022)

Ivy didn't know where she was, not exactly anyway. She knew she was still in Woodstock, or close to it, because the ride from her house had only taken about ten minutes. They had turned off Water Street at Cemetery Road and wound their way uphill to a stop sign at Riverview Park, a community playground with a kids' baseball field at the front. They took a left turn, and then fairly quickly a right turn onto a dirt road that hadn't seen much use in recent years. The man who brought her had stopped their vehicle to open a cow gate, then closed it behind them after they went through. They arrived momentarily at an abandoned barn that looked across the river below to the magnificent Blue Ridge Mountains. Ivy had never been there before, but the man said she'd be safe and would only have to stay a few days.

He helped her up a ladder to the haymow, where she was surprised to find a mattress and pillow, some blankets, an old leather chair, and a card table. He had brought some food for her and said he would bring more when he came to check on her the next day. He had also brought her backpack with her drawing tablet and colored pencils.

Ivy quickly developed a routine in her new life at the barn. She sat by the window for a couple of hours each morning, enjoying the sounds and sights of the birds: the soft cooing of the mourning dove, the muted jackhammer of the downy woodpecker, the brilliant red of the cardinal that perched in her window, staring back at her and cocking its head as if trying to figure her out. She particularly loved the graceful glide of the red-tailed hawk that soared on distant thermals in its own version of the "stitutional" Ivy had built her days around.

She didn't mind being at the barn; in fact, she liked it. The quiet and contentment were food for the soul. She could think, and she could draw, and she had a wealth of new material to engage her in both pursuits. *What am I doing here?* she wondered. *Who is this man who has become my keeper, my jailer, my protector, and my savior? Why did I go with him? What does he want from me?*

His name was Balthasar. That's what he had said, anyway, but Ivy had her doubts. Who names a kid Balthasar? It didn't really matter because he had told her to call him Bart. Whatever. If he wanted to be called Bart, she would call him Bart.

It was in her mind—maybe from her early days in Sunday school when she was only seven or eight—that Balthasar was the name of one of the three kings who went to visit the baby Jesus at the stable in Bethlehem. Maybe it was a Middle Eastern name, but this man didn't look Middle Eastern. He was fair skinned with alert blue eyes and short blond hair cut close to his scalp, almost shaved. He was less than average height, around five nine maybe, and had a lean, muscular build. Not like a bodybuilder, though—Bart's muscles were more subtle than that. If you were thinking animals, you wouldn't think lion or tiger. More like a cheetah. Yes, definitely a cheetah. Bart looked sleek, strong, and very fast.

Ivy barely knew Bart before he came to her house two nights earlier. She had met him the previous month when she was returning home from her daily walk. He was mowing the small plot of grass in her yard.

"Excuse me, sir," she said, "but what are you doing?"

"I was cutting the grass next door, and yours looked like it might appreciate a little trim. I hope you don't mind."

"I don't, but I'm afraid I don't have any money to pay you."

"Don't worry about that. Your yard only takes a minute. Consider it my good deed for the day."

"Thank you. And I know you'll feel better if you repeat your good deed every week, so I'll tell you in advance that would be OK with me. Tuesdays would be wonderful."

They both laughed, and she said, "My name is Ivy."

"Yes, ma'am," he said. "Everyone around here knows who you are, and I'm happy to meet you. My name is Balthasar, but please call me Bart."

"OK ... Bart. You haven't been in Woodstock very long, have you?"

"No. I was in the army, but I had enough. I had two tours in Afghanistan. Too much fighting, too much killing, so I got out when my commitment ended. I grew up in this area and recently came back. I'm staying in the apartments down the street while I look for a job."

This was a long conversation for Ivy, and she felt it was bordering on personal. Time to cut it off. "Well, it's nice to meet you, Bart. I'll see you around, and don't forget about next Tuesday." They laughed and shook hands, and she headed toward her small house.

She had seen him a few times since then, usually in the afternoons when she was coming back from her walk. He seemed to have picked up some work at the dairy farm across the street. He always waved, and she lifted her crutch in reply.

It was not in Ivy's nature to be trusting. There was little in her past to justify trust, especially where men were concerned. But there was something about Bart she couldn't put her finger on, a kindness in his eyes, a sincerity in his smile. She instinctively believed in him. And that was why she unhesitatingly left her home when he knocked two nights earlier and urgently said, "Ivy, we need to move you out of your house for a few days. It isn't safe for you here. We have to go. We need to leave right now. Your life may depend on it."

CHAPTER FIFTEEN

Ivy (1980-97)

Ivy sat by the barn window and thought about her mother. She hadn't seen Rosaria de la Rosa for twenty-five years. Even if Rosaria was still alive, Ivy knew she would never see her again. Nothing, not even her mother, would take her back to the Philippines.

She had never known her father. Rosaria said he was a good man who had joined the army and died fighting a communist group in northern Luzon, but Ivy didn't believe it. Rosaria carried a sadness and suspicion of men that could only have come from a bad relationship, perhaps involving some mistreatment and certainly some deception. A hero? Ivy didn't think so. Her father was just another love 'em and leave 'em kind of guy.

How unfair life had been to her mother, Ivy thought. Rosaria had named her only daughter Estella, or star, and called her Stellie. She raised her in a densely populated and crime-ridden district of Manila called Tondo. It wasn't easy for a single mother to bring up a child in that predatory environment, but Rosaria loved little Stellie and kept her safe.

Rosaria's only mistake had been loving her daughter too much. She knew a beautiful young girl, bright but undereducated, had no future in Tondo or even in greater Manila. Stellie's would be one more wasted life in a world overcrowded with them. The thought of being separated from her daughter was agonizing, but Rosaria felt she had no choice. Whatever the personal cost, she had to give Stellie the opportunity for a better life than hers had been. She had to get Stellie to a place where she could be happy and safe, could hopefully marry and have a family.

One day as she bicycled to work along the Pasig River, Rosaria saw a billboard that gave her hope. It had a picture of a beautiful Filipina girl, smiling happily, next to the words, "Want a better life, with education and a good job?" Yes, that was exactly what Rosaria wanted, not for herself but for Stellie. She called the number on the billboard as soon as she had a private moment. Jaime Roxas, who answered the call, was cheerful and confident. The job was in a suburb of Los Angeles, and it would consist of working in the home of a wealthy couple named Brown. They would take Stellie in and treat her as their own, enrolling her in the well-regarded public high school in their district. Stellie would do domestic work for the Browns after school and during vacation periods. She would be paid for her work, and after three years, the Browns would fly Rosaria to the States for a monthlong visit with Stellie.

It sounded perfect, all but the separation, and Rosaria had long since accepted that as a necessary sacrifice. Her only hesitation was the cost; Rosaria had carefully saved what money she could but was well short of the required payment. Jaime suggested a workaround.

"Your payment would leave you owing about fifteen hundred dollars. Could we agree to deduct a small amount from Stellie's pay until that debt is paid?"

That seemed reasonable, but Rosaria didn't like owing people money and told Jaime she wanted to think about it.

"Sure," said Jaime, "you need to be comfortable with your decision. By the way, I'll be sending you reference letters from the last two Filipino children who worked for the Browns under this kind of arrangement."

When the letters arrived, they were glowing. Carlos Bersa and Lita Campos had worked for the Browns for two and three years, respectively, before going on to college. Both said they had their own room in a "large house in a nice neighborhood," which even "had a swimming pool" that they were free to use. They spoke of the Browns as "kind" and "generous" people who had raised them out of the poverty they knew in Manila and given them opportunities to have far better lives. Their gratitude to the Browns was effusive.

This was everything Rosaria had wished for, and more. She contacted Jaime and signed the agreement. In three weeks, she would take Stellie to the airport, where Jaime would meet them and accompany Stellie on the flight to Los Angeles.

Their parting was heart-wrenching. Saying goodbye to her seventeen-year-old daughter was the hardest thing Rosaria had ever done. But she left the airport with joy and peace, knowing she had done the right thing. She had gotten Stellie out of the filth of Tondo. She had given her a better life. She began counting the days until their visit in Los Angeles.

CHAPTER SIXTEEN

Ivy (1997-2007)

S tellie was one of an estimated fifty thousand victims of international human trafficking in the United States that year. Jaime Roxas was her captor, overseer, and pimp.

She lived in a private home in greater Los Angeles for almost ten years. She didn't have her own room but shared a small space with five other girls. She didn't go to school but was forced to work twelve hours a day. Some was domestic work for the Browns, or whatever their name was; the rest was in a crowded sweatshop in East LA, where she made children's clothing that generated a lot of money for someone, presumably the Browns, because it was inexpensive for clothing that carried a "Made in the USA" label. She worked as a prostitute several nights a week.

She was paid a pittance and told the rest of her salary was being applied to her mother's debt. She got no answers to her questions about when the debt would be fully paid. She was not allowed to call her mother and, as the three-year mark approached, she was told what she already knew in her heart: the promised visit from her mother would not happen.

Jaime Roxas was not a cruel man, but it was his job to make money for the Browns. He did it well because he didn't allow feelings to be part of the equation. He treated Stellie and the other girls as chattel. He was indifferent to them most of the time. He disciplined them harshly when they stepped out of line.

The prostitution was the worst part. Most of the johns were OK, some were even kind, just guys who were horny or looking for diversion, but every now and then there was a sadist, and that was big trouble. On one occasion, a brawny, bald-headed pig of a man slapped Stellie hard three times and tried to make her commit an act that was way, way over the line, an act she knew even Jaime wouldn't tolerate. She broke a bottle to defend herself, but the man turned it on her and opened a frightening gash below her left eye. He thought he had killed her and ran away, but Jaime tracked him down and used a *balisong*, a butterfly knife common in the Philippines, to end his days of sexual activity.

Stellie didn't see much of the Browns. They owned several homes and were away most of the time. Human trafficking and whatever else they did was clearly profitable. Stellie and the other girls tried to avoid Mr. Brown because he had an annoying habit of brushing his body against theirs as he walked by and pretending not to notice, but he was essentially harmless. Mrs. Brown was the brains of the outfit. She had a job with a big company in England, or maybe Ireland; her business in LA was a side venture. She once showed Stellie a softer version of herself, going to the hospital to visit her as she recovered from the sadist's attack. Stellie thought that was very kind.

After eight years of slavery and imprisonment in the Browns' home, Stellie tried to escape. She had tried once before, and Jaime had warned her there would be serious consequences if it happened again. She was gone two days before she was spotted by one of his informants and taken back home. Jaime hit her left knee with a baseball bat, just once but with enough force that she was never able to use that leg again. He calmly put the bat down and said, "That will make it harder for you to walk out the next time you're thinking about it."

Stellie did keep thinking about it, though, as she carried out her work duties as well as she could on one leg and a crutch over the next two years. One day, she saw her chance. Someone had left an outside door open. She walked through it. *I can't do this anymore,* she thought. *I know Jaime will kill me if he catches me, but death would be better than the life I'm living. I've got to take my shot. Please help me, God.*

She made her way three blocks to a CVS store, where she saw a kindly-looking white-haired man getting into a car. She didn't know him, and she had learned, from Jaime, the risks of trusting someone she didn't know. But she was living in hell, and she didn't have much time to make a decision. She rapidly approached the man. She was out of breath and trembling with excitement and fear. This was her make-or-break moment, when her life would either change for the better or come to an end.

"Can you please help me, sir? I need a ride. It's very important." She blurted out the words, her efforts to be calm unavailing. She had a fleeting thought about the risk she was taking. Who was this man? Where might he take her? What might he do to her? Would he report her to the authorities, which would inevitably lead her back to Jaime? She struggled to suppress her fears. The man looked kind, and she had to believe her chances with him were better than her other alternatives.

Startled at first by her unexpected approach and physical condition, the man collected himself and gave her a smile. "Sure. Hop in. What's your name?"

Stellie was prepared for the question. She had been planning her escape for a long time. She knew she had to change her identity if, somehow, she managed to get away. She could no longer be Stellie.

She looked back at the man and uttered the words she had practiced so many times. "Ivy. Ivy Villanueva."

"Nice to meet you, Ivy." As they pulled away, the man looked at her with concern. "Those are nasty wounds. What happened, and where are you going?"

"As far away from here as you can take me. Someplace where these things won't happen to me anymore."

"I can take you a long way. I live in Woodstock, Virginia."

Ivy leaned back in her seat and began to relax, just a little. "Woodstock, Virginia. That's where I'm going too."

CHAPTER SEVENTEEN

Jaime (2007)

Jaime Roxas was not a happy man when he learned that Stellie was gone. He had taken a liking to her, and he admired her grit, but he didn't have a successful operation if his captives escaped. Anyone who ran away had to be caught and pay a severe price. The integrity of his program depended on it. He knew the other captives were watching closely and would be emboldened if he didn't bring Stellie back to face the consequences. Finding her was a top priority.

He decided not to tell the Browns of her escape, not at first anyway. It would reflect badly on his stewardship of the program. He was confident she would be quickly found and returned. After all, he had built a strong network of informants throughout the greater Los Angeles area; they had located the four previous escapees, including Stellie herself on her first two attempts, and returned them to Jaime within two days. She would be easier to find this time because her mobility was severely limited by her unusable leg. The Browns need never know she had gone missing.

With each passing day, Jaime's concern and agitation grew. He checked in with his informants constantly, but there were no sightings. He didn't know how that could be. She couldn't have gotten very far on foot, and public transportation wasn't an option since she had no money or credit cards. She had to be in the area, hiding out. If so, it was a matter of time until she was found. But if, God forbid, she had gotten out somehow, past Jaime's network of informants, she could be anywhere. Jaime intensified the search effort by tripling the usual bounty he paid for locating missing captives.

Two weeks went by. No results. Jaime's concern and agitation hardened into anger and resolve. He was convinced there were only two possibilities. She was either hiding in the area, dug in deep with someone committed to protecting her, or she had used her considerable intelligence and charm to persuade a kindhearted stranger to give her a ride. In either case, Jaime could no longer rely on his network to find her. He needed to broaden the search by using social media, and, distasteful as it was, he needed to tell the Browns.

Social media was an obvious play because of its international reach and broad appeal among the Filipino people. Jaime was active on Facebook and Twitter and had a significant following, including a large Filipino following. He could be easily tracked through those accounts, however, so he used the dark web to post a notice of a $20,000 reward for anyone providing information that led to finding the Filipina woman whose photograph accompanied the notice. The photograph was ten years old and taken for his use in pimping for Stellie when she was eighteen and new to the program. *She was beautiful,* he thought, looking at the photograph. *I touted her as Stella, our star. And she was.* But she didn't look that way now, so he cautioned that the woman in the photograph had acquired a scar below her left eye and probably walked with a crutch or a cane. He was optimistic that the sizable reward, along with Stellie's picture and highly distinguishing characteristics, would produce solid leads in short order.

Jaime then contacted Mrs. Brown, who was away on business, to tell her Stellie had escaped. Mrs. Brown ran a tight ship, and Jaime hadn't looked forward to the call. He described the actions he was taking to find Stellie and, despite his serious doubts, led Mrs. Brown to believe her capture was imminent.

"Which one was Stellie?" asked Mrs. Brown.

"The one you visited at the hospital after she was attacked," said Jaime. "The pretty one."

"Oh yes, I remember. Send me her photograph, will you?"

"Of course. I'll email it to you right now."

"Thanks," said Mrs. Brown. "Do whatever it takes to find her because you know the damage this causes our business. Let me know if I can help."

"I will, I promise you that." Jaime sighed with relief that the call was ending without his having gotten the tongue-lashing he expected and probably deserved.

"I like Stellie. She's tough, and she's smart. We can't have her running around loose. Sooner or later, she'll blow the whistle on us. I want her back, or I want her dead. Keep me posted."

CHAPTER EIGHTEEN

The Investigation (May 2022)

Duane Foskey drove out to see Steve Loudermilk and quickly eliminated him as a suspect. Yes, his blood was AB negative, and yes, he sometimes did business with the dairy farm on Water Street, but no, he didn't know Ivy, and no, he hadn't heard anything about the incident at her house. Most importantly, he didn't have any visible wounds; he certainly hadn't shed recent blood in quantities that would account for the scene at Ivy's house. On top of that, his eyes were blue.

Angelo took Duane's call and listened to his report. "That means the victim isn't local, or at least isn't in the hospital's database. If he is a local, he isn't a blood donor and hasn't been injured seriously enough to require medical attention. I guess we do it the hard way, knocking on doors, talking to people, and hoping we catch a break."

"That's where I'm going now, back to the Water Street neighborhood," said Duane. "Beth is meeting me there. We'll divide up the work."

"Good," replied Angelo. "I'm about to interview Chris Lloyd, and after that Sam Picken. Let's get together at four this afternoon to compare notes."

Chris Lloyd arrived a few minutes later. Angelo waved him into the conference room at the sheriff's office and felt apologetic about its appearance. It could accommodate eight without crowding, ten in a pinch, and was standard government issue—the eyesore pale green walls that brand and degrade government offices everywhere, fluorescent lights, a ceiling fan, and cheaply framed photographs of the president of the United States and the governor of Virginia. *Oh well, it is what it is. I'll have to add some personal touches to give it warmth and character when things settle down, but for now we have more important things to worry about than the office décor.*

Angelo greeted Chris as a friend. "I'd like to spend some time with you, and I look forward to getting to know you and Sam. I'm afraid we'll have to defer that though. There's urgency to this investigation because we need to find Ivy. Do you mind if we jump right in?"

"Not at all. You've got your priorities in exactly the right place."

"Thanks. Let's begin with this: How well do you know Ivy?"

"She was already here when Sam and I moved to Woodstock a decade ago. We started seeing her almost immediately as she took her daily walks. She always smiled and said hello, and we did too."

"Did you ever get to know her more closely than that?"

"No, not really. Sam did because she helped her with a legal matter. They became friends, as I told you yesterday. Sort of friends, anyway. But we never saw her socially. My relationship with her continued to be one of exchanging pleasantries when we saw each other on the street."

"Who are Ivy's other friends in town?"

"Just George Johnson, as far as I know. You'll want to talk to George. He's an art consultant and has a small gallery. He and Ivy had a business relationship and seemed to genuinely like each other. George called me out of concern when Ivy missed their last monthly meeting, and that's what triggered my asking Chief Betterman to see if he could find her."

"Did she ever get into any trouble, as far as you know?"

"No, not at all. Frank would know better than I, but I'm sure he would have told me if there was anything there. She was a model citizen."

"Did she have any enemies, or people who might want to hurt her?"

"I can't imagine it. She's a peaceful and private person. Of course, no one here knows her very well. I suppose it's possible she has a dark side we don't know about."

"Thanks. That's all I need for now. I'll get back to you if I think of anything else."

Angelo barely had time to refill his coffee cup before Sam arrived. She was attractive in a plain sort of way, with straight brown hair pulled back in a ponytail and freckles she had long since accepted and now wore as marks of distinction. She bore the facial lines and features of someone who's content and aging well. It registered with Angelo that she and Chris must have a happy marriage.

"I'm Sam Picken," she said, extending her hand. "Welcome to Woodstock. We're glad to have you here. Sorry it's been a rough start."

"Good to meet you, and thanks for the welcome." Angelo poured Sam a cup of coffee and said, "I understand you're one of the few real friends Ivy has around here."

"Yes, I think that's right. She came to me for legal help several years ago. She wouldn't say much at first, but I told her I couldn't help her if she didn't confide in me. She understood that in principle but still found it hard to talk about herself. She got there eventually, and it became easier once she came to trust that I was on her side and wouldn't use anything she said to hurt her. She told me a lot, a lot for her anyway. More, I suspect, than she's told anyone else around here. I grew very fond of her."

"Apparently, you haven't shared what she told you with anybody?"

"No."

"Not even Chris?"

"No. I told Ivy I wouldn't disclose what she told me, and I've honored that. Chris knows I would tell him anything I could, and he respects my privacy enough not to put me in a difficult situation by asking."

"Good for you both." Along with their apparently happy marriage, Chris and Sam got high marks for integrity. There was little question one had a lot to do with the other. "Are you willing to disclose what she told you now?"

"Yes, within limits. But only because her life may be at risk. If she's still alive, that is."

"I'll keep things as general as I can," said Angelo, "and nothing you tell me will become public unless it needs to. Let's start with this. Ivy is unusually secretive. Do you know why?"

"She was a victim of human trafficking. Instead of being given a job and an education, as she and her mother were promised, she spent almost ten years doing forced labor and prostitution. This was in the Los Angeles area."

"Jesus God," whistled Angelo.

"To say nothing of the physical abuse she suffered. Some truly bad people took advantage of her mother's trust. They lied to her, knowing she would do anything to help her daughter. They were pure evil. It's little wonder Ivy has trust issues. Anyone with her background would."

"That explains an awful lot. What can you tell me about her legal problem?"

"She believed she was being stalked."

"Was she? I heard you made the case go away. How did that happen?"

"There was a young Filipino man who was watching her. She caught him at it twice when she was taking her daily rest outside the Café, and another time he was hanging around her house."

"Did he ever approach her or attempt to communicate with her?"

"No, but she had good reason to be concerned. Her human trafficking captor, a man named Jaime Roxas, was Filipino and very vindictive. She knew he would never stop looking for her and would kill her if he found her. There isn't a Filipino community in Woodstock, so she thought it was more than a coincidence when a Filipino man showed up and seemed to be watching her. She believed he was connected to Roxas."

"How did you stop it?"

"I didn't. Chief Betterman did. I asked him to stake out Ivy's house for a couple of days. The stalker showed up the first night, and Frank brought him in."

"And?"

"He admitted he wasn't from this area. He said he was passing through and saw Ivy on the street. He thought maybe she was his sister, who he hadn't seen for years. He decided to hang around for a few days to watch her and try to figure out if she really was his sister."

"That's lame. Why didn't he just ask her? Does Ivy have a brother?"

"It was ridiculous, and no, she doesn't." Sam paused for a sip of her coffee. "Frank thought he was just a screwed-up kid, so he gave him the hard-ass treatment and scared him half to death. Told him to leave town and if he ever showed up here again, he'd be looking at serious jail time. No one saw him after that."

Sam tried to hide her look of disapproval, but Angelo caught it. "I take it you didn't agree with Chief Betterman's handling of the matter. Was any connection established between the young man and Roxas?"

"No, none that we could figure out. I never completely ruled it out, though. From what Ivy told me, Roxas was a very bad dude. She was right to be afraid of him. There were many stories about him cutting people up with a Filipino butterfly knife that he carried around. And the people he worked for, who went by the name of Brown, had the resources to track her down. Even across the country, she wasn't safe. She never will be."

Sam hesitated, then added, "I don't mean to be critical of Frank. He's a good man, and he's done a fine job as our police chief. I don't know what I would have done in his place. It's hard to argue with the way he handled it since the stalker never returned."

"But?"

"But things aren't always as they seem. Roxas had a clear motive for harming Ivy. He had tracked down runaways in the past, including Ivy, and punished them severely. He never used the knife on Ivy, but he busted up her leg with a baseball bat when she tried to escape once before. My instincts tell me he was involved in whatever happened at her house. Maybe I'm too close to her, but I just can't imagine anyone else wanting to hurt her."

Angelo nodded thoughtfully. "Here's my problem with that, Sam. Even if Roxas, or maybe the Browns, sent that young man here, he's never come back. Maybe they've given up—or maybe, as I think more likely, the attempt on Ivy was someone else's doing."

"Or maybe they haven't given up. Maybe they just got smarter. The stalker got caught, so they wouldn't send him again. If you were in their shoes, would you send another Filipino into a non-Filipino community, or would you send someone who looks more like you and me?"

"That's a fair point." Angelo recalled Chris saying Sam had been a prosecutor in her earlier life, and her investigative instincts and familiarity with criminal enterprises were evident. She and Chris were class acts. He would enjoy getting to know them. "Just a few more questions. Is Ivy Villanueva her real name?"

"I doubt it, but I didn't ask. To me, she's Ivy Villanueva."

"Do you know how she happened to come to Woodstock?"

"She slipped out of the Browns' house somehow and hitched a ride at a nearby CVS. The man was coming to Woodstock. She wanted to get as far away as she could and rode the entire way."

"Did she tell you who the man is?"

"No. I don't have the impression she knows him or has seen him since the ride."

"Final question. Has she said anything to you recently about being afraid or having feelings of particular concern?"

"Nothing specific, no. But she is wary, as I am. She doesn't believe she'll ever be clear of Roxas or the Browns."

"With that in mind, has she made any preparations to protect herself in her home? Could she defend herself if she had to?"

"She's an artist. She has strong hands. She knows how to use a palette knife, although that's not a very sturdy weapon. But to answer your question directly, no. With only one good leg, she wouldn't have much of a chance."

CHAPTER NINETEEN

The Investigation (May 2022)

Angelo studied his team as they gathered in his office to discuss their respective findings. He was getting to know something of their personal lives as well as their work habits and capabilities. In both respects, it was a patchwork bunch.

Duane was the most solid member of the team, a smart and serious police officer who, out of instinct and need, Angelo was coming to trust deeply. Duane's only weakness was his lack of experience in dealing with homicides and other violent crimes. Angelo chuckled as he acknowledged the same weakness in himself, except for the Worthy case, which was purely providential. Perhaps because of his serious nature and complete dedication to his job, Duane had never married and didn't seem inclined to pursue a social life. The one exception was his passion for bingo—unless a work emergency got in the way, he played every Wednesday night at the fire station in Toms Brook. Angelo thought that odd but harmless; he was glad to have Duane and grateful to Chief Betterman for detailing him to the team.

Beth Lasker remained a question mark. She was a deputy sheriff with a good record, and her observations at their last meeting showed a curious and active mind. Angelo's hesitation was due to her long service and evident loyalty to his predecessor, Sheriff Beamer. That wouldn't be an issue except Angelo's gut told him there was history between Beamer and Scott

O'Hanlon. Angelo would have to see whose side Beth came down on. She would have to earn his trust. She evidently felt the same way, because she seemed determined not to show Angelo anything of her private side. The standoff didn't affect her performance, but it was uncomfortable. At some point, as he got to know Frank better, Angelo would try to learn what went down between Beamer and O'Hanlon.

Finally, there was Frank. He was an unofficial team member. He didn't actively work the case, but he came to meetings out of loyalty and concern for Ivy and the town he had served for so long. His participation, insights, and local knowledge were invariably helpful, and Angelo was glad to have him. Frank was a team player, and, despite an initial wariness, Angelo did not feel threatened by him. In fact, he enjoyed Frank's company, largely because of their shared fondness for bourbon and murder mysteries. They were both devotees of Louise Penny and her wonderful lead character, Inspector Armand Gamache.

Angelo had no complaint with his team except that it was way too small to handle a case like this, particularly if the investigation was to spread to California, as Sam Picken clearly thought it should. They would need serious cooperation from law enforcement organizations in faraway communities.

"OK, what have we got? Duane, you've eliminated the dairy farmer as a suspect. That's a start. What did you learn from talking to Ivy's neighbors?"

"Beth and I covered the neighbors in a two-block radius of Ivy's house. We got the usual—no one saw or heard anything. People go to bed early around here, and whatever happened that night wasn't loud enough to wake them."

Beth jumped in. "There was one exception. I talked to an elderly woman, a Mrs. Billings, who lives two doors down from Ivy. She was watching a rerun of *NCIS* and heard some noise outside her house after midnight. She said it was a thumping noise, like someone falling or running into a wall. Then a buzzing sound about forty-five minutes later. She said it sounded like a swarm of bees."

Angelo was listening intently. "No screams? Did she go outside?"

"No screams. She was too afraid to go outside. She double-checked that her door was locked. Then she turned down the TV and closed the blinds.

She tried to look through them but didn't see anything. She showed me exactly where she was watching from. You couldn't see Ivy's house from there."

"Anything else?"

"She saw a car turn onto Water Street maybe twenty minutes later. It could have come from Ivy's house, but she wasn't sure."

"Did she see a license plate? Could she identify the car?"

"Just that it looked dark, and she thought it was an SUV. That's not very helpful because there aren't any streetlights in that area, and all cars would have looked dark."

"Not much, but something," Angelo said. "Thanks, Beth."

Frank was puzzled and frustrated. "How the hell could there have been a fight as violent as this one had to be, and a body hauled out of the house and presumably dumped into a car, and no one saw or heard anything?"

Everyone sat quietly for a moment, trying to put the little bits of information into something meaningful. But there wasn't enough there.

Angelo broke the silence. "Let's write down what we know and use that to develop some working assumptions. I'll go first. The blood at the scene was AB negative and came from a male. It wasn't Ivy's. I can't get myself to see how she could have been there and not shed any blood. I think we need to assume, for present purposes, that she wasn't there."

"That seems reasonable," replied Frank. "But it opens a whole new can of worms. If she wasn't at her own house after midnight, where the hell was she? She's a quiet person who never goes anywhere. If she wasn't there, she must have been given a warning, or else someone got her out of there ahead of time. But who? When? Why? Where is she now?"

"Those are all valid questions. Duane, you look like you want to add something. Go ahead."

"Thanks, boss. I just wanted to add to the list of what we know. There was blood on the palette knife. There were prints on it, too, prints other than Ivy's. We haven't been able to identify them, but I think we have to assume the palette knife was one of the weapons used that night. It couldn't have been the only weapon, though; palette knives aren't very substantial and would be unlikely to have done this kind of damage. Besides, whoever came here wouldn't have come unarmed. This wasn't a social call."

Angelo nodded, still thinking about Duane calling him boss. "Right. So why was the palette knife used at all? Was it an expedient because it happened to be there? Or was someone trying to frame Ivy?"

"I don't know," said Duane, "but knives, including the palette knife, were clearly the weapons used. No one heard gunshots; there was a small hole in the window screen at the back of the living room which could have been made by a bullet, but we took a good look around and couldn't find any bullets in the room. No shell casings, either, but of course those would have been outside if a shot was fired through the window."

"Also, and I guess this is stating the obvious," said Beth, "there's no indication that robbery was the motive. Or sex, for that matter."

Frank nodded and moved to a new subject. "I keep thinking about the paintings in that room. Do you think they were paintings of different men, or were they all the same man?" Grunts, nods, shrugs—the jury of four was split right down the middle. "For what it's worth, I think they were the same man, and she was using different paintings to show him at different stages and in different attitudes. If that's right, Ivy seemed to have a fixation with him. I wonder who he is and whether he has anything to do with this."

"That's an excellent thought, Frank," said Angelo. "I can tell the rest of you don't know any more about art than I do. Maybe George Johnson can help. He's at an art show in Miami right now, but I have an appointment to see him when he gets back."

"One other thing for the list," said Duane. "There was no body in the house, even though someone was badly injured. Whoever removed the body had to be very strong. Or else there were two of them."

"OK, here's what I'm writing down as our working assumptions. First, Ivy wasn't there during the fight. Second, the palette knife was used as a weapon, and one or more other knives probably were too. Third, guns don't seem to have been a factor. Fourth, the motive didn't involve money or sex, at least not directly. Fifth, there were two or possibly three people involved; if there were only two, one of them had to be strong enough to carry the other." He looked at his list thoughtfully and put a shorthand version of it on the whiteboard. "Anything else?"

The room was quiet. "I have one more thing," said Angelo. "You need to know this to do your jobs, but it was told to me in confidence, and I expect all of us to honor that confidence." He told the team about Ivy's years as a human trafficking victim, and Jaime Roxas and the Browns, and the likelihood Roxas would try to track Ivy down and do her harm. There was a stunned silence, accompanied by looks of horror.

Finally, Frank spoke. "That poor woman. I remember the creep who was stalking her. I thought he was just a punk and scared him off, but obviously, I didn't dig deep enough."

"That was then, and this is now," Angelo replied. "He may or may not have had anything to do with this. But there are two things we need to do now. Beth, see if you can track down Roxas or the Browns, who would have lived at the same address in Los Angeles fifteen or twenty years ago. There's probably little chance of finding them, but we need to try."

"On it." Beth was crisp, clear, and businesslike. Angelo responded in kind. "Thanks." Turning to Duane, he said, "We're going to need a list of everyone who's new around town, let's say people who have been here six months or less. We need to know who they are and what they're doing here. They may be working for Roxas or the Browns. They may have come to hurt Ivy."

"Got it, boss," said Duane. Boss again, Angelo thought. He liked it. "Here's a head start," Duane continued. "The dairy farm hired a guy recently for some part-time work. He hasn't been here long."

"Any connection between him and Ivy?"

"The person I talked to saw him waving to her once or twice when she was getting home from her daily walk. And she waved back."

"That's interesting. Got a description? Or a name?"

"Blond hair. Medium height. His name was Bart."

CHAPTER TWENTY

Laura (2007)

Laura Marcus didn't need to work. Someone in her ancestry—her great-grandfather, maybe?—had invented the bobby pin after World War I and made a fortune. It was enough for the family to coast, quite comfortably, for generations. But that wasn't the Marcus way. When it was his turn at the trough, Laura's father accepted his sizable share, said thank you very much, and quadrupled it through wise investments.

Laura's ambitions took her in a different direction. She wanted to be a trial lawyer. After law school at Yale, she clerked for the Second Circuit Court of Appeals and then the Supreme Court. When the United States invaded Iraq in 2003, she put her intention to be a prosecutor on hold and joined the army. She despised what Saddam Hussein had done to the Iraqi people and wanted to contribute to ending his regime. She was highly decorated for her work as a sniper in Baghdad and Fallujah but became disillusioned when the United States didn't leave Iraq after Saddam's fall from power. She left the army when her service commitment ended.

Upon her return to New York and the law, Laura walked quickly past the long line of big-name firms bidding for her services and into the arms of Crowell LLP. Her choice wasn't dictated by money or prestige—she already had plenty of both. What she wanted was the culture, the commitment to diversity, and the innovative and winning litigation practice for which Crowell was known. She never regretted her decision.

Laura was almost a year into the job when her favorite partner, John McGoohan, asked if she'd be willing to help him out on a pro bono project. "You know I'd never say no to you, Gooey," Laura said, "but just for a moment, just for the sake of pretending I might have a choice, tell me what it's about."

McGoohan didn't blink at her use of his nickname. People had called him Mags for as long as he could remember, and those closer to him sometimes used the more affectionate Gooey. He was fond of Laura and welcomed the familiarity.

"We'll be representing an up-and-coming painter named Pablo Ingersoll. I haven't met him—that will happen next week—but I'm told he's a rising star with a dedicated following. Will you be able to join us Tuesday at three p.m.?"

Laura made a quick entry in her phone. "It's on the calendar. What's the case about?"

"We'll have to hear what he has to say. This is a referral from a friend of mine who collects Pablo's work. It seems Pablo's behind on something he promised a gallery in New Jersey. He told my friend the gallery's been hectoring him and threatening a lawsuit. My friend suggested he talk to me."

"Did he actually use the word hectoring?"

"It's a legal term. You passed the bar exam—you should know it." Mags liked flirting with Laura; he could do it endlessly. "Anyway, the case doesn't sound too complicated, whatever it is. I'd like you to take the lead and make it go away without our having to put too much time into it. Think you can handle that?"

"I can. And I will because you'll hector me if I don't."

When Pablo arrived the following Tuesday, he was shown into a conference room, offered coffee or a soda, and told that Mr. McGoohan would be there presently. He took a moment to admire this small slice of a world he did not know: the stunning city view, which extended west down 57th Street to the Hudson River, the ash-blond conference table and credenza that quietly rejected the stuffiness of the old-line firms, the wonderful *Burning Elegy* lithograph by Robert Motherwell.

Pablo had just taken a seat when Mags arrived and greeted him. Laura entered the room seconds later and stopped momentarily as her eyes met his. *For a guy his age, he's gorgeous,* she thought, taking in his playful dark eyes and neatly trimmed blond hair that was losing its battle with gray. *He's very fit for someone who sits around on his ass painting all day.*

The playful dark eyes reciprocated her interest. *This is one beautiful woman. Her face and features are stunning, very classic. I would like to paint her.*

Mags stayed long enough for pleasantries and to hear Pablo recount his situation with the gallery, but he excused himself at the earliest opportunity to get back to billable work. "I'll keep an eye on things," he said, shaking Pablo's hand, "but I won't be needed much. Laura is as good a lawyer as there is. I almost feel sorry for the gallery owner."

With some difficulty, Laura and Pablo resisted the magnetic force between them and focused on the case. She asked a few questions to be sure she had the facts right, then sat quietly for a moment, looking down at her notes. Pablo watched her and wondered what she was thinking when she finally spoke.

"I'm going to give you my legal analysis. This is bullshit. The gallery owner doesn't have a leg to stand on. He's just bullying you, and he's probably enjoying it. With your permission, I'd like to take him off the grid."

"I like the sound of that. Do whatever you think is best."

Laura sent the gallery owner a letter that turned him every which way but loose. It was professional, firm, and left no doubt about what the gallery would face if it didn't cease and desist from hectoring—yes, she did say hectoring—Pablo. Neither she nor Pablo heard from him again. No bluster, not even a whimper. Like all bullies, he turned and ran when confronted by someone with equal power.

Laura had learned in Iraq to remain motionless after taking the kill shot until she determined the target had been neutralized. She waited three weeks after sending her letter, decided the gallery owner was gone for good, and called Pablo. "I think we can declare victory on this one. It was a pleasure to work with you."

She played it as cool as she could, and Pablo responded as she hoped he would. "That's great news! Can we meet for a drink to celebrate? I'd like to thank you in person."

"I'd enjoy that very much," Laura said. They agreed to meet the following evening at a bar Pablo suggested in Chelsea. He was already there when Laura arrived. He had secured a table by the second-floor window that overlooked the West Side Highway and the river beyond. The leather furniture was comfortable and subtle, as was the music from the piano in the corner of the spacious room. Everything about the place was designed to highlight the artwork that graced the walls and quietly showcased the artists who were showing in the outstanding galleries on the streets below.

Pablo and Laura ordered drinks and quickly fell into a conversation that was easy and warm. The time interval had not diminished their initial attraction, and now they were free of the constraints of a lawyer-client relationship. As they inevitably drifted closer to personal matters, Laura said, "I must confess I've been reading up on you and looking at some of your work. All for professional reasons, of course, so I could represent you as effectively as possible."

"I'm not offended. I might have studied up a little on you too."

"Your paintings are very good. If I'm not being too intrusive, why do you only paint one woman, and only her face?"

"I've always been drawn to painting faces. I find them fascinating. The woman I paint is my wife, Sally Sullivan. There are infinite variations in the landscape of her face. I enjoy trying to capture them. It makes my painting personal, and I like to think that makes it better."

"Do you ever paint other women?"

"Funny, I was asked that by someone in London a couple of years ago. She gave me a commission to paint another woman, and she instructed me to paint her in the style of the great Alexej von Jawlensky."

"That raises so many questions. Who is the woman? Why Jawlensky? Why did you accept the commission? Have you found it difficult to stray from your wife?"

Pablo looked up sharply and decided to give Laura's final question an innocent read. "She only said that the woman is important to her, and that she admires Jawlensky's work. I accepted the commission because the money is generous and will provide a steady income. It relieves the pressure, sort of like an author being freed from having to write dime novels under a pen name to make a living while working on *The Great Gatsby*. And, I suppose, I was curious to see what my reaction would be to straying from my wife, as you put it. It's still a work in progress. I'll let you know how it goes."

"If you find you're comfortable with painting other women, maybe you'll agree to paint me one day. Maybe I'll be your *Gatsby.*"

"Maybe. I've always thought my *Gatsby* would be Sally."

Pablo did love Sally Sullivan. But Laura Marcus was in his head.

CHAPTER TWENTY-ONE

The *Lydia* Painting (2006-08)

Pablo studied the photograph of Lydia. She looked to be in her mid-sixties. Short white hair rimmed her angular face. She had the confidence to look straight at the camera with blue eyes that were unafraid. The lines in her face gave evidence of past battles, and the turn at the corner of her mouth betrayed the satisfaction of having won most of them. Her face conveyed strength, and that was what Pablo wanted his painting to show as her essential quality.

Jawlensky was a favorite, and Pablo knew his work well. He wanted to know it better, though, and he researched the artist more broadly and studied his work more deeply. Ann had said the painting wouldn't be in the public domain; nevertheless, Pablo knew it had to be good. He knew he could never compete with the Russian master, but for Ann's sake and his own, the work had to stand up. He wanted it to be mistaken for a real Jawlensky and not be dismissed as a cheap imitation.

Pablo's favorite Jawlensky paintings were from his later years, when he concentrated on large heads with faces that were essentially reduced to geometric forms. They typically featured a vertical line down the center that served as a nose and two simple slits or arcs for eyes. Pablo wanted to paint Lydia in that style, but Ann's instruction that she be recognizable as Lydia effectively precluded it. He painted her with the open eyes of earlier Jawlensky portraits but kept her features simple and geometric, and he laid on the texture and splotches of color that were Jawlensky trademarks.

He did a more than creditable job. Ann was delighted with the result. She hung the painting in the center of a wall she had cleared in the great room of her London home. Above the painting and stretching well beyond its width was the title, *Important Women in My Life*. The size and scale suggested there would be four more paintings, two on either side. The words, *Lydia, My Teacher,* were etched on a tasteful acrylic label below the painting.

The painting of Lydia and the wall on which it hung were the backdrop for a small dinner party Ann hosted for the art crowd in 2008. The select group of museum curators, major gallery owners, and art critics in attendance knew only that Ann had an important announcement to make. They didn't know what it was, and they didn't know about the painting. Neither did Lydia Tomlinson, the guest of honor.

The excitement about the painting grew with the arrival of each new guest.

"What a marvelous painting."

"I didn't know Ann Merriman had a Jawlensky."

"It can't be a Jawlensky—I know his work well, and I've never seen this piece."

"Maybe it was recently discovered. It must be a Jawlensky—there's no mistaking the geometry and the use of color."

"Surely a work of this quality and importance can't have been unknown."

Ann was thrilled as she listened to the buzz. It was exactly the reaction she had hoped for. "Ladies and gentlemen," she said, clinking her glass. "I'm sorry to interrupt, and I'm even sorrier to tell you that, regrettably, this is not a Jawlensky. I'm flattered, and I know the artist would be, that you think the work good enough to raise the question."

There was a murmur of disappointment among the dinner guests. "Nevertheless, the work is extraordinary," one of them said. "Who is the artist?"

"I'm afraid I can't tell you that," Ann replied. "The anonymity of the artist is an important part of what I hope to accomplish with this painting and others to come. With your permission, I'd like to tell you about the project that begins with this unveiling. I call the project *Imagine*."

The room fell into respectful and expectant silence. Ann went on.

"First, I'd like to introduce my friend and greatest teacher, Lydia Tomlinson. Many of you will have recognized her as the woman in the painting. Lydia was the president and CEO of Ashford Global when I worked there many years ago, and we subsequently served together on two public company boards. She taught me about leadership, compassion, curiosity, and the importance of always being prepared. I honor her by making her the centerpiece of my project."

Ann and Lydia looked at each other with heartfelt warmth. There was an unaccustomed mist in their eyes.

"Alexej von Jawlensky is a favorite of Lydia's, as he is of mine. He could not have made this painting because Lydia was still a young girl when he died. But this is the painting he would have made of her had the timing of their lives been more coincident. It is a tribute to one of the greatest women of our generation to have her memorialized by one of the greatest painters of any generation. The fact that it is not a real Jawlensky is unimportant to the proposition *Imagine* seeks to advance.

"The reality is that greatness transcends time. It transcends gender. Tom Brokaw wrote a book called *The Greatest Generation*. It was a wonderful book, and the people in the generation he wrote about, his father's generation, deserved to be honored. *Imagine* has a different focus. It doesn't compare generations, but rather pulls out the greatest from different generations and treats them as contemporaries. It strives to shine a light on the unfair underrepresentation of women in our historic assessments of greatness.

"As you look at the wall behind me, you will notice that there is room for four more paintings. I will add a painting every two years. Each will be of an important woman whose achievements or qualities have challenged me to be better. As with *Lydia*, each will appear to be the work of a great artist I admire and see as a fitting complement to the woman in the painting. In ten years, I expect to be in partnership with one of the outstanding museums represented here tonight. I will donate the five paintings to that museum, which will house them in a space devoted exclusively to great women and great artists and their 'interaction' with each other. The museum will carry *Imagine* forward by commissioning paintings of great women by great artists for a minimum of ten additional years. Those women and artists will be chosen by a panel on which the museum and I will agree.

"My hope, quite obviously, is that *Imagine* will shine a spotlight on women whose qualities and accomplishments make them truly important. The increased attention *Imagine* brings them would be achieved not only by their public recognition, but also by their linkage to leading artists, living or dead. I believe the common greatness of the women and the artists, underscored by their 'interaction' with each other, will be inescapable."

The room was deathly quiet as Ann returned to her seat. Was the initiative that big a flop? She was in agony. She had put so much into this. Then the applause started, and grew, as the guests rose to their feet, one by one, until the entire room was standing in enthusiastic approval. Finally, Ann felt the soothing hand of relief and vindication. She had to call Pablo and let him know. It was his work that had made this possible.

Elated by Ann's report, Pablo called Laura Marcus at his first opportunity. He gave her the news and asked her to meet for a drink. Two hours later, they were back at the bar in Chelsea.

"I've learned something from all of this," Pablo said. "I *can* paint women other than my wife. I've just done it, successfully. More importantly, I loved it."

"And?" Laura asked, having a pretty good idea where this was going.

"I want to paint you." Pablo said it without apology or embarrassment. Only hunger.

CHAPTER TWENTY-TWO

Laura and Pablo (2008)

They met the following evening at Laura's condominium in the East Village. Her family's wealth liberated her from the constraints of a law firm salary, and she enjoyed a three-bedroom spread with a view of the East River. She liked a contemporary feel and an absence of clutter, and her apartment reflected her taste.

The kitchen and dining area were small, but Laura didn't care because she didn't like to cook and seldom ate at home. The living room was out of Roche Bobois and very comfortable. Laura occupied the largest of the bedrooms and and used the next largest as an office and library. The remaining bedroom was given over to various weights and exercise equipment; she had considered making it a guest room, but she didn't want to encourage family visits and valued fitness more than family in any event.

Laura's anticipation of her evening with Pablo peaked when the doorman rang to say he was downstairs. As he was buzzed up, she realized she had no idea what to expect—after all, she had never been painted before—but she did know she was eager to see him.

"Hey," she said, welcoming Pablo into her home. He was in blue jeans and a polo shirt. He carried a camera.

"Hey," he replied. "It's good to see you. I figured it was OK to come casual since this is a working session."

"That's great. I didn't make dinner, but I can offer you tortilla chips with salsa and a nice cabernet."

"Perfect." Pablo sat down as Laura emptied a bag of chips into a bowl and opened a Col Solare cab from Washington state.

"I'm surprised at your gear," Laura said, pouring the wine into two Riedel tumblers. "I thought you were a painter, not a photographer."

"I am, but it will be a while before I start to paint." He sniffed, swirled, and tasted the wine she handed him. "This is very nice, I must say. Your place is very nice too." He looked around appreciatively, then raised his wineglass to Laura. "Cheers. Let me tell you how this will go. It's important for me to know my subject well before I paint. That enables me, hopefully, to capture certain character and personality traits that I can use to create depth and feeling in my work. I also like to take photographs, lots of them, so that I have images of my subject from various angles, images that will be with me in my studio when I do begin to paint."

"Just how well do you need to know your subject before you begin?" Laura teased.

Pablo smiled. "Let's not get ahead of ourselves. As you know, I have had one primary subject through my years of painting. I know her very well."

Laura admired his frankness but didn't respond. Pablo broke the awkward silence. "I brought the camera to take a few preliminary photographs. Mostly, I want to talk to you, tonight and for several additional sessions after tonight. I want to know who you are—what you like and don't like, who you're close to, how you think about work, and God, and things that matter, what causes you would fight for, your travel and wine preferences, those sorts of things. Only when I really know you will I be able to paint you."

"OK. I'm in."

"I propose that we meet every Wednesday evening, except, of course, when work obligations get in the way. Can we do it here?"

"Sure. I'm putting it in my calendar. Hump days with Pablo. My place at seven."

He just smiled and shook his head. "Grab your wine and give me a tour. Let's see what's the best place for me to take some photos."

As they stood, she turned to him, cocked her head, and said, "Are you really all business all the time?"

"No. I'm done with business." He placed his index finger under her chin and gently guided her mouth to his. Their kiss was fresh and tender. Tantalizing. An amuse-bouche.

"Let's start the tour in the bedroom," Laura said, taking Pablo's hand.

"If you think that's necessary," parried Pablo.

"The evidence suggests it would be a good place to begin," countered Laura. "Besides, it will be the highlight of the tour. We may as well start at the top."

Their lovemaking was frantic, that first time, because their want was urgent. They both knew there would be other times, many of them, when they could explore in depth the nooks and nuances that slipped by undiscovered in their frenzied rush to make their separate imaginings a single reality. Afterwards, Laura lay on her side, caressed and sheltered by Pablo's long arm. Her head was on his chest, and she smiled as his heartbeat slowed, gradually yielding to a relaxed and contented calm. "I think I'm going to enjoy Wednesdays," she said.

"So am I," whispered Pablo, gently stroking her hair. But the elephant was in the room, and he knew he had to acknowledge it.

"I'll never leave Sally."

"I'll never ask you to."

"Wednesdays then?"

"Wednesdays."

CHAPTER TWENTY-THREE

The Investigation (May 2022)

Angelo called the team together. He had a feeling he was having too many meetings, that he should let his people do their work, but he wanted to know what progress had been made and where things stood. He promised himself he would keep the meeting short.

"Let's start with the scientific stuff. Duane, you had pegged Saturday, May 14, as the date of the crime. Have we been able to confirm that?"

"Affirmative. I got the medical examiner to go to the house. It wasn't easy because he's an old fart, and he kept saying his job is to examine dead bodies, not bloody walls. He told me to find a body and he'd be right over. I finally took the low road and said I'd buy him a beer, then he said OK, he'd take a look. He assessed how the blood had dried and concluded the bleeding occurred the night of May 14, possibly early morning on May 15."

"OK, that's a step forward. Any developments on the prints on the palette knife?"

"Nope. Sorry."

"Is there anything else we need to do at the house? We should take one last look around, take more photographs if we need to, but after that, I'm inclined to release it as a crime scene."

"I'd hold up on that, Angelo, and I'll tell you why," drawled Frank. "I've got two concerns. One is that hole in the window screen. We can't rule out a gun until we know what made that hole. We should take another hard look around to see if we can find a bullet or any shell casings. But even if we don't, it doesn't prove a gun wasn't used. What if someone shot the victim through the screen and the bullet lodged in the victim's body? We can't know one way or the other until we find the victim, or the body. If that's what happened, it explains why there's no bullet in the house."

Beth wasn't buying it, not all of it anyway. "Wait a minute. There's too much blood in that place for a simple shooting. Even if the victim was shot, there had to be substantial knife wounds as well."

"Maybe. Probably." Angelo was trying to square Frank's legitimate theory with Beth's legitimate observation. "Frank's right that we can't release the crime scene yet. Let's think about what he said. If the victim was shot and the bullet left the house lodged in his body, we can't prove or disprove the use of a gun without finding the victim. The best we can do is eliminate the possibility that there's a bullet somewhere in the house, or a shell casing outside, and we just missed it. We need to take another hard look. Will you take that on, Duane?"

"Sure, boss."

"Thanks." Angelo grunted. "This thing is getting harder rather than easier. You said you had two concerns, Frank. What's the other one?"

"I'm afraid this is going to make things harder still. We didn't find any bone fragments in the house, but we weren't looking for them. There was no reason to. But I keep thinking about what that neighbor lady, Mrs. Billings, said about hearing a buzzing sound. Let's assume the victim was killed, either by gun or knife, it doesn't matter. What if the killer had a bone saw and cut the victim's body up? That could have been the buzzing Mrs. Billings heard. It also could explain, at least partly, all the blood in the room and why it was splattered all over the place. And if the victim's body was cut up, the killer could easily have removed it by himself. Just bring in two or three trash bags and take the body out in pieces. A couple of trips and he's done."

"Jesus, Frank." Angelo didn't usually swear, but this was a gruesome possibility that made sense in a lot of ways and couldn't be dismissed. "Duane, when you go to the house to look for bullets, look for bone fragments too."

No one knew what to say. They hated the fact that Frank's hypothesis was more plausible than any other scenario they could come up with. And they wondered who the people at the house were, and what they had to do with Ivy.

Beth was feeling snarky. "Just to close the loop, Frank, Mrs. Billings also said she heard a thumping noise before she heard the buzzing noise. Do you have a theory about what caused that?"

"Well, the furniture had been thrown around. That tends to make noise, and it's my theory for what Mrs. Billings said she heard." Frank was testy. Beth had gotten to him. They were all frustrated and on edge.

"Let's move on," Angelo said, looking for a way to return to productivity. He hoped the exchange between Beth and Frank wasn't a sign of friction between the sheriff's office and the police department. They didn't have time for that. "Beth, have you had any luck trying to track down Jaime Roxas or the Browns?"

"Not much, sorry to say. I'm afraid the Browns are a dry hole. Brown is one of the most common names in the United States, and we don't even have first names to work with. And Brown almost certainly isn't their real name anyway. There's just nowhere to go with that."

"I'm sure you're right, but damn! And Jaime Roxas?"

"When you go on Facebook and into the search world, there are at least fifty people named Jaime Roxas. We found four who were Filipino and lived in the Los Angeles area fifteen years ago. One was a florist, one a computer programmer, one a doctor, and one a retired lawyer. None of them fits the profile of the Roxas we're looking for."

"Tell me something good, please."

"I'm getting to that," said Beth. "We were able to get some help from the cyber unit at LAPD. They found a posting on the dark web that might have come from Roxas. It was a reward notice, several years old, for information leading to the location of a Filipina woman. The photo accompanying the notice could have been a younger version of Ivy, before she was all beat up."

"Bingo!" shouted Angelo. "Let's track him down and pick him up."

"Can't do that," said Beth. "One of the reasons people use the dark web is that it protects their identity. We're not going to be able to get the sender's identity, at least not without going to court. And I don't think—"

Angelo cut her off. "We don't have time to go to court. To say nothing of resources. Could you tell if there were any responses to the reward notice?"

"There were not. No online responses, anyway."

"Well, at least we know someone out there, almost certainly Jaime Roxas, is looking for Ivy. That moves him way up on the list of persons of interest. Looks like Sam Picken was right to believe he was involved in whatever happened at Ivy's house."

Frank muttered under his breath, "I hope the sonofabitch is AB negative."

Angelo looked at him. "Why?"

"Because that would mean he's dead."

Frank rarely showed emotion, and no one knew what to say. Angelo quickly turned the page. "Duane, did you track Bart down and talk to him?"

"I tried. He quit his job at the dairy farm. He didn't give notice or anything. Didn't collect his pay. He just left, and nobody's seen him since."

"When was that?"

"His last day was Friday, May 13. The last workday before all hell broke loose at Ivy's house."

CHAPTER TWENTY-FOUR

Pablo, Sally, and Ann (2008)

Pablo was still savoring the success of *Lydia* when Ann called. "I'll be in New York on business next week," she said. "I'd like to take you and Sally to dinner if you're agreeable to renewing our arrangement for another year."

"I am, and we'd enjoy that very much."

"Good. Meet me at Jean Georges on Wednesday at eight. Be prepared to talk business. I'll see you then." She hung up.

Pablo was disappointed that he would miss his Wednesday evening with Laura, but it had to be done. He knew Laura would be disappointed too, but she would understand. That was one of the many things he liked about Laura—and Sally, for that matter. They gave him room. If something came up, they accepted it, probably because they had busy lives of their own and could easily find something else to do.

"Boo-hoo," said Laura when Pablo called to explain. "I'll miss seeing you, but it's probably a good thing. I have a trial starting the following Monday, a patent infringement case in Boston, and I can use the extra time to prepare. I'll have to cancel for the Wednesday of that week and possibly the following Wednesday as well. Sorry."

"See you whenever. This is going to be a long three weeks. Good luck with your trial."

"Good luck with your dinner. I'll be interested to hear who you'll be painting next. After me, of course."

"Of course."

As Pablo thought about Ann's call and what lay ahead, he was grateful their arrangement gave him two years before his next painting was due. He was very busy right now. He had another solo show coming up at Stockbridge in three months and was still two paintings short of what was needed for that show. He had framed out the first of those paintings. It would be Sally in drag, with a wry, come-hither smile breaking at the edge of her mouth. He was amused as he thought about it, knowing Sally would be less amused. He would have to make his final painting something that honored her by conveying her generosity and enjoyment of life.

Sally was also very busy. She had a group show at a gallery in Chelsea the following month. She painted in a distinctive style that had notes of Dubuffet and Penck but was more colorful. Her following was regional but dedicated; her work didn't command Pablo's prices, but it generally sold out.

Pablo and Sally were both in the business of making and selling art, but they were mutually supportive and not at all competitive with each other. They worked hard and didn't allow for distractions when a show was coming up and they were on deadline. The one exception was Ann Merriman. Her commissions gave them an important cushion. If she was coming to town and wanted to have dinner so she could hand Pablo another $100,000, they would be there. Italian, Chinese, pizza—it didn't matter. They would be there.

And this was Jean Georges! Pablo donned his Zegna sport coat and Eton shirt, Sally slipped into a simple black outfit from Jil Sander, and they hopped on the subway to Central Park West. Their spirits were soaring as they entered the high-ceilinged temple of culinary bliss. The décor was modern and tasteful, with free-standing tables and banquettes set in pastels, a palette of grays, beiges, and whites with an occasional accent wall of light or dark brown. The tall white drapes were drawn at night to cover the large windows and provide a sense of intimacy, and a simple but sprawling metal chandelier graced the ceiling.

Sally and Pablo greeted Ann at a nice corner table, and three glasses of

Dom Ruinart champagne magically appeared. "Congratulations in person for your excellent work in creating *Lydia*," Ann said, raising her glass. "The work was extremely well-received. As you know, it is the cornerstone of my Project *Imagine*, which seeks to remedy the underappreciation of the accomplishments of women on the world stage. It does that by exhibiting paintings of women I consider important, paintings that appear to have been done by some of the world's leading artists, in this case Lydia Tomlinson by Jawlensky. I intend the project to be taken over and carried on by an important museum in ten years' time. I'm pleased to say I've had some expressions of serious interest since the unveiling."

"What a fantastic idea!" Sally raised her glass to toast Ann and wish the project success.

"It was your painting that gave *Imagine* the launch it needed, Pablo. There were serious art people at the event, and many of them were convinced that *Lydia* was the real thing: an undiscovered Jawlensky."

Pablo gave it the old aw shucks smile, and said, "I really enjoyed doing it. I look forward to my next assignment."

"That's a nice segue to the reason for this dinner. But first, let's enjoy the egg toast. It's one of the chef's specialties and absolutely to die for."

The server placed before each of them a small, delicious-looking rectangular sandwich of toasted brioche with three egg yolks as the filling and a generous dollop of caviar on top. Sally loved to cook and was mystified that the yolks held their shape; she was curious to know what possible preparation could work that miracle. Pablo just dug in. Biting down through the layers of caviar, brioche, and egg yolks was a life-altering experience.

"Good?" asked Ann, knowing full well what the answer would be.

"Unbelievable," grinned Pablo, pointing upward towards heaven.

"Unreal," said Sally. "This is an extraordinary treat. Thank you, Ann."

"Right," replied Ann. "I thought you'd like it. Well then, to the business at hand."

They paused for a moment to allow the server to present them with another Jean Georges specialty, black bass *en croute*. It was accompanied by a delightful Chassagne Montrachet which Ann sniffed, tasted, and unhesitatingly approved. She then turned to Pablo.

"For your next effort, you will be Vincent van Gogh." Ann handed him a photograph. "You will paint this woman. Her name is Claire."

Pablo looked at the photograph and smiled. "I know who this is, and I know just what I want to do with the painting. I can't wait to get started."

CHAPTER TWENTY-FIVE

The *Claire* Painting (2008-10)

Pablo looked at the photograph with admiration. Claire Shanahan was amazing. The most famous American woman astronaut since Sally Ride, she was a test pilot in the Air Force, had commanded a space shuttle mission, and had taught physics at Stanford. She currently served as the administrator of NASA and was widely credited with turning the agency around. She was mentioned in some quarters as a long-shot vice presidential candidate. Not bad for an Irish lass whose parents moved to the States from Derry in 1962 to escape the Troubles.

The photo was a three-quarter shot, undoubtedly set up to show Claire looking up and away, toward the heavens. A good look for a NASA administrator and former astronaut. Her chestnut hair was shoulder length and framed a face dominated by clear eyes, a strong jaw, and a smile that was friendly but determined. It was a face that invited you in but drew a line: *I'll work with you, but don't mess with me.*

Pablo thought back to the van Goghs he had seen in Paris many years before. He knew exactly what he wanted to do. He would channel van Gogh's self-portrait and make Claire's face as expressionless as he could without giving away the determination that was her calling card. She would be looking toward the heavens, quite literally, because the background would be alive with the motion of van Gogh's swirling *Starry Night.* Pablo worked hard to do the artist justice and was pleased with the result. The painting was a tour de force.

Two years after the unveiling of *Lydia* and the announcement of *Imagine*, Ann Merriman brought the London art crowd together again at her London home. The van Gogh painting of Claire Shanahan was hanging on the wall, right next to *Lydia*, and was accompanied by a tasteful acrylic label with the words, *Claire, My Inspiration*. Ann stood before it and quieted her dinner guests.

"Friends," she said, "we had a lot of fun with the Jawlensky two years ago, but now you're on to me. You know this isn't a real van Gogh, though I daresay you might think it was if I hadn't given the secret away. I'm sure you'll agree that it's a marvelous painting and a fitting tribute to our guest of honor tonight, the remarkable Claire Shanahan."

Claire stood, smiled, and nodded in appreciation of Ann's warm introduction.

"Claire's achievements have been extraordinary. She would have been a clear choice to be part of *Imagine* in any event, but my admiration for her escalated when I had the privilege of spending time with her at Stanford. She was teaching physics, and I was giving a guest lecture at the Stanford Arts Institute. We chanced to have dinner one night, and I was deeply impressed by what she had done and the strength of her commitment to do more. She has a unique combination of humility, approachability, and determination. Our friendship has continued and flourished, to my enormous delight and honor."

Claire smiled again, put her hands together as if in prayer, and gently bowed her head to Ann and her guests.

"I won't take much more of your time," continued Ann, "but I have a thought I want to share with you about the rationale that undergirds Project *Imagine*. How many of you know who Dr. Gachet is?"

Virtually every hand in the room shot up.

"Of course you do. Everyone in the art world knows of Dr. Gachet. He was a doctor in Arles with whom van Gogh resided following his stay in an asylum. In gratitude, van Gogh painted the famous *Portrait of Dr. Gachet*, which sold at auction in 1990 for 82.5 million dollars. It was the most expensive painting in the world at the time. Now let me ask you this: How many of you would know who Dr. Gachet is if it weren't for the painting?"

No hands were raised.

"That's the power of a van Gogh. That's the recognition it gives. Many of you, perhaps all of you, would know who Claire Shanahan is without the painting behind me. But think how many more will know her because van Gogh painted her, and that work will be available for the public to view at one of the outstanding museums represented here tonight.

"Just one final point, an update really. I'm pleased to report that several of you have expressed interest in Project *Imagine* and have asked for meetings to discuss the terms under which your museums would be willing to take it on. I am eager to begin those discussions and will be in touch with you soon. Thank you, very much, for coming tonight."

After the guests left, Ann poured herself a glass of whiskey. She had once preferred a single malt from Scotland, Lagavulin in particular, but she had spent time in the United States and had acquired a taste for bourbon, Blanton's in particular. She took a deep sip and sat back on her chaise. Then she called Pablo.

"You did it again," she said quietly. She could almost hear his smile. "I'm so pleased, and so committed to this project, that I'm going to increase the amount of your commission. We will meet soon to talk about the next painting, for which I intend to pay you one hundred twenty-five thousand dollars. The commission will increase by twenty-five thousand dollars for each painting thereafter."

"I don't know what to say, Ann. That is way beyond generous. Thank you."

He walked into Sally's studio to tell her. He brought two glasses of champagne. They laughed and hugged and sipped champagne, then laughed and hugged again.

Then Pablo went to his own studio to call Laura.

CHAPTER TWENTY-SIX

Pablo and Laura (2008-12)

The affair was comfortable and uncomplicated. Pablo and Laura had both had lovers before, but there was a physical connection between them, a familiarity, a talent for pleasing each other sexually that neither had experienced with anyone else. That was an important part of why they kept coming back for more, but it was by no means all of it. They genuinely enjoyed each other's company, in and out of bed.

With Sally, the common interest in art and artists was a unifying force. With Laura, it was the opposite. In their many, many Wednesdays of talking, as Pablo sought to know Laura well so he could capture her essence when he painted her, he became fascinated with different aspects of her life. Her growing up wealthy, her ambivalence toward her family, her time in Iraq, her experience at the Olympics, her being a lawyer—he wanted to know about it all. She had lived a life so different from his; he was enthralled by those differences and wanted to understand what it was like to be Laura, why she had made some of the choices that shaped her life.

The reverse was also true, even though Pablo's reluctance to talk about himself made the conversations about growing up on a farm and spending a life making art more abbreviated. Still, he said enough for Laura to see that he trusted her, that he gave up more of himself to her than to anyone else except Sally. She liked that he didn't care what anyone thought of him other than

Sally and her. She knew it was a strange and wildly unconventional notion, but she admired his fidelity. For Pablo, there were only the two of them. He wanted no one else.

The strength of their relationship was the truth of what Pablo and Laura had said to each other that first night. He would never leave Sally, and she would never ask him to. That made it easy for Pablo. But what of Sally? And Laura, for that matter? They each knew of the other woman in Pablo's life.

Sally hadn't known it initially. She knew, of course, that Pablo was being harassed by a gallery owner in New Jersey back in 2007. She knew Pablo was represented by a "very beautiful" lawyer named Laura Marcus. She knew Pablo had drinks with Laura to thank her when she made the case go away. She knew because Pablo told her. She knew in 2008 that Laura had asked Pablo to paint her, and that he had agreed. She knew he would be away on that assignment on most Wednesday nights for the foreseeable future. Pablo had told her that too.

Perhaps alarm bells should have gone off, but Sally knew Pablo's recent experience making a serious painting of a woman other than herself, when he did *Lydia,* had set him free to paint other women, and Laura just happened to be the first of those women. Sally was happy for him: she had no claim and no desire to be the only subject of his paintings. The arrangement seemed purely business. She knew Pablo loved her.

The arrangement went on, seemingly a little longer than such an arrangement should, then clearly too long, with no evidence of the painting he was supposedly working on. Perhaps Sally should have stepped in, asked to see the painting, asked to meet Laura. But she didn't. She loved Pablo and knew he loved her. Then it was too late. She knew in her heart that Pablo was having an affair with Laura. She accepted it. They had a good marriage, and Pablo was with her six days a week. He was a good man. She didn't want to lose him.

Laura had told Pablo she would never ask him to leave Sally, and she meant it. But she could have been forgiven, as their relationship intensified, for wanting more of him, for changing her mind. It would have been the natural reaction. She adored Pablo, looked forward to seeing him, and was happy when they were together. But she had a life apart from him, a demanding job she loved, an ambition to be the best at what she did, a desire for independence, and negative memories of a short marriage years earlier.

Jonah was a good man and remained a friend, but he and Laura had been terrible together. He was wealthy and charming, a confirmed member of the country club set. He lacked Laura's drive, and neither understood nor accepted her desire for space. He stifled her, and she left him after three months of marriage. She vowed never to marry again. She wanted a lover, a friend, someone she cared about and who cared about her, but someone who respected her desire to pursue her own ambitions and interests. Pablo was perfect. And so was Sally; she was what made Pablo perfect.

Laura's one frustration was that Pablo still had not painted her. His exclusive bond to Sally had been severed when he did *Lydia* in 2008, and shortly thereafter he had agreed to paint Laura. They had talked, made love, and talked some more as he sought to know Laura in order to paint her. That took time. And he had been busy with other paintings to meet deadlines for various shows. Then he had devoted himself to becoming van Gogh and painting *Claire*. Laura had been occupied with trials, general work demands, and a series of personal ventures that included climbing Mt. Kilimanjaro and running several marathons. The painting of Laura kept being put off.

Pablo took photographs of Laura—lots of them. The affair went on, and the years went by. Laura became a partner at her law firm in 2011 and celebrated in 2012 by moving from the East Village to a fabulous three-bedroom condominium on Park Avenue near 79th Street. The new building had its own gym, so Laura used the third bedroom as a studio for Pablo. He had been working to finish his third commission for Ann; when that was done, conditions would be perfect for him to paint Laura. Finally.

But he didn't. He couldn't.

CHAPTER TWENTY-SEVEN

Angelo (May 2022)

It had been another long day with little progress. Angelo didn't look forward to his spartan room at the Comfort Inn, but he needed a change of scenery. He was getting up to leave his office when the phone rang. He heard Frank's unmistakable drawl.

"Care to spend a couple of hours with another bachelor? I know you like bourbon, and I'm buying."

"Sure, Frank. That sounds great. But I haven't seen too many great bars in town. Where does one go to get a bourbon around here?"

"In this case, one goes to my house." Frank gave Angelo his address. "I have a selection that I believe will satisfy your requirements. If you're ready to go, I'll see you there shortly."

Fifteen minutes later, Angelo pulled his F-150 into the driveway of a one-story brick duplex with a well-tended yard. It was in a development of identical duplexes that the builder had believed, correctly, would appeal to older couples who were looking to downsize after their children had left home. The development was affectionately referred to around Woodstock as Wrinkle City.

Frank met Angelo at the door and welcomed him into his tidy home. "I moved here six years ago after my wife died. Cancer. I liked the larger place we lived in for twenty years, but there were too many memories there. This is much less to take care of, yet big enough for my three grandchildren when they visit. It's all I need."

"I can see why you like it," Angelo said, looking around appreciatively. "And I can assure you it's far more enjoyable than my room at the Comfort Inn. Thanks for having me."

"My pleasure. I'm glad to have a chance to get to know you better. Now let's choose a bourbon and have a seat."

From an impressive array of fifteen or eighteen bourbons, Angelo chose a Noah's Mill. Frank opted for a Henry McKenna. It was a splendid Shenandoah Valley evening, and they sat outside on the deck.

They spent an hour or so on the basics: Frank had grown up near Woodstock, married a local girl he knew from Central High School, had a couple of daughters, tried working in Washington, DC for the better pay but hated the commute and missed the Valley, loved to hunt and fish, started an appliance repair business but didn't like the management end of it, and ultimately stumbled into law enforcement, where he found his true calling. Angelo was born to a first-generation Italian family who lived outside of Roanoke, went to Old Dominion University where he was the starting quarterback, couldn't decide what to do after college and kicked the can down the road by going to business school at UVA; then at the last minute, with an offer in hand from Chase, he couldn't face the prospect of living in New York and surprised his family and everyone else he knew by taking a deputy sheriff job in rural Bath County.

Frank poured them each another bourbon. "How are you getting along with Beth?" he asked. "I sense some aloofness between you. Not hostility, more like wait and see."

"You're perceptive. I'm not sure what it is. It's not personal, not from my end anyway. We were both loyal to our former bosses, and I think it has something to do with that. Was there a problem between them, do you know?"

"I never knew Scott O'Hanlon, but I knew of him through Jim Beamer. I knew Beamer very well, of course. We worked alongside each other in this small community for many years. He was a wonderful guy who inspired great loyalty among his subordinates, including Beth. He was a real go-getter in his younger years but dropped off quite a bit as he got older. Started taking shortcuts and enjoying the good life, from what I could tell."

"How did he and Scott know each other? What went down between them?"

"Jim was originally from Bath County. He and Scott were deputies together, and best friends as I understand it, in their younger years. It didn't sit well with Jim when Scott got the sheriff's job down there. He left, moved to Shenandoah County, and ultimately became sheriff here. You'd think that would have squared things between them, but it was clear, to me at least, that Jim still held a grudge."

Angelo reflected on that. Scott had hinted at the possibility of corruption when he spoke about Jim Beamer. Frank's account made no mention of anything that would explain that reference. Angelo decided to put out a little more line. "That seems like old news and small potatoes, Frank. There must have been more to it."

"There was. I don't know the specifics, and whatever I do know I know from Jim, so you need to take that into account in evaluating what I'm about to tell you."

"Fair enough."

Frank shifted position in his chair, took a sip of Henry McKenna, and waded in. "There was a situation that brought Jim and Scott back together seven or eight years ago. Scott was investigating a former executive at the Homestead for embezzlement. It was a serious amount of money, hundreds of thousands of dollars as I recall. The guy had moved to Shenandoah County, had a big house on the river, and was living a lifestyle that was way more than his job here could support. Scott asked Jim to help investigate, since this was his jurisdiction, and bring the bastard to justice."

"That all sounds reasonable," said Angelo, aware that he was sounding defensive about Scott.

"Yes, it does, and that was Scott's side of the story as Jim told it to me. But Jim says it was all bullshit, that he investigated the matter, met with the guy at length, and there was nothing there. He told Scott he wouldn't proceed further and wouldn't recommend prosecution. That effectively ended the matter. Scott was furious, according to Jim, and accused him of taking money from the guy to make the investigation go away."

Angelo could picture Scott's reaction. Principle was a part of his DNA. If he thought he had a suspect dead to rights based on the evidence, and suddenly the case was shut down, he would be irate. Angelo could see Scott suspecting a whitewash; after all, he knew his former friend's tendencies, and if the case was as airtight as Scott thought it was, he would have had to believe money had changed hands. That would explain his corruption reference. "And that was it?" Angelo asked, hoping to keep Frank talking, hoping he would provide his take on the matter.

"That was it, except for the shouting," Frank said thoughtfully. "Part of Jim's charm was his openness with the people in his office. He didn't take kindly to Scott's accusations, and I'd be surprised if he didn't talk about the situation with his subordinates and bad-mouth Scott in the process. Beth was there at the time. She would have heard whatever he said, and based on her loyalty to him, she would have believed it."

There was a moment of silence as each man sipped his bourbon and thought about the damage pride and jealousy can cause. Such a waste. Finally, Frank spoke. "Out of curiosity, what did Scott say about the situation at your end?"

"I wasn't there when it happened. I came to the office a couple of years later. But I never heard a word about any of this. I sensed there was something between Scott and Jim, but I never knew what it was."

"I wouldn't worry about Beth," Frank said at length. "She's a good person, and she doesn't suffer from whatever integrity problems Jim might have had. She's wary because of what she heard, but this will all sort itself out as you get to know each other."

"Thanks, Frank. I really appreciate the conversation and the guidance. And, of course, the bourbon. I'd better be going. We have an early morning."

As Angelo got ready for bed—and had a short glass of Elijah Craig, just to compare it to the Noah's Mill—he thought about what Frank had said. He felt better about the situation with Beth. She was smart, and he liked her. More importantly, he was going to need her.

CHAPTER TWENTY-EIGHT

The *Lucy* Painting (2010-12)

Pablo's third commission was Justice Lucy Williams, an African American who had been a civil rights leader before being elected to the House of Representatives by the people of her district in Georgia. In her third term, she led the unsuccessful effort to secure passage of the John Lewis Voting Rights Act. She now sat as the junior member of the United States Supreme Court.

Ann had met Lucy but didn't know her well. That was not disqualifying for inclusion in *Imagine*. Ann's commitment was to selecting women she admired, women who were important to her, and Lucy certainly met that test. Despite her accomplishments, Lucy was still a youngish woman with a raw-boned beauty. Her photo showed dignity, grace, intelligence, and toughness. From the moment Ann gave him the photo, Pablo was eager to paint Lucy.

"I want this to be a painting by Laura Wheeler Waring," Ann had said. "It has a special importance because Lucy is *Imagine's* first woman of color. As I studied the artists who have made significant paintings of women, the portrayals of African American women that most resonated with me were made by African Americans. That led me first to Amy Sherald, but I find her official portrait of Michelle Obama too staid and regal for what I have in mind for Lucy. I think Waring is a perfect choice."

"I totally agree," said Pablo, nodding and smiling.

"You know Waring's work?" Ann was impressed.

"I do. When I was at Pratt, I used to go to the Brooklyn Museum. Waring has a piece there. I think it's called *Woman with Bouquet*. It captivated me. I can see in it some of the Manet and Cezanne influences Waring picked up when she lived in Paris. I think she's a great choice for Justice Williams."

Pablo finished the painting in 2012. He was proud of the result. It had energy and movement and displayed the vivid colors, light, and atmosphere that are characteristic of Waring's work. He shipped it to Ann at her London home.

Pablo now had time to paint Laura and no more excuses for not painting her. He wanted to, and he tried to, but something held him back. He knew he could paint women other than Sally, and he found it an enjoyable diversion. But Lydia, Claire, and Lucy were just faces to him. He did not know them. He did not have feelings for them. Laura was different. When he tried to paint her, every brushstroke was an act of love, and betrayal.

Laura observed his painfully slow progress and said, "I guess maybe I'm not your *Gatsby* after all." Pablo dissembled. "You may be. I don't know yet. I want to get it just right. I want the painting to capture all I know and love about you. Producing a *Gatsby* takes a lot of work, and time."

Laura knew better. She had a good idea why Pablo was struggling. She didn't begrudge Sally. And she didn't begrudge Pablo for loving Sally. She just had to be patient and let Pablo work through it. Hopefully—one day—a Pablo Ingersoll painting of Laura Marcus would hang in her living room.

Ann asked Pablo to visit her in London the day after her unveiling of the *Lucy* painting. She didn't want him at the unveiling itself because he was bound to be recognized by some of her dinner guests, and that would start the public speculation that he was the unnamed artist of the *Imagine* works. But she did want him to see the *Lydia, Claire,* and *Lucy* paintings all hanging together. It would give him a better appreciation of the contribution he was making. She also wanted to give him the next photo.

The unveiling went well. Ann stood before the three paintings, the most recent labeled *Lucy, My Conscience,* and introduced an appreciative Justice Williams to her guests. Then she teased the art crowd, asking if any of the gathered guests could identify the artist.

There was a low murmur, accompanied by some evident confusion and head shaking. Finally, the art critic for the *New York Times* spoke up. "It looks like a Laura Wheeler Waring."

"It is. Good for you."

Then a representative of the Tate Museum said, "I must say it's a brilliant painting and captures Justice Williams beautifully. But I had understood that one of the purposes of your project is to enhance the reputation of the chosen women by having them painted by some of the world's greatest artists. Waring is a fine painter, but she's not in the same league as Jawlensky and van Gogh."

"That's a fair point, and I initially went back and forth about choosing her," Ann responded. "But think about it. Waring is not recognized as being in their league, but maybe in other circumstances she would be. If her work is on a wall next to a Jawlensky and a van Gogh, as part of a project that claims to feature important women painted by leading artists, it will significantly advance her reputation. So as a side benefit, *Imagine* will not only boost the reputation of some strong women but also the reputation of some outstanding African American painters. The challenge lies in the balance between the acknowledged great artists and the lesser-known ones. That balance must heavily favor the acknowledged greats if we are to achieve our goals. I assure you that you will recognize the painter who does the fourth painting, which we will unveil two years from now."

Ann's explanation made sense and satisfied the art crowd. The evening ended on an upbeat note. She kicked off her shoes and poured herself a Blanton's. She looked forward to seeing Pablo in the morning.

Pablo rang the doorbell at ten on the dot. Ann showed him into the living room. He had not seen *Lydia* and *Claire* for four years and two years, respectively, and he loved, loved, loved seeing them again, hanging side by side with each other and with *Lucy*. They stood up well and looked beautiful together. Ann's curator, a fit young man named Barry Thomas whom Ann had hired to assist with *Imagine* and its coming transition to a museum, had done a masterful job with the presentation. Pablo was gratified, and proud.

Over tea, Ann told Pablo about the previous night's unveiling. He was not surprised that including a painting by Laura Wheeler Waring had sparked some mild controversy and was pleased to hear that it had been put to rest in a positive way. He personally thought Waring was top-notch and felt that having her as part of the project sent all the right messages.

Then Ann handed Pablo an envelope. "This is a photograph of Christina. She is a fitting subject for Picasso."

"I'm in, but can we narrow it down?" said Pablo. "Which Picasso? The blue period? The cubist? The rose period? The…."

"The Picasso who painted the *Portrait of Dora Maar*."

"That's one of my favorites. I'll enjoy this one immensely."

Then Pablo opened the envelope and looked at the photo. Christina was the most beautiful woman he had ever seen. The painting of Laura would have to wait a little longer.

CHAPTER TWENTY-NINE

Jaime (2012)

As he began his second term, President Obama implemented a series of initiatives to combat human trafficking. He convened a White House forum on the subject. He declared a national human trafficking month. He pushed out statistics to demonstrate the scope and horror of the problem. He encouraged the American people to say something if they saw something.

Jaime Roxas followed the reports in the media and chuckled. He wasn't worried. Obama's programs might make a small dent, but nothing more. The human trafficking business was too big, too profitable, and too deep underground. It would never be stopped, so long as the people in the business were careful.

Unfortunately, Jaime hadn't been careful enough. Stellie had escaped on his watch. He hadn't been able to find her. Five years, and she was still out there somewhere. One of these days, she would talk. She would name names, give addresses. She couldn't stop human trafficking, but she could bring the operation run by the Browns and Jaime to a standstill. He had to find her.

The dark web wasn't working. It had produced only one result, in 2010. Jaime had been tending to other business when the call came in. When he checked his messages, he heard a voice say, "If you're the person who's offering a reward, I think I'm on to something. I'll give you the details when we talk. I'll call you at nine tomorrow morning. Filipino Freddie."

But at nine the next morning, Filipino Freddie couldn't call. He was being interrogated and run out of town by Chief Frank Betterman of Woodstock, Virginia. He had never been in trouble before and was scared to death. He decided the reward money wasn't worth it and threw away his burner phone. Jaime never heard from him again.

Jaime tried calling back but got no answer. He wasn't surprised—by now, the burner phone would be in a dumpster or sewer somewhere. There was no way to track Filipino Freddie. A golden opportunity missed. Jaime fell back on his mother tongue to invoke the ultimate Tagalog expression of frustration, despair, and disgust. Then in English, he added, "Shit, shit, shit, shit, shit!"

Jaime did the only thing he could think of: he increased the amount of the reward. He had done that once before, and with the current increase, the reward stood at $40,000. That was serious money. He hoped it would talk.

There was one other thing Jaime had learned from Stellie's escape. He wasn't sending a tough enough message. He busted up Stellie's leg when she had escaped once before, but it wasn't the deterrent he intended. Painful though the punishment was, it didn't stop Stellie from running away again. He needed to get the attention of the other captives. It wouldn't bring Stellie back, but it would sure as hell serve notice to those who remained.

The unfortunate victim of Jaime's new get-tough policy was a sweet young girl named Consuela Flores. She had fallen under the spell of a john named Ben. Prostitutes aren't supposed to let feelings interfere with their work, Jaime had told them that again and again, but it happens. Ben was smitten too. Over time, his sessions with Consuela evolved from sexual function to deep emotion. They fell in love. He promised to get her out of there so they could have a life together.

It was a brazen and dangerous idea. Ben was a trusted regular, and he and Consuela were typically assigned a "special" room on the first floor of the Browns' house. One night, they slipped out the window, crossed the lawn, jumped a fence, and drove away in Ben's Dodge Charger to an apartment he had rented a mile away. Jaime put the word out to his informants about the Charger, and it was easily spotted. Jaime showed up at the apartment the following morning.

"Good morning, Ben. You've taken something that doesn't belong to you. I want it back."

"Are you talking about Consuela? She doesn't belong to you, man. She wants to be here, with me. I intend to pay for her, to buy her out. What would you consider a fair price?"

Jaime smiled and shook his head. "You just don't get it, do you, Bobo ka?" The *balisong* was in his hand. A couple of flicks of his wrist and it was open, ready for use. And then it was in Ben's chest. A few deft strokes, and Ben sported a Colombian necktie.

Then Jaime turned to a screaming, sobbing, and flailing Consuela. He lifted the *balisong* and went for her eyes.

The captives in the Brown household quickly learned what had happened. No one tried to escape after that. But Stellie was still out there.

CHAPTER THIRTY

Jaime and Mrs. Brown (2012)

It was a long call by Mrs. Brown's standards. She wanted a report on the operation, but mostly she wanted to know if there was any progress in finding Stellie.

"Business is profitable," said Jaime. "The workforce is stable, and we're seeing record earnings. The clothing side is booming, but the real money is in the extracurricular activities. We have a strong group right now."

"And Stellie?"

"Nothing to report, I'm afraid. I had that one call I told you about a couple of years ago. That's been our best chance so far. The guy must have gotten cold feet. Either that or he realized his information was bad. In any case, I never heard from him again and couldn't track him down. The reward's up to forty thousand now. I'm sure something will turn up soon."

"I've been hearing that from you for several years, Jaime, and we've got nothing. I must tell you I'm disappointed. I depended on you to be better than this. The business is at risk. I've made some decisions."

Jaime didn't like the sound of that. He waited apprehensively for whatever was coming next.

"I haven't been in Los Angeles much lately, particularly since my husband died. I don't have any reason to keep the house there. And with Stellie on the loose and getting more comfortable with her freedom each day, the risk of having that house is too great. If she decides to talk, and she will eventually, she'll provide the address, and the authorities will be there in a heartbeat. The cops will find you, and you can lead them to me. I can't risk that."

Jaime jumped in. "I would never—"

"I've sold the house. You have two weeks to vacate and get the operation moved. I've rented a warehouse in Long Beach. It's suitable for you to live in, to house the girls, to set up the clothing business, and to run the rest of the operation. It should be a moneymaker since it's near a major port and not far from one of the country's busiest international airports." She gave him the address. "You'll pay the rent from the proceeds of the business. I expect you to make this work, Jaime. And I expect you to find Stellie."

That was bad, but at least he still had a job. "Where will you be?" Jaime asked.

"You don't need to know that. I'll check in with you as needed, and we'll be able to communicate electronically, as we do now."

"What if I need to call you?"

"You can call a special number I've reserved just for you." She gave him the number. Area code 202. Washington, DC.

CHAPTER THIRTY-ONE

Ivy (May 17, 2022)

Ivy was worried. It was Tuesday, her fifth morning at the barn. She continued to enjoy the scenery and the solitude, but she was fretting about Bart. When he dropped her off, he said he would visit her every day. He did come the first two days, but he had missed the last two. She wasn't worried about food, not yet anyway. Bart had left her an ample supply. She could get by for at least another week.

She had placed her trust in Bart. When he came to her house and said, "We've got to go," she went without hesitation. That was uncharacteristic; she had been guarded and wary of strangers since her experience with Jaime. She surprised herself by leaving with Bart, who was, for all intents and purposes, a total stranger. But there was an uncommon sincerity about him.

She thought back to their conversation during Bart's second visit to the barn. He stayed for an hour and had coffee with her. She was more open with him than she was with most people. He expressed interest in her paintings.

"They're very good," he said. "We were in a hurry, and I only had a quick glance, but they were stunning. They had depth and richness and showed their subject in different and interesting lights. If you don't mind, I'd like to see them again once this is over. Where did you learn to paint like that?"

"Thanks." Ivy considered whether to say more. The question bordered on the personal and could lead to even more personal follow-up questions, but it was about her art. She didn't have anyone to talk to about that except George, and she had never told him about her paintings. She decided to trust Bart, and went on.

"I just kind of figured it out. Mostly, I do small drawings. That's how I make my living. I sell them to George Johnson, and he sells them at art fairs. The paintings are my passion, though. I like the process of painting, the feeling it gives me. I do the drawings quickly, but I spend a lot of time on the paintings. I work hard to get them just right, so they show a person's character and not just his face."

"Well, they're terrific. Who is George Johnson?"

"He has an art gallery in Woodstock. I've worked with him for about ten years. I like him. He's one of my two real friends in town. Well, three I guess, counting you."

"Thanks. Who's your other friend?"

"Sam Picken, my lawyer. She got me out of a situation once. I trust her, the same way I trust you."

"Tell me about yourself, Ivy. What happened to you?"

That took the conversation over the line. Ivy had to shut it down. "I worked in California before I came to Woodstock. I had a rough time there."

That was it. That was all Ivy was going to give him. Bart began to make his exit.

"I've enjoyed our conversation, Ivy. Just one more question: Who's the man in your paintings?"

"Just some guy. I saw his picture in a magazine."

Shutdown complete.

Bart smiled and rose. "You're a good person, and I'll see you tomorrow." But he didn't see her tomorrow, or the day after.

Where is he? she asked herself as she sat by the window with her morning coffee and engaged the bright red cardinal, who had become a regular visitor. *Something must have happened to him. I know he'd have come if he could. He's been careful and even tender with me, and he looked me in the eye and said he'd come to see me every day. Something must have gone wrong.*

She tried to imagine what that could be. *What was the urgency in getting me out of my house? There was clearly some danger involved in my staying there—Bart said we had to go right away, that my life might depend on it. What did he know? How did he know it? Something was going to happen at my house, and he wanted to get me out of there to protect me. Why? What am I to him? Did he go back to my house after he brought me here? To the danger? Was he hurt or killed? He must have been. Otherwise, he would have come back.*

Her worry about Bart and what might have happened to him turned her thoughts to her own predicament. She didn't have a phone. She didn't want a phone, or a computer for that matter, because of her fear that it would make it easier for Jaime to find her. Now she wished with all her heart she had made a different decision.

Bart's my only communication with the outside world. He's the only one who knows I'm here, wherever here is. If something's happened to him, how am I going to get out of here? When is it safe for me to go? Whatever the danger, I have to go one week from now. That's when I run out of food. I don't know about getting down that ladder with one leg, but I have to. Next Tuesday, if Bart hasn't come back, I'll have my morning coffee, leave a message in case anyone ever comes to this place, throw my crutch down to the barn floor, and go down that ladder however I can. I'll leave the other stuff here for later. There's no way I can take it with me. I'll have to come back for it.

But where will I go? I don't know where I am. It's not far, I know it's not far because it only took us ten minutes to drive here. I can walk that once I get myself pointed in the right direction. It'll be a good walk, but not much longer than my daily walk around town. Maybe someone will see me and help me. But where will I go? I can't go home—it might not be safe yet. I know. I'll find Sam. She'll help me. It's going to be OK.

Where is Bart? He's a good man, a kind man, and he protected me. I couldn't live with myself if he's been hurt because of me.

CHAPTER THIRTY-TWO

The Investigation (May 2022)

"Got any leads on this Bart guy?" Angelo was all business. He had an appointment with George Johnson, now back from the art show in Miami, in an hour. His gut told him it would be an important interview, and he had more preparing to do. He didn't have time for a team meeting, but he wanted to get the latest.

"Not a thing," Duane replied. "He was only at the dairy farm a short time. The people there don't know much about him, other than he served in Afghanistan in some sort of special ops unit. He was looking for permanent work and asked around to see if the other employees knew of any job openings. That's all they could tell me. We found the apartment he was renting and talked to the manager. Bart left with everything he had, which wasn't much, on May 15. He had paid his rent up front and in cash. He left no forwarding address."

"We need to find him. He knew Ivy, and he disappeared the day after the crime. Two coincidences too many. If he left May 15, he wasn't the victim, but he could still be the killer. We need him if we're ever going to know what went down here. It's possible he didn't have anything to do with it, but all my instincts say otherwise."

"Agreed," said Frank, changing the subject. "Did you find any bullets in the house, Duane?"

"No bullets, I'll swear to that. We made a very thorough search. The place is clean." Duane saw the frustration on Angelo's face and continued. "We did take a close look at the hole in the living room window screen. The screen was fairly new and not rusted at all. No evident wear and tear anywhere on it. It could have been a bullet hole. The size is right, and the broken mesh elements are facing inward, indicating that whatever force made the hole came from the outside, pushing in."

"Looks like you might have called that one, Frank." Angelo tipped his cap to Chief Betterman, who nodded without changing expression and said to Duane, "How about bone fragments?"

"That's the big news. We did find what appeared to be very small bone fragments in the center of the room. The area had been vacuumed and stood out from the rest of the room because of that. It was clean. We never would have seen them if we weren't looking for them. Just a few crumbles, sort of like a coarse sea salt. We bagged them and sent them to the lab. We should have the results tomorrow." Duane looked pleased with these findings, as if looking for bone fragments had been his idea. He wasn't one to take credit, though. He was all about the mission—he was pleased because the bone fragments represented progress, however slight. They provided a new avenue of pursuit.

Angelo smiled. "Maybe we finally caught a break."

Frank bored in on Duane. "Let's assume they are bone fragments, and that the killer used a bone saw to cut up the dead body of Mr. AB negative. It's not likely he would have moved the body before using the saw. He would have cut it where it lay, which was where you found the fragments. Where was that in relation to the window with the hole in the screen?"

"Toward the center of the room, but dead in line with the window."

"So the killer could have shot the victim through the window screen, then entered the house to cut him up and carry him out. That would explain why we only found one blood type. There wouldn't have been a fight at all. The source of the blood was the victim being sawed into manageable pieces."

"Let's go with that as our working assumption," said Angelo hurriedly.

"Let's also assume he used a silencer since no one heard gunshots. Good work, Duane, and Frank. Anyone have anything else?"

Silence. "Sorry, but I've got to run. I've got to get to the art gallery to interview George Johnson."

The gallery was just down the street. It was a modest space, but freshly painted and brightly lit to make it seem larger and show off the current exhibition. George was a small man with wavy gray hair, a demure but distinct potbelly, and traces of an Eastern European accent. He greeted Angelo at the door and led him to his small and cluttered office. A quick handshake, and George asked anxiously, "Any word on Ivy?"

"Not yet. We're doing everything we can. We do know the blood at the scene isn't hers, so that's good. But we don't know where she is, or when and why she left her house. Tell me about your relationship with her, and when you last saw her."

"I'm very fond of Ivy," George replied. "I almost said I was fond of her, but I'm going to keep speaking in the present tense until we know she's gone. I refuse to believe she won't show up one of these days with her smile and her backpack full of drawings.

"Sorry for getting sidetracked," he went on. "I've known Ivy for ten years or so. I had seen her around town before then, taking her daily walks, but it was about ten years ago that she showed up at the gallery one day and asked if she could talk to me. I said sure, come on in.

"Then she pulled ten or twelve drawings out of her backpack and showed them to me. I was blown away. I thought she was some poor woman down on her luck who liked to walk around Woodstock. I had no idea she was an artist, and she really is a good artist. I told her I'd buy them all if she was looking to sell them. We agreed on a price of one hundred dollars a drawing. I told her to come back again when she had more drawings to sell. And we sort of fell into a routine where she'd come on the second Friday of each month. She missed our May meeting—that's why I called Chris Lloyd—so I guess the last time I saw her, to talk to anyway, was the second Friday in April."

"Had she ever missed a meeting before?" asked Angelo.

"Never. Not once. That's why I was so concerned."

"Did you try to contact her after she missed the meeting?"

"There was no way to do that. Ivy doesn't have a phone. She says she enjoys her quiet life and doesn't want electronics interfering with it. She just wants to live peacefully, to take her walks and draw."

"What were your meetings with her like? Were they all business? Did you ever get to know her?"

"All business at first. She's very private, as I'm sure you've learned. I would say guarded even. But bit by bit, she became more comfortable with me, and opened up just a crack. I know she grew up in the Philippines, then came to the States to work out west somewhere, southern California, I think. Then she came to Woodstock. I never could get her to tell me why. I wouldn't say we became friends, but we became friendly. We grew to trust each other. I like and admire her very much."

"What do her drawings look like?"

"She's totally self-taught. She doesn't know anything about art, or artists, or the art world. She just likes to draw and has a God-given talent for it. She draws what she sees, some street scenes, but mostly faces of people she sees around town. They're small, tablet-sized, and mostly done in pencil, usually black and white but sometimes in color. Those are the tools she has to work with, a tablet of drawing paper and some pencils. Her work isn't very detailed, more like line drawings. Spare. Clean. She gets great movement and depth out of a single line. Reminds me of the line drawings Matisse made of women's faces for a time. Her work is simple but compelling. Extraordinary, really."

"Did you recognize any of the faces she's drawn?"

"Yes, here, I've kept a few I particularly like. Here are two of Sam Picken. And here's one of me. She gave it to me as a gift."

Angelo didn't know anything about art, but he could see these were good. George had chosen accurate words to describe them—simple, compelling, extraordinary.

George went on. "There were many others I recognized. Some I know, and some I've seen but don't know. There's one of a white-haired man, for example. I've seen him around but don't know him. Ivy drew him with a kind face and a nice smile, driving a car, for some reason.

"Then there were faces I didn't recognize at all. Whoever they are, they aren't Woodstock people. They must be from her past. There were several of a woman I'm guessing is Ivy's mother, at least as she remembers her. There's one of a pleasant-looking, middle-aged woman—no idea who that is. And there's one that particularly stood out because it's out of character for Ivy. Almost all her drawings are positive, because she sees the best in people, but this was a drawing of someone, a man, who looked evil. I had the sense it was more a caricature than a real likeness, almost as if she didn't want a clear record of him. It was so out of character that I asked her who it was. She said something like 'someone I knew once,' but that's all she would say."

Jaime Roxas! It had to be! "Do you still have that drawing?" asked Angelo excitedly. A picture of Roxas, even a caricature, would be a big step forward.

"I'm afraid not. I generally sell Ivy's work in New York, out of a booth at an art fair. She has real talent, but these are small pieces, unframed, by an artist no one has ever heard of. People walk in off the street to look at the art, are struck by these, and buy one as an inexpensive souvenir that will be a conversation piece in the right spot. They pay cash, and I don't keep records. Saves me from having to deal with the IRS."

"What do you sell them for?"

"Two hundred bucks."

"That's a tidy profit, particularly tax free."

"It works for me, and Ivy's happy with the arrangement. I guess you'd say it's a win-win."

"Do you remember who you sold the evil man drawing to? Is there any way to track it down? It could be very important."

"No, unfortunately," said George. "It was years ago, and the buyer was a face in the crowd. I don't even remember if it was a man or a woman. I want to help you find Ivy, but I just don't have a clue."

"If anything comes to you, let me know. Thanks for your time." Angelo shook George's hand and turned to go. Then he stopped.

"Oh, one other thing. Do you know who the man is, or maybe it's several different men, in the paintings at Ivy's house?"

"I've never been to Ivy's house. And I didn't know she did paintings. All I've ever seen were drawings. She never talked about paintings. I'd like to see them, if I could."

"Hop in," Angelo said, motioning George toward his truck. "Let's go over and take a look."

They made the short drive to the Water Street house. The yellow police tape was still up. "This is a crime scene, George. Please don't touch anything. There's a lot of blood around, some of it on the paintings. I'm afraid the place is a mess."

They walked into the living room. George ignored the blood. He was fixated on the paintings. "These are superb," he said. "Truly superb. I had no idea. These are world-class."

"Look at them closely. Five men, or one man?"

"One man," said George. He couldn't take his eyes off the work.

"Do you know who he is?" asked Angelo.

"A well-known artist in New York. His name is Pablo Ingersoll."

CHAPTER THIRTY-THREE

The Investigation (May 2022)

There are many reasons to know about Brooklyn. Angelo's reason was his father. He loved the Brooklyn Dodgers. He loved all the Dodgers from the 1950s—Peewee Reese, Gil Hodges, Duke Snider, Roy Campanella, Don Newcombe, Sandy Koufax—but he especially loved right-fielder Carl Furillo. It was an Italian thing.

Angelo couldn't count the times he had heard his father say, "Did I ever tell you about the time me and Danny Frescobaldi hitchhiked from Roanoke to Brooklyn to see the Dodgers at Ebbets Field? Great game! The Dodgers beat the Phillies in the ninth. One out, and Reese scores from second on a single by Junior Gilliam. But Brooklyn! What a place!" He thought it was a betrayal when the Dodgers moved to Los Angeles in 1958, and he stopped following them.

Now Angelo was in Brooklyn, just across Prospect Park from the old Ebbets Field site. He had called in advance and was promptly buzzed up when he rang the doorbell at a building of loft condominiums in the Park Slope neighborhood. A lively, mid-fiftyish woman with a busy face greeted him, brushing frizzy black-gray hair from her left eye and trying to wipe her hands and clothes free of paint splatters.

"You must be Sheriff Jones. I'm Sally Sullivan. I've been working, and I'm a mess, so I won't shake your hand. Please come in."

"Thank you, ma'am. Please call me Angelo." He pulled out his ID and showed it to her. "Is Mr. Ingersoll available?"

"Yes, of course. He's in his studio. I'll get him. Please have a seat," she said, gesturing toward the living room sofa. "Would you like a soda, or maybe some coffee?"

"Coffee would be great. Just a little milk, please." Angelo looked around the room. Eight paintings adorned the exposed brick walls. They were clearly by two different artists, Pablo and Sally, Angelo supposed. Four were paintings of Sally's face, in different aspects and attitudes; those would be by Pablo. The others, more abstract, were more to Angelo's taste. The styles were quite different, but the paintings coexisted beautifully.

"Angelo, this is my husband, Pablo Ingersoll." The men shook hands. Angelo's quick reaction was that he was indeed the man in Ivy's paintings, but he looked older in person. Ivy had left out the crow's-feet and thickened his hair. He was trending toward a fuller version of the fit image Ivy had depicted.

Sally interrupted his mental comparison of the man before him to the man in the paintings. "I'll get the coffee. Angelo, do you mind if I sit in?"

Slightly embarrassed at having been jolted back to reality, Angelo used his easy smile as an apology. "Thanks, and no, not at all."

Angelo tried to get a read on Pablo while Sally was out of the room. "I'm afraid I don't know much about art, but I like these paintings. Tell me about them." Pablo gave him the three-minute verbal tour. When Sally returned with the coffee and all were served and seated, Pablo and Sally looked at Angelo expectantly. "We're a little mystified," Pablo said. "You're here as part of a murder investigation?"

"Yes. I can't say for sure that there was a murder because we don't have a body, but we do have a lot of blood, and all indications are that someone was killed and the body was removed. This occurred at the home of a local artist in Woodstock, Virginia. She doesn't appear to have been there at the time, and we don't know where she is."

"I can't imagine what this has to do with me, but I'll help if I can." Pablo sipped his coffee and exchanged glances with Sally.

"Thanks, I appreciate that." *No time like the present,* Angelo thought. He put his mind into interrogation mode and looked Pablo in the eye. "Do you know a woman named Ivy Villanueva?"

"No. The name means nothing to me."

"Ivy is the artist I mentioned. She's a poor woman of Filipino descent, very reclusive. I wish I had a picture to show you, but we haven't been able to find one. She does have some distinctive features that might jog your memory. She has a bad scar beneath her left eye, and she walks with a crutch."

"Sounds like she's had some hard luck. But no, I don't know her."

"Have you ever been to Woodstock?"

"Only Woodstock, New York. I didn't know there was a Woodstock, Virginia."

"Does the name George Johnson mean anything to you? He owns an art gallery in Woodstock."

"No, sorry," said Pablo. "I can't see how any of this connects with me. Yet something led you here. What was it?"

"Ivy typically makes small drawings of local scenes and people. George sells her work at art fairs, including New York art fairs. No one knew she made larger paintings, but we found five of them when we went to her house to investigate the crime. They were all paintings of one man, shown in different ways, sort of like what you do with Sally. We asked George if he knew who the man was. He identified you."

Angelo handed Pablo photographs of the five paintings. He watched intently as Pablo studied them and handed them to Sally. "I must say these are good. Very good. I'm flattered. But I'm totally stumped. I don't know the woman. Why is she painting me?"

"That's what we're trying to figure out. Understanding that may be a key to solving this case."

CHAPTER THIRTY-FOUR

The *Christina* Painting (2012-14)

Pablo's schedule was relatively light when he got back from visiting Ann in London, and he immediately turned to his latest commission. He knew the *Portrait of Dora Maar* well, but he pulled it up to study closely as he considered how he would paint Christina to channel Picasso's tribute to the woman who was his lover and muse.

Picasso and Dora Maar met in 1936 and found common ground in their leftist activities and fierce opposition to Franco's efforts to upend Spain's democracy, which led to the Spanish Civil War. A photographer, she memorialized his work on the monumental *Guernica*, perhaps his most famous painting, which graphically denounced the Nazi bombing of the Basque village of the same name. In *The Weeping Woman*, a contemporaneous painting, Picasso attempted to convey the suffering of the people of Guernica through a tormented and sobbing Dora Maar.

Picasso's affair with Dora Maar began while he was still living with Marie-Therese Walter, the mother of his daughter. He seemed to delight in pitting the two women against one another; not surprisingly, his relationship with Dora Maar was tempestuous. It nevertheless endured for nine years, and he often used her as his model during their time together.

In the *Portrait of Dora Maar,* Picasso painted his lover seated in a chair, in a relaxed posture, with long red fingernails, her right arm resting on the arm of the chair, and her right hand touching her cheek. As with many of his paintings, he displayed her face both frontally and in profile, a technique that enabled him to show two aspects of her personality at the same time. It was a strong and thought-provoking piece.

Pablo looked at the photo of Christina. She was reclining slightly, and her easy smile contrasted gleaming white teeth against light brown skin and thick black hair. Her eyes were green, calm, playful, and inviting. *My, my,* Pablo thought, smiling at the photo as if Christina could see his appreciation and welcome his approval. *She is proof of God's perfection. Or at least a demonstration of what two extraordinary sets of genes can produce when they collaborate on a project.*

Pablo's instruction was to paint Christina as Picasso would have, and he would do that. He admired Picasso for his imagination and abstraction, for the breadth and depth of his body of work, for his unparalleled genius. But Pablo knew, as he looked at the *Portrait of Dora Maar,* that he wanted something different for Christina, something more, something to show her beauty not in an abstract way but as a perfect reality, something of his own. What that would be, and how he would accomplish it, was constantly on his mind as he strove to make the Picasso version of Christina so good that it would be mistaken for the real thing.

The *Christina* painting, labeled *Christina, My Courage,* was hung on the left side of the *Imagine* wall in Ann's living room. It more than held its own at the 2014 unveiling. The sighs and gasps were audible as the art crowd gathered around, jockeying for the best viewing position.

"This is the best yet," said one.

"We know it isn't a real Picasso," said another, "though I would have sworn it was."

"I'm not so sure it isn't," said a third. "I can see that little bald-headed bastard rising from his grave, with a sly grin and chewing on a cigar, to paint this as a demonstration of his immortality."

A fourth chuckled. "He just may have. Whoever the real artist is, he—or she—has outdone Picasso."

Ann listened approvingly to the chatter. She loved it. And she had to agree. She found all the paintings Pablo had made for her project amazing, but *Christina* was in a class by itself. Ann stepped to the front of the room and clinked her glass.

"Our guest of honor tonight is Christina Cruz. Unfortunately, she can't be with us. She works undercover and is often on assignment, as she is tonight. I met her once when she was in a difficult situation and was impressed with her bravery in the face of extreme danger. I won't say more because we need to protect those who do right in the shadows as well as those whose work is more visible.

"Our previous honorees have resumes that are public testaments to their greatness. Christina's accomplishments are private. They bespeak a strength of character—standing up for what is right, with courage and quiet humility, without regard for the consequences. Picasso portrays her well in the relaxed alertness of her seated body, the resignation on her face in profile, the defiance in her frontal gaze.

"We talked the last time, in the context of Laura Wheeler Waring, about whether including artists who are less well-known than Jawlensky and van Gogh somehow diminishes or devalues what this project strives to do. We could have the same conversation about the inclusion of lesser-known women, and I would come out at the same place—public recognition is neither the only, nor the most valid, measure of greatness. Christina belongs on this wall.

"Now let me update you on where things stand in our plan to transition *Imagine* to a worthy museum in the next two years. Actually, I have asked my curator, Barry Thomas, to do that. As you know, Barry will go to the museum, along with the paintings, when the time comes. I will miss him dearly. But tonight, in the interest of full disclosure, I must show you another side of Barry before he takes over."

Ann placed a large, framed photograph on the right side of the *Imagine* wall. It showed Barry and Prince Harry in the combat fatigues of the British Army. They were laughing and drinking beer together.

The art crowd roared its approval. Ann couldn't resist adding to the hype. "We could caption this with the words of the American country singer Garth Brooks, 'I've got friends in low places.'" The art crowd cheered.

"Sorry, Barry," Ann said. "Just having a little fun with you. Please come on up."

"No worries, Ann," said the trim young man, patting down his short hair and smiling to show he could take a good ribbing as well as enemy fire. He adjusted his wire-rimmed glasses and approached the mic. "You never know who you'll meet when your father sends you to Sandhurst. Harry's my mate, a fine soldier and a better man." More applause from the crowd. They liked this guy. His knowledge of art was accompanied by an appealing humility and sense of humor.

Barry took a moment to straighten his tie and gather his thoughts. "Now, let me tell you where we are with the transition of the *Imagine* project. Ann and I have been working hard and are now down to a short list of three museums. I will not disclose who they are, but our due diligence shows them all to be well-qualified from both a reputational and financial perspective. We will continue our efforts through a series of interviews with each of the three. I'm confident we will be in a position at the 2016 unveiling to tell you who will carry the project forward as of that date."

Ann rose to speak. "The truth is that Barry's done the lion's share of the work on this. I don't know where this project, or I, would be without him. Thank you all for coming tonight. It's been lovely to see you, and I especially appreciate your very warm reception of the Picasso."

It was time for her customary Blanton's. Ann called Pablo. He was clearly pleased by her report and said all the right things, but he seemed distracted.

CHAPTER THIRTY-FIVE

Annabel's Eyes (2015-16)

Pablo had worked hard on the *Christina* painting. He was proud of the work and pleased by Ann's report of its embrace by the art crowd. But he was glad it was done. Now he could concentrate on his own painting of Christina. He knew it would be different and special; he owed such a beautiful woman his very best effort. He had allowed himself to think Christina might be his *Gatsby*.

When he had first shown Sally the Christina photograph, she reacted as he had. "Ooh, she's unbelievable. Her features are perfect, and so are her colors. Pablo, you have to paint her in your own way, as an Ingersoll, and not just in the manner of someone dictated to you, even if that someone is Picasso."

"I know. I want to, and I'm going to. Do you think I need to ask Ann's permission?"

"Why? Because she gave you a photograph? She told you what to do with it, and you've done that, magnificently I might add. She never said you couldn't do something else with it. The arrangement with Ann is silent on that score."

"I agree. But Ann's been good to us, and I wouldn't want to do anything she might think was underhanded, even if it isn't contractually prohibited."

"Why would she care? It isn't going to cheapen the value of the Picasso

Christina. The public doesn't know you did that work, and anyway, your painting won't look anything like the Picasso version. Ann will see it, of course, and she'll know it's Christina because she's seen the photo, but she's not going to tell anyone. Obviously, you'll have to change the name. You can't call your painting Christina."

"I was thinking of Annabel. Poe's most beautiful poem has been going through my head lately. It puts me in mind of you."

Sally beamed. "How so?"

"Not to interject Browning into a discussion of Poe, but 'let me count the ways.

'...we loved with a love that was more than love, I and my Annabel Lee....
'... can ever dissever my soul from the soul of the beautiful Annabel Lee....
'... my darling—my darling—my life, and my bride....'

"Shall I go on?"

"You goof. I do love you."

"Then it's done. I'm not going to ask Ann. If she said no for some reason, it would complicate things. I'm going to do this painting come hell or high water. I'm going to do it for me, and also for you."

"Better to ask forgiveness than permission," Sally grinned, locking her arms around Pablo's neck.

"Always."

Pablo thought the reclining and seductive pose Christina effected in the photo was perfect, and he adopted it as the framework. There was something about that pose that triggered a memory. *Olympia!* It was Manet's *Olympia* painting he had seen in Paris a decade earlier. Christina's pose wasn't all that Manet brought to *Olympia*, but it captured an essential piece of it.

The pose was Pablo's only reference to the Manet work, that and the flower he placed in her hair. The woman in *Olympia* was a prostitute, and Manet showed her full body, naked, reclining casually on a bed. The photo showed Christina only from the waist up, modestly covered by a top with a scoop neck. Pablo found that more seductive than Olympia's naked body. He wasn't trying to show the indifference of a prostitute, but rather the beauty of an engaged and fully engaging woman.

He achieved that by painting the photo largely as it was. It had struck him with its beauty the instant he saw it, and he didn't want to chance ruining the image by trying to improve on it. Olympia's hair was up. Too business-like. Pablo let Christina's hair flow, as it did in the photograph. He also left out Olympia's earrings and bracelet, which were seen as signs of prostitution when the Manet painting was made, and the thin ribbon tied in a bow around her neck. These were all distractions; Pablo wouldn't chance any diminution of Christina's natural beauty by including them. The biggest changes were in the face. Olympia was unsmiling and expressionless; she bore a slight hint of defiance, maybe even a sneer. Her face said, *I am what I am. I don't care what you do to me. I don't care what you think of me. Come on if you want to. Don't if you don't. I don't care either way.* Christina was smiling, coy, inviting. Her face said, *I'm a beautiful woman. I want you to see that. I care what you think about me. Please be my friend.*

The work went on for weeks, months, a year. Pablo painstakingly did the underpainting, then lovingly did the painting. He was obsessed. He worked on nothing else and thought of little else. When Ann gave him the fifth photo and said, "This is Farah; please paint her as if you were Frida Kahlo," he put it aside. He found reasons to cancel most of his Wednesday nights with Laura. His mind and heart were with Christina, Sally, and their apotheosis in Annabel.

Finally, it was finished. He did some overpainting, adding texture, depth, character. He knew it was a masterpiece, but the eyes weren't quite right. They were magical in the photo. He had to make them better, more alive, in the painting. They were the best part of Christina. He had to make them the best part of Annabel. He worked on the eyes alone for another month. He even flirted briefly with the notion of bringing them to life by somehow affixing human eyelashes to them, but dismissed that as ghoulish. He finally got them just right. They were an impossible green, sparkling and sensitive, defining.

Pablo knew he had done it. He had created something extraordinary, a work that would mark his career. He had written *Gatsby*, at last.

He called the painting *Annabel's Eyes*.

CHAPTER THIRTY-SIX

Laura (2015-16)

Laura was less than enchanted. She didn't like the changes in Pablo and their relationship. She didn't like having so much less of him than she had in their first eight years, with his mind somewhere else on the Wednesdays he didn't cancel.

When he had first shown her the Christina photo, she had been excited for him. It would be a test of his painting skills to create a Picasso. She knew Pablo loved a challenge and was energized by rising to meet it. She was supportive and encouraging. She wasn't a student of art, but of course, she knew of Picasso. Everyone did. She decided to learn more. She read about Picasso. She read about Dora Maar.

As she began to sense a fade in her relationship with Pablo, Laura was struck by the disturbing parallels between her situation and that of Dora Maar. For starters, they each loved a man named Pablo. They each began an affair with their Pablo while he was living with another woman, Marie-Therese Walter in Dora Maar's case and Sally Sullivan in Laura's. Dora Maar's relationship with Pablo Picasso ended after nine years. Laura first noticed the distance in her relationship with Pablo Ingersoll after eight years; it could easily be done after nine.

Still, there were differences, critical differences. Pablo Ingersoll was not Pablo Picasso, not as a painter—he was great but not a genius—but more importantly, not as a man. Picasso was totally self-absorbed and set his two lovers against each other. Her Pablo was not of that ilk. He was a good man who loved both Sally and Laura; he wanted them to understand each other and forgive him for loving them both. Laura decided her Pablo was worth fighting for. He would get through this.

Then the *Christina* painting was finished. Laura was proud of Pablo's accomplishment. She was relieved that things would now return to normal. But they didn't. They got markedly worse. Laura could see that when Pablo told her he would now be doing his own painting of Christina. She could see it when he began to beg off their Wednesday evenings together, often for the flimsiest of reasons. She could see it in his total obsession with his painting, his inability to find interest in what she was doing or engage with her in any meaningful way.

As Pablo told Laura about Annabel and his work on the painting, his satisfaction with her pose, his decision to add a hibiscus to her hair, his difficulty in bringing her eyes to life, Laura could see she had lost him. She had lost him to a painting. He would never paint Laura Marcus. When he proudly told her he had finished *Annabel's Eyes*, she knew it was his *Gatsby*.

Laura loved Pablo, but she had too much going for her, and too much pride, to allow herself to be taken for granted. She did what she had to do. She told Pablo it was over.

CHAPTER THIRTY-SEVEN

The *Farah* Painting (2016-17)

"I'm so, so sorry, Ann." Pablo had been unforgivably late with the *Farah* painting.

"You let me down, Pablo. For the first and only time, you let me down. I had a schedule that was public knowledge. I will suffer a reputational hit for not keeping that schedule. Worse yet, *Imagine* has lost important momentum at the very moment of its transition to a museum."

"I feel badly about that, mostly for letting you down. I have an excuse, but I know it won't fly with anyone but Sally and me. I was working on a project of my own. It was highly personal and terribly important to me. It was all-consuming. I couldn't leave it, even for you. I'm sorry. It's done now, and I won't let this happen again."

"I won't say it's all right, because it isn't. I'll do what I can to calm the waters. We're late with the unveiling, but you did a nice job with the *Farah* painting."

A "nice job"? That was well short of what Ann had said about the other paintings. A gut punch. Still, Pablo guessed he deserved it. He knew he had shortchanged *Farah*. He didn't give it the attention he had given the others. That was mostly because he didn't have the time; all his time was going to *Annabel's Eyes*. It was also because he didn't like Kahlo's work as much as he liked the work of the other painters Ann had asked him to be, and he just couldn't get into it. And, after *Annabel's Eyes*, it was a letdown. He was spent. But a "nice job"? It was better than that. He thought it was passable as a Kahlo even if it wasn't his best work. *Get over it, Pablo*, he said to himself. *Ann's the customer, she's paying you handsomely, you weren't at your best, and you were late. What do you expect? Praise? If anything, Ann was gentler than she had a right to be. Do better next time—if there is a next time.*

The unveiling of the *Farah* painting in 2017 was greeted with murmurs and polite commentary, but no real excitement or enthusiasm. The art crowd could see what Ann saw, and what Pablo had to admit to himself. It was a nice job, but not nearly as good as the others.

Ann clinked her glass and held her head high. "Welcome, friends, and apologies for our tardiness with this unveiling. There were unavoidable complications. These things happen. But our slippage, for which I take full responsibility, should in no way detract from our guest of honor tonight and this wonderful Kahlo painting of her." She looked at the painting and its label, *Farah, My Hope.* Then she looked at the unmistakable subject of the painting, a woman in her late forties with a determined face, a ready smile, and glistening black hair.

"I am so pleased and privileged to introduce tonight's guest of honor," Ann said, "President Farah Rashidi of Barmakistan." The woman rose, smiled, and bowed in appreciation. "Farah's story is one that gives us strength and hope, and many of you already know it. She grew up in a poor family in Iran. Her mother was from Bijar, from people who made village rugs for centuries. Her father was a fisherman in Bandar Abbas. She did well in school and was the first in her family line to attend college.

"While studying at Tabriz University, Farah developed an intense hatred of her government's repressive treatment of women. Her opposition grew over the years following her graduation, as she taught history and culture to Iranian schoolgirls. Believing she could make a difference and determined to try, she began to organize and lead protests that defied compulsory hijab laws. It became a movement, and she became an enemy of the state. She was captured but managed to escape and seek asylum in Barmakistan, a small country that borders Iran but has more enlightened policies. Farah was admired there for the stance she had taken in Iran. Running on a platform of securing equal rights for women, she was elected president of Barmakistan two years ago."

The art crowd stood and applauded heartily, clearly more enthusiastic about the person than the painting. There was no doubt that Farah Rashidi was dynamic and inspirational. Ann thought her presence and her connection with the dinner guests might have saved the day.

Ann called the room back to order. "We now come to a very important part of tonight's meeting. We have made our selection and agreed on terms. I am very pleased to tell you that the Hemphill Museum of New York will be home to *Imagine* for at least the next ten years, and hopefully far longer than that. Barry Thomas will move to New York to carry on his important work as curator of the project. The museum and I have agreed that Barry will also chair the panel that will determine the next five great women and the artists who will paint them. Please join me in congratulating Barry and the Hemphill Museum by giving them both a well-deserved round of applause."

The art crowd was generous. Its constituency had come to know, like, and respect Barry. Ann added a personal note.

"I had harbored a secret and selfish hope that *Imagine* would find its permanent residence in London, where I could and would be a frequent visitor. I have to acknowledge, however, that New York is the center of the art world. That is where the project belongs. I will simply have to increase my visits to that great city.

"Thank you, Farah, for your astonishing work on behalf of women and for taking the time to be with us tonight. Thank you all for coming. I look forward to seeing you in New York at the 2019 unveiling."

Ann retired to her chaise, kicked off her shoes, and poured herself an extra finger of Blanton's.

She did not call Pablo.

CHAPTER THIRTY-EIGHT

The Investigation (May 2022)

The investigation was at a standstill. Everything was slippery, uncertain, elusive. Angelo and his team still didn't have a solid lead. There had almost certainly been a murder, and they didn't even have a body. They desperately needed a toehold. Anything would do at this point.

Angelo wanted updates on the different elements of the investigation. Grasping at straws to find something to build on, he called the group together. What were the lab results on the bone fragments? Had the fingerprints on the palette knife been identified? Any news about Bart, or anyone else who had shown up in Woodstock recently? What other ideas or leads did they have? Of most pressing concern, where the hell was Ivy?

Everyone could feel Angelo's frustration as Frank, Duane, and Beth took their seats. "Bone fragments. Duane?"

"The lab couldn't do much with them. They were too small. But they contained trace elements of blood that the lab picked up. Not surprisingly, it was AB negative. We now know there was a dead man in Ivy's house who was AB negative. We just don't know who he was."

"Fingerprints on the palette knife?"

"Nothing, boss."

Angelo reported on his interview of George Johnson and the art dealer's identification of the man in the painting as Pablo Ingersoll. He told them about his meeting in Brooklyn with Ingersoll and his wife.

"Do you believe the guy?" Frank asked.

"I do. He knows nothing about this. That can't be the end of the story, though. Ivy painted him for some reason. In one way or another, he's connected to what happened at her house. He has to be. We need to find out what that connection is."

Everyone nodded. Angelo went on. "Beth, you're good with computers. Better than the rest of us, anyway. Can you put a trace or tickle or whatever they call it on your computer so that it tells us everything there is to know about Pablo Ingersoll and anything that comes up on him in the future?"

She smiled and made a note. Angelo felt her aloofness starting to slip away, just as Frank had predicted it would. "Sure, happy to. I'm always up for an easy assignment. I'll have the everything-there-is-to-know-about-him part to you this afternoon."

"Thanks."

"By the way," Beth added, "do you mind if I call you Angelo? Duane calls you boss, but I'm older than you are, and it doesn't feel right to me. Duane's older than you are, too, but he's a natural suck-up, and he can overcome his discomfort if he thinks it will score points."

Angelo broke into a grin. "Sure, call me anything you want." He noticed that Duane was grinning too. This was more like it.

"Now that that's settled, do we know any more about Bart? He may be involved in this thing. We have to figure it out."

"No more. I've asked around, but nothing," said Duane.

Beth added, "Without a last name, the computer won't be any help on this one. Doing a search of 'Bart,' or even 'Bart, Woodstock' or 'Bart, Afghanistan,' would only give us a ton of irrelevant stuff. It's the old garbage-in, garbage-out thing."

"Right," said Angelo. "Keep asking around. Maybe someone talked to him or even saw him. Try the public places—the Café, the brewpub, the bakery, the tattoo parlor, the barbershop. Long shots, sure, but maybe we'll get a miracle. We're due for one. Check the hospital and the urgent care centers.

If he was involved and was injured, he might have gone to one of them for treatment."

Angelo looked around the room. The welcome breakthrough aside, he knew he was being short and demanding. Duane, Beth, and Frank were doing all they could. It wasn't fair to take his frustrations out on them. He was relieved that the team seemed solid, and that Beth was coming around. Still, he wanted to give them something to reward their patience and commitment. "I'm going to put Julie Jarrett on the team as an added resource," he said. "You know Julie—she's a junior deputy in my office. She's good. Smart. She has a full plate, but she'll make time for this."

It was a welcome offering. They could use all the help they could get. They relaxed a bit, enough for Duane to venture the inappropriate observation that "it will be good to have another body on this case, particularly a body like that."

No one expected that from Duane, who was way too serious and focused to make such a comment. The others were startled, and there was a quiet moment before Beth punched a hole in the awkwardness.

"Eww, Duane, did you really say that?" Beth was going into middle age kicking and screaming, still attractive, but the muscle of her twenties and early thirties was sagging at forty-three. Her loyalty to Sheriff Jim Beamer had made her wary of Angelo, and she hadn't given away much of herself, but she was far enough past that to reveal a sauciness Angelo enjoyed and had not suspected.

"Angelo, I apologize for the childish utterance we just heard from the boys' locker room. I, for one, am grateful for the extra help, and particularly the addition of a woman. Julie will not only move the investigation forward but will add some much-needed maturity to the team."

Duane looked at Beth and grinned broadly. He knew her well and liked her. They had once had a thing, briefly, after a night of celebrating their cooperation in tracking down and arresting a scumbag who was dealing meth. They both knew the night had been a mistake, but neither regretted it.

This was good, Angelo thought. If the team could laugh when things were aggravatingly slow, they would focus effectively, support each other, and solve this case. Angelo knew he had to show disapproval and tried to give Duane a stern look, but it only produced an outburst of laughter from Beth and Duane. The best plan was to move on.

"One other thing," Angelo added. "I've decided to release the crime scene. I talked to Sam Picken, and she's agreed to take responsibility for the house for the time being, at least until Ivy comes back or we need to make another arrangement. She'll get it cleaned up and put straight."

"Seems like the right call," observed Frank. "I don't think there's anything else the house can give us at this point."

"Good. Thanks, guys. That's all I've got for today. Let's meet again at nine Monday. That's May 23, nine days since the crime. Do what you can tomorrow. I know it's Sunday, and I hate to ask you to work, but we need to keep the pressure on."

There was no objection. Duane said, "It's OK, boss. If Ivy's still alive, we're running out of time. We've got to find her."

As it turned out, circumstances brought them together again before Monday.

CHAPTER THIRTY-NINE

The Investigation (May 2022)

The North Fork of the Shenandoah River originates in Rockingham County, Virginia, and flows north about a hundred miles through the Shenandoah Valley, along the west side of the Blue Ridge and Massanutten Mountain. At Front Royal, it joins the South Fork to form the mighty Shenandoah River, which continues northward until it becomes the principal tributary of the Potomac at Harper's Ferry. The North Fork isn't a large river, but it's beautiful, serene, and provides a sought-after playground for people who like canoeing, fishing, and camping.

Aptly named, The Friends of the North Fork is a nonprofit organization headquartered in Woodstock whose mission includes keeping the river clean, healthy, and beautiful. Its active volunteer program helps the environment by taking tons of trash out of the river each year. The trash comes in many forms: bottles, cans, plastic bags, the occasional toy that got away from a child or a dog, even a mattress every now and then.

Dan Kendall and Greg Geraghty were working the river on Saturday, May 21. Lawyers with big firms in Washington, DC, they were good friends who journeyed out to Star Tannery in Virginia every month or so when the weather was right. They had a favorite campsite there, and they loved to canoe. Star Tannery gave them access both to Lost River in West Virginia and the North Fork of the Shenandoah. It also gave them access to some inexpensive Virginia wineries that produced surprisingly decent wines.

The North Fork had been good to Dan and Greg, and they believed in giving back, so they spent a day every three months doing clean-up. On Saturday, May 21, they were collecting trash in an area near the low water bridge at Pughs Run, wading or rafting as circumstances warranted, filling bags with the debris they found, and using a johnboat to float the trash to a dump site. It was hard but rewarding work.

They were getting ready to call it a day when Greg saw a black trash bag that had lodged against a fallen tree near the riverbank. He waded over to it, noticing that an air pocket caused the bag to billow up above the water's surface. The bag was closed with a plastic tie. Greg called Dan, who guided the boat over. Something about the bag didn't look right, and it had an unpleasant smell. Greg had no desire to open it, but he grabbed it and felt around to try to get a sense of what was in it. He thought the contents might be a couple of small branches, but they were softer. Fleshier. Whatever it was, it wasn't good.

"Dan, I don't know what this is, but it feels like an arm. Maybe two arms. We'd better call the sheriff's office."

Dan had his cell phone out in a minute. Beth was on the computer, finding out everything she could about Pablo Ingersoll, and happened to answer the phone. Dan gave her a quick report and described where they were on the river. "We're on our way," Beth said. "Don't go anywhere, and don't let that bag get away from you."

Moments later, there were flashing lights on the low-water bridge. Beth and Duane jumped out of one car and raced along the riverbank to where Dan and Greg were guarding the bag. Angelo got out of the other car and was right behind them. Duane pulled the still-floating bag out of the river. It had taken on some water and was heavy, but still manageable. Breathlessly, Duane began to open the bag.

"Holy shit," said Greg, taking a step backward.

"No kidding," said Dan.

Reminded of their presence, Angelo turned to them. "We'll take it from here, guys. Thanks for your help. Please call my office and leave us information about how to contact you."

He turned back to the bag, then back to Dan and Greg, and added, "Please don't talk about this, not for a few days anyway." *Fat chance*, he thought, and gave his full attention to the matter at hand.

The bag gave up its contents grudgingly. First out was a human arm, a man's right arm that had been severed just below the shoulder. It was mottled blue and white from its time in the water, and the smell intensified with its exposure to air. Then came a leg, cut off below the left buttocks. The bone saw had cut through the femoral artery. There had been a lot of blood, much of it sprayed around Ivy's living room and most of the rest washed away by the river. But there would be enough left for the lab to test, to confirm that it was AB negative, that it came from the man who was killed in Ivy's house.

"Call the lab," Angelo said to Beth. "Tell them we're on our way with some human appendages for them to examine. It's an emergency. They'll have to cancel their Saturday night plans. We need the results by tomorrow morning."

Duane was removing the last item from the trash bag. It was the left arm, severed at the same location as the right, just below the shoulder. This arm was different. It was wearing a wrist sheath. Snapped into the sheath was a butterfly knife.

CHAPTER FORTY

The Investigation (May 2022)

They met at noon the following day, Sunday, May 22. They needed answers, and that was the soonest answers would be available. Julie Jarrett had joined the team. It was her first meeting, and she didn't look happy about it. This was a grisly business.

The results started rolling in. The blood was AB negative. *No surprise there*, Angelo thought. The victim appeared to be of Asian descent. *Jaime Roxas? Had to be.* The grumpy old medical examiner confirmed the death: "There must have been a death because these limbs are all from the same body, and that body can't be walking around out there without them." *No shit, Sherlock.*

The report may not have been sophisticated, but no one questioned the bottom line. A man had been killed and cut up. His blood was AB negative. He was apparently Asian. This wasn't absolute proof that he was the person killed in Ivy's house, and it wasn't proof that the body parts had once belonged to Jaime Roxas, but it sure looked like it. Ivy had told Sam that Jaime's favorite weapon was a butterfly knife. Circumstantial, but strong. Case closed. Almost.

"Methinks Jaime came to kill Ivy and got himself killed instead," said Angelo after hearing the various findings. Elated by finally having caught a break, he felt a little playful.

"Couldn't happen to a nicer guy," muttered Frank.

"Yes, but it doesn't tell us anything except that the dead guy looks Asian and has AB negative blood." Angelo's moment of play was over. "We don't know it's Jaime and I shouldn't have said that it is. The signs point to Jaime and we want it to be Jaime, but we don't yet have proof of that. Whoever it is, we don't know who killed him, or why. We don't know who protected Ivy by getting her out of the house, or why. We don't know where Ivy is, or if she's all right. We really don't know much at all."

"Yeah, but we do know an evil piece of crap has been removed from the face of the earth, and that's a good thing." Frank continued his theme. "Assuming it is Jaime, how do you suppose he managed to track Ivy down, after all these years?"

"We know he had posted a reward for information about her on the dark web," Beth said. "At least we assume it was Jaime's post. Maybe someone spotted her, called Jaime, and claimed the reward money."

"That's as good a guess as we can make at this point." Angelo was thinking hard. "I can't believe that artist in New York, Ingersoll, would have been part of something like this. What would that kind of a guy have to do with the likes of Jaime Roxas? How would he even know him? We still need to connect the dots between Ingersoll and Ivy, but I don't see him as having been at the crime scene."

"Seems right, for now," said Frank. "And we don't know enough about Bart to make a judgment about whether he was involved."

Angelo's frustration was mounting again. "The only people we can link to Jaime are the Browns. He worked for them, and they presumably had the same motive he did to get even with Ivy for running away. Maybe they even ordered it. The problem is they're deep underground, and we don't have a clue how to find them. That's the only link I can make, but damn, where do we even start?"

Angelo could feel the heat rising in his neck. He and his team were getting nowhere. He was angry at their impotence. His frustration over the lack of progress was clouding his reason.

"Let's back off a bit, slow down, and update the assumptions you wrote down a few days ago," said Frank, calmly and deliberately. He knew focused analytical thinking was needed now, not emotion. "Let's take a look at your whiteboard, Angelo."

Angelo took a deep breath and immediately felt better. "Thanks, Frank," he said, reaching for the whiteboard. "That's a good suggestion."

Just at the right moment, just as Angelo was about to let his Italian impatience render him ineffective, his old mentor, Scott O'Hanlon, had spoken to him in Frank Betterman's voice. Angelo clearly recalled a critical point during the Worthy investigation when he was about to lose it, and Scott had said, "Get a grip on yourself, Hotshot. You won't get anything done by being mad." So true. He was fortunate to have had Scott, and now Frank, to save him from himself.

"OK," he said with a quiet determination. "Our first assumption was that Ivy wasn't there during the fight. We can't confirm that yet, but I think we know it in our guts. Let's keep that assumption." Everyone nodded in agreement.

"Second, the palette knife was used as a weapon, and other knives probably were too. Well, the palette knife may or may not have been a weapon. There's blood on it, as well as fingerprints other than Ivy's that are still unidentified. There are no knife wounds in the three limbs that came out of the river, but we don't yet have the rest of the body to check."

"Maybe there were other knives, maybe not," Duane added. "We know Jaime's wasn't used because it was still strapped into its sheath, unopened, when we found it. This looks more and more like a gun killing, like Chief Betterman was saying."

"Agreed," said Angelo. "So, let's keep the assumption about the knives but put a couple of large question marks next to it. Our third assumption was that guns weren't a factor. That no longer seems right. We can't say they were because we haven't found a bullet. My guess is we'll find one in the victim's head or chest if those body parts ever turn up. For now, let's change this assumption to say he was probably killed, or at least badly injured, by a gun fired from outside the living room window."

"Good," observed Frank. "By the way, have you got someone dragging the river to find the rest of the body?"

"Yes. That started this morning and is underway as we speak. Our next assumption was that the motive didn't involve money or sex. No reason to change that one.

"Finally, we said there were two or possibly three people involved; if two, one had to be strong enough to carry the other. With the bone saw fragments and body parts, the three-person theory loses its validity for me, and there's no reason to think the killer had to be overly strong to remove the vic. Hell, even Duane was able to pull the bag with two arms and a leg out of the river, and that's a third of the body right there. Two or three trips for an average man and the body would be gone. Right?"

Frank was pleased that Angelo had regained his sense of humor. It would serve him well to keep his emotions in check if they were going to solve this crime. Beth looked at Duane and grinned. He smiled self-deprecatingly. "C'mon, boss, there was water in that bag. It was heavy."

"OK, so let's scrap that assumption and put in that the victim was killed by a lone actor, who cut up the dead body with a bone saw and removed it from the house. Anything else to add?"

People looked around at each other. Frank said, "You might want to add that the victim was a male, Asian, and appears to have been Jaime Roxas, a man who had previously hurt Ivy and had reason to want to kill her."

Angelo fiddled with the whiteboard, erasing and adding until it reflected the team's current thinking. "I wish we could confirm that Jaime Roxas was AB negative, just to pin down the victim's identity, but I doubt we're going to find any records of his blood type."

"I'll check the LA hospitals," Beth volunteered. "Long shot, because if Jaime ever went in for treatment, he's not likely to have given his real name. There's no point contacting the Red Cross. He doesn't seem the type to have been a blood donor."

"I dunno. He did a good job of donating blood at Ivy's house." Everyone smiled. The return of Angelo's lighter side was a good sign. He smiled back, knowing he had his team's loyalty. They wanted to work with him, for him. He had to be patient with them, not drive them away.

"We've got a lot of work to do," he said. He looked at Julie. "Welcome to the team. I want you out there talking to people. Learn things. Break this case open for us." Then to the group, "Let's meet at nine tomorrow, as previously scheduled. With any luck, the search of the river will be done by then."

"One thing before we go," Duane interrupted. "I've been putting together a list of people who are new in town in the last six months. I had a message at home last night when we got back from the river. It was from the manager of one of those fast-food places on Reservoir Road, up near the interstate."

Angelo's head snapped up. "And?"

"He said they have a new employee who showed up a couple of weeks ago. He's been sweeping up. Nice guy, apparently. He gave his name as Chico Santos. His job application gave an address at an apartment on Water Street, just down from Ivy's house, but the apartment manager never heard of him."

"Let's pick him up and talk to him," barked Angelo.

"We can't. He hasn't been at work this week."

CHAPTER FORTY-ONE

Pablo (2018-19)

Pablo's reputation as an artist had enjoyed a rapid ascent. It wasn't because of the paintings he had made for the *Imagine* project because his role in those was not publicly known. There had been speculation in some quarters that he was the artist behind them, but it had never been confirmed. He was on the rise because he excelled at his day job.

He was still painting Sally, and his work was getting better and better. It was richer, deeper, more imaginative, earthier. He was introducing elements of some of the world's great artists into his paintings, not enough to detract from their identity as Ingersolls, but enough to strengthen them and broaden Pablo's reach.

The art world responded. In the years immediately following his first solo show at the Stockbridge Gallery in 2001, he occasionally had short reviews in the back sections of the major art magazines. By 2015, he was a recognized name, not a Warhol or a Basquiat, but solidly in the third or fourth tranche of American artists. People wanted to read about him, and once or twice a year, he was the feature story in a leading art magazine. People wanted to see his art, and he had added galleries in San Francisco, Santa Fe, and Miami to New York's Stockbridge Gallery. People wanted to collect his art, and his work now sold regularly in the six figures. His paintings came up at auction from time to time and unfailingly did well. He was shown at museums, university art museums initially but eventually the large, prestigious museums that exhibit the work of leading artists.

Despite overtures from better-known New York galleries, Pablo had remained loyal to Jennifer Stockbridge. She had been good to him in the early years, had given him his first real chance, and promoted him relentlessly. His loyalty to her was tested in 2016, when the Upton Gallery approached him about representation. Located in midtown, Upton was one of the leading contemporary art galleries in New York and, for that matter, the world. He was tempted but kept putting them off. *Annabel's Eyes* changed everything.

Pablo loved that painting. It was a piece of his soul, and he didn't want to part with it. He did want it to be seen, however, and appreciated for what it was. After all, *Gatsby* wouldn't have been *Gatsby* if no one had read it. The challenge was to get the painting into the hands of a leading museum or a world-renowned collector of contemporary art. That would give the work stature, provenance, and the critical acclaim he thought it deserved. The Upton Gallery played its trump card. It had an anonymous buyer with impeccable credentials in England, southeast of London in Sussex, who was willing to pay 5 million pounds for *Annabel's Eyes*. The deal was made, quietly and privately, and Pablo moved his business from Stockbridge to Upton.

Pablo and Sally would never want for money again. They certainly could have moved out of Brooklyn, but they loved Brooklyn. They contented themselves with the purchase of a charming eighty-acre farm in the Hudson Valley. Their plan was to get out of the city and spend weekends and holidays there.

Pablo had done exceedingly well, particularly with *Annabel's Eyes*, but he also suffered a setback. Ann called him some months after the unveiling of *Farah* to express her displeasure.

"As you know, Pablo, *Imagine* has undergone a transition. It is now housed and overseen by the Hemphill Museum. I still have some influence, I'm sure, but I no longer call the shots. That is done by Barry Thomas, who you know. He curates the project and chairs the panel that will determine the women to be painted and the artists to paint them going forward."

"Yes, Ann, I read about that. Good for Barry. I'll make it a point to call on him."

"I'm sure he would enjoy seeing you, but as a friend and not in the *Imagine* context. You know we were deeply disappointed by your performance on the *Farah* painting. You let us down, and Barry has decided to go in a different direction for the next painting. Frankly, I agree with his decision. In fact, I suggested it. You did some wonderful work for us, and I'm sorry."

"I am, too, Ann, very sorry. I never wanted to disappoint you."

"Well, that's water under the bridge. As you can imagine, I now know what you were working on that kept you away from *Farah*. I haven't seen *Annabel's Eyes* yet, but I'm told it's an exceptional painting. I'm also told it has landed in very good hands. I'm anxious to see it in person. Congratulations!"

"Thanks. I think you'll like it. May I ask who the artist is who will be taking over for me?"

"You know the rules. The artist must remain anonymous. All best, Pablo." Ann rang off.

Shut down and shut out. Pablo was crushed. It wasn't the loss of Ann's generous commissions—he and Sally now had plenty of money. It wasn't because he had chosen to paint *Annabel's Eyes*—he would never regret that. Ann had been good to him, and he had let her down. He had been an integral part of Project *Imagine*. He had celebrated its successes, his successes, with Ann and Sally. Now he was an outsider.

Barry and the panel engaged a fine artist named Jane Dorsett to do the sixth painting. She was an up-and-comer whose work was widely admired. For her first assignment, Barry gave her a photo of a stern-looking woman named Helen. His instruction was to paint Helen in the style of the great Dutch master, Johannes Vermeer.

Jane took to the project with relish. She loved Vermeer's *Girl with a Pearl Earring,* one of the world's most famous paintings, and worked tirelessly to depict Helen as Vermeer would have. Unfortunately, Jane was not Vermeer and Helen was not the *Girl*. The *Helen* painting was a fizzle at its New York unveiling in 2019.

With the addition of *Helen*, the *Imagine* wing of the Hemphill Museum beautifully displayed six paintings of leading contemporary women made by some of the world's most esteemed artists. It was a stunning site for the unveiling and accommodated a larger art crowd than had the great room at

Ann's London home. The biannual presentation of a new *Imagine* painting had become a highly sought-after ticket in the art world.

As the various critics and lovers of art filed in to see the *Helen* painting, their reactions uniformly deflated from high anticipation to benign acknowledgment.

"This isn't as good as the others," one said.

'Not even *Farah*, which was the least impressive of the opening five," said another.

"A far cry from Vermeer," said a third. "I love Vermeer, but this is no Vermeer."

"They must have changed the artist who did these," said a fourth. "This isn't the same hand that did the others. I wonder why they would do that. They were riding a winning horse."

Listening to the comments, Barry and Ann were dismayed. They were not surprised—they were art experts in their own rights, and they knew this work wasn't as good as Pablo's. They suspected the project was going to suffer as a result. There would be long discussions about what changes needed to be made.

Barry stepped to the mic and clinked his glass. "A very warm welcome, ladies and gentlemen. On behalf of the Hemphill Museum, I am delighted and proud to be able to show off this wonderful new venue." There was a hearty round of applause. The *Imagine* wing of the Hemphill was truly magnificent.

"Thank you," continued Barry. "I know you're eager to get to the business at hand, so let's do that straightaway. It gives me the greatest pleasure to introduce tonight's guest of honor, the remarkable Helen Baldridge."

A stout woman of sixty peered at the dinner guests from her seat and smiled stiffly. Her poorly chosen eyeglasses did nothing to soften her severe facial features. Her untamed gray hair resembled a cowbird's nest. Barry looked at her and realized that Vermeer was all wrong for her. He should have gone with Whistler. *Oh well, we are where we are.* He soldiered on.

"As you know, Helen has been a leading physician and educator. She has taught at two of the finest medical schools in the world. Those are signal accomplishments, but what truly sets her apart is her relentless fight against cancer. Over the past five years, her contributions to the war against that killing disease have exceeded the contributions made by any other person over any five-year period in recorded history. We honor her tonight with a painting by the incomparable Johannes Vermeer."

Polite applause, no more. Tepid at best. The *Farah* painting had been Pablo's weakest effort, but it was better than this. Besides, Farah Rashidi was a dynamic personality, and her compelling presence rescued what could have been a real stumble for *Imagine*. The *Helen* painting was degrees weaker than *Farah*, and whatever the enormity of her accomplishments in fighting cancer, Helen Baldridge didn't have the presence to save herself, let alone the evening.

This is a disaster, Barry thought, trying to hold his smile and a shred of poise. He could see the momentum of *Imagine* not just slowing but braking to a near halt as contributions dried up and the art crowd looked around to find the next new thing. He had to do something to save the project. Ann's head was down; she couldn't help him now. He made a bold decision.

"Thanks for your attendance tonight. Before you go, I have an important announcement to make. We lost a year when the *Farah* painting was late, and we are determined to get back on schedule. I am pleased to tell you that the unveiling of the seventh painting will happen one year from now. Mark your calendars. I promise you something truly extraordinary."

As the guests filtered out, Ann joined Barry in his office down the hall. He knew she enjoyed Blanton's and poured them each a glass.

"I'm sorry to have gotten out ahead of you, Ann. I couldn't think of anything else to do."

"No apology necessary. That was an all-star save. Quick thinking and pure genius."

"I promised something extraordinary, and in a year's time. I hope we can deliver."

"You've kept us in the game. We need to take advantage of that. We have no choice but to deliver."

"Do you think we can get Pablo back?"

"We have to."

CHAPTER FORTY-TWO

Laura (2019)

Laura and John McGoohan left Big Law to start their own firm in 2018. They had worked long hours for many years and wanted a more controllable pace, which would give them more time to pursue their respective outside interests. They weren't concerned about getting business. They each had a substantial book of their own, and they knew their clients would follow them with any litigation that didn't require armies of associates and paralegals. It didn't matter anyway because they weren't practicing law for the money. Mags had done well and was set, and Laura was born wealthy.

They formed Marcus, McGoohan and leased a gorgeous suite overlooking the Hudson River in the emerging Hudson Yards project. A year in, they were ten lawyers strong and had a steady but manageable stream of interesting work. Everything was turning out as they had hoped.

Over coffee one morning in the late summer of 2019, Laura said, "I need to ask you a favor, Gooey. I'm going to London next month. Would you mind looking after things here while I'm away?"

"Sure. Happy to. What's in London?"

"There's an auction at Sotheby's that I want to attend. Pablo has a piece coming up, and I'm thinking about bidding on it."

"Say no more." Mags knew all about the saga of Pablo and Laura. He never could understand why this beautiful, smart woman of untold wealth had gotten herself into a long-term relationship that wasn't going anywhere. He knew about the estrangement Laura felt when Pablo was working on *Annabel's Eyes*. He supported and comforted her when she ended it with Pablo—it was the right thing to do—but his heart ached for her because he knew she still loved Pablo and probably always would.

"How long will you be gone?" he asked.

"A week if all goes well. Much longer if it doesn't."

"That sounds ominous. Want to tell me about it?"

"I'll tell you when I get back. Thanks, Gooey. You're a prince."

Prince or not, Mags was unquestionably a sucker for Laura. He was curious about what the "much longer" scenario might look like and how long it would last. He knew he would be minding the store for an extended period if that scenario prevailed, but that was OK—he enjoyed managing the firm and was happy to do it for as long as was necessary.

With her professional responsibilities under control, Laura contacted her good friend Jane Parks, one of London's leading barristers, to make the necessary arrangements. Could Jane provide her with a pistol upon her arrival, preferably the kind she had fired at the Olympics?

"What?" exploded Jane. She was not amused.

Laura detailed her plan. No, she wasn't going to hurt anyone. She was only going to shoot a painting, and she would own the painting when she shot it. Yes, she would be civil and courteous at all times. Yes, she understood she would almost certainly be arrested. No, she wouldn't kick up a fuss with the constabulary. She would be a perfect gentlelady until Jane got there to spring her.

"I'm glad you told me about this in advance," Jane said. "It will take some time, and all my wits, to come up with a defense for this madness. You know my fees are high. This will cost you a pretty penny."

"How much?" asked Laura, smiling.

"Drinks at the back end."

"Done!"

The plan worked to perfection. Jane and Laura played their roles masterfully. They relived every moment with great satisfaction over their martinis at Duke's.

"You know, there's one aspect of this I'm afraid we haven't planned for," Jane said with a mixture of amusement and concern. "We have very active tabloids here in London. They're curious, inventive, and unmerciful. I should think you'll be the toast of the town by noon tomorrow."

Jane was an accurate fortuneteller as well as a fine lawyer. When Laura rose for a leisurely continental breakfast in her suite at the Lanesborough the following morning, coffee was served with a copy of *The Dirty Laundry*, the nastiest and most successful of the British tabloids. "You'll want to have a look at this, mum. You're famous," her server said, stifling a grin and excusing herself.

Oh, dear, Laura thought as she unfolded the paper. *What have I done?* Spread across the front page was a picture of her standing before *Annabel's Eyes*, glaring at it with a slight smile on her face. Her right arm dangled at her side, still holding the smoking pistol. Laura remembered the moment—it was just after she fired the shots and just before she placed the gun on the chair to await her arrest. People were scared and diving for cover, but there was always someone who managed to get a picture. Laura imagined *The Dirty Laundry* had paid handsomely for this one.

The headline blared: "ANNABEL WIDE-EYED!!!"

The sub-headline declared: "Madwoman Buys Ingersoll Painting for Record Price, Then Shoots It!"

Laura shook her head in a mix of amused recall and serious regret. She turned the page and began to read. "Laura Marcus, a name partner in the New York law firm of Marcus, McGoohan, stunned the patrons at Sotheby's and the art world generally yesterday when she…." *Gooey isn't going to like this.*

It was an amazing story, unbelievably juicy stuff, and by the next day, it had been picked up by newspapers everywhere. It was gleefully covered in Europe by *Le Monde*, the *Daily Mirror*, *Der Spiegel*, the *Irish Times*, and *Corriere della Sera*. In the United States, readers of the *New York Times*, the *Washington Post*, the *Boston Globe*, the *Los Angeles Times*, the *Chicago Tribune*, the *Miami Herald*, the *San Francisco Chronicle*, and *USA Today* devoured it.

Mags McGoohan faithfully read the *Times* from cover to cover each day, but he liked to begin with the *New York Post*. He went straight to Page Six, the celebrated gossip column, to chuckle over the latest gaffes, controversies, and exposes. "Oh shit!" was all he could say when he saw the shocking news about his law partner and friend. "Shit, shit, shit," he added when he came to the mention of their law firm.

Jane Parks saw the coverage on the telly and roared with laughter. She went to the source to read the article. She was delighted that she was not only named but identified as "a prominent barrister who had the madwoman back on the street in the blink of an eye."

At her London home, Ann Merriman read about it in the *Daily Mirror* and the *New York Times*. She had never met Laura but knew of her and her affair with Pablo. She shook her head sadly. *Why would Laura do something like that?* she thought. *She must really hate Pablo, or really love him. Poor Pablo. Annabel's Eyes was his crowning achievement.*

Pablo was in Miami for a gallery opening and read the account in the *Herald*. He understood Laura and forgave her, but he was heartbroken.

Laura stayed in her suite at the Lanesborough, removed from the public eye and absorbing the nonstop media coverage of the shooting of *Annabel's Eyes* until she couldn't bear it any longer. She pulled her collar up and put on a baseball cap to effect a makeshift disguise, then embarked on a long and thoughtful walk that took her around Green Park, down Birdcage Walk, along the Victoria Embankment all the way to Blackfriars Bridge, then back up busy Fleet Street and the Strand, past Charing Cross Station and across Trafalgar Square to St. James Park, and finally up lovely Jermyn Street, through the Picadilly arcade, and safely back to the sanctuary of her hotel. She had made some decisions and wanted to review them over a quiet dinner in her suite.

She had planned to be in London for a week but decided to stay for two more. The unwanted publicity risk was intense in London, but it would be worse in New York. Better to hunker down in place until this blew over. A modest effort at disguise would be enough to throw off most of the passersby. She would revert to being a brunette—hadn't Jane said she preferred her as a brunette anyway?—because the splash of her blond hair was the most memorable identifier in the now-viral photo from *The Dirty Laundry*. As she thought about that photo, she was glad she had worn her blue hat to the auction; her face was partially hidden in its shadow.

After dinner and a cup of tea, she decided to call Gooey and get it over with. It was mid-afternoon in New York, and he would be at his desk. She wanted to apologize for dragging the firm's name through the muck of her scandal, and she needed to know he would cover for her at the office for another fortnight.

"Gooey?" she said tentatively, as he answered his phone.

"What the hell were you thinking?" he blurted out without preamble.

"I'm so sorry. I knew this would draw some attention, but I didn't account for the tabloids."

He softened immediately. He had made his point and was too fond of Laura to beat her while she was down. "Are you alright?" he asked.

"Yes, I will be. How bad is it at the office?"

"We'll talk about it when you get back. Lie low and take care of yourself." He rang off.

The following morning, Laura went to Sotheby's to apologize for the incident and arrange for the painting to be shipped to her home on Park Avenue. The nice people there suggested she might wish to have the painting restored first; they knew an excellent restorer and would be delighted to manage that for her. She thanked them for their kindness but declined, saying she wanted the painting just as it was, and asked if they would be so good as to send it on forthwith.

Laura rarely left her hotel during the rest of her stay. She made brief visits to Waterstones to pick up two books she had been meaning to read and Berry Bros. & Rudd to buy three bottles of claret. She went to Harrod's to buy gifts for Jane and Gooey. She went to the theater twice but couldn't keep her mind on the shows. She treated Jane to dinner at Le Gavroche.

She thought endlessly about what she had done. On balance, she felt it was right, but she had regrets. She was sorry for the negative impact her actions had on Gooey and the law firm, but her biggest regret had to do with Pablo. She knew the pain she must have caused him. He deserved it, but she still loved him and was truly sorry to have hurt him.

Everything had died down when she returned to New York. She and Gooey had orchestrated her return to the office. He told her she would have to meet this head-on and arranged for a session with the staff on the morning of her return. He greeted her somberly upon her arrival and led her to the large conference room. The halls were eerily quiet, as if everyone were in hiding. She entered with trepidation and was met with a roar. The lawyers and staff who disapproved expressed their disdain by staying away; those in the room cheered wildly. A brightly colored sign that hung from the ceiling screamed the words, "Welcome Back, Badass."

CHAPTER FORTY-THREE

Pablo (2019-20)

Pablo was devastated by what Laura had done, but he didn't have time to feel sorry for himself. He had been given a chance to make amends for his failure on the *Imagine* project and was determined to make the most of it.

Following the catastrophic unveiling of *Helen* and his bold promises to the art crowd, Barry had called an expedited meeting of his blue-ribbon panel. It was a tense and protracted session, but the panel ultimately ratified his commitment to regain the lost year and approved his recommendation, supported by Ann, that they reengage Pablo Ingersoll to do the painting—if they could get him. The panel understood the stress that pulling things together in one year would entail, and it had little appetite for the groveling that would be necessary to bring Pablo back, but they had no choice if the project was to survive. It took only a short discussion to get to yes on Barry's motion that Ann be deputized to approach Pablo. Her relationship with Pablo gave the project its best chance for success.

When she called, Ann opened with an invitation. "Can I interest you and Sally in celebrating the holiday season with me over dinner at Per Se?"

Pablo was delighted to hear from her. "We'd love to, Ann. When will you be in New York?"

"I won't be coy, Pablo. I'm coming to New York to see you. Sooner is better from my perspective, but let's select a date that suits your schedule." They agreed to meet the following week.

Pablo was reasonably confident he knew the reason for the dinner. He had read the negative commentary about the unveiling of *Helen*. He felt badly for Ann and Barry, who had worked so hard to make *Imagine* a success, and he felt particularly badly for the artist, whoever he or she was. He was aware that Barry had promised to get the project back on schedule and deliver something extraordinary in a year's time. He had worked with Ann and the project long enough to be able to read between the lines. Other than *Farah*, his work on the project had been outstanding. They wanted him to come back. He was their hope for saving *Imagine*.

In the days before their dinner, Pablo thought about how he should respond to Ann's request. It was a wonderful opportunity to take his revenge for having been terminated. He could easily decide to be petty; he could say no, in the nicest way, of course, pleading that he was just too busy to take it on right now, or he could make Ann beg, and he knew she would. Tempting as the prospect was, Pablo's better angels prevailed. He would not do that to Ann. She had been good to him, and in fairness, he had no one to blame but himself for his termination. He resolved to help Ann and the project in any way he could.

Ann was already seated when Pablo and Sally arrived at Thomas Keller's beautiful Columbus Circle restaurant for dinner. They greeted each other with affection and toasted their reunion with perfectly chilled flutes of Taittinger Comtes de Champagne Blanc de Blancs. Ann wasted no time with preliminaries.

"Pablo, *Imagine* needs your help. I need your help. You've doubtless read about our last unveiling. It was a disaster. We're on a downward slide and face a serious risk of failure. We want you back. You are not only our best hope for redemption. You are our only hope."

"Of course, Ann. How can I help?"

Not hearing the words because she didn't expect to hear them, Ann went on. "You have every right to be angry with us, and certainly with me. You have every right to say no. What I am asking of you will turn your life upside down. I hate that, but I ask it anyway because this project means to me what *Annabel's Eyes* means to you."

"I understand, Ann. I'll do it."

Ann heard him clearly this time. "Thank you," she said, taking a moment to gather herself and let her emotion subside. "You understand this must be your best work yet, and you must do it in half the usual time. It cannot be late, even by a day. There is no margin for error."

"I will never disappoint you again, Ann." Sally squeezed his hand under the table. He was taking the high road. This was the man she loved.

"Good, then it's settled," said Ann, relaxing slightly with heartfelt relief. She took out a photo of a beautiful woman and handed it to Pablo. "This is Grace. You are Andy Warhol."

It was a brilliant choice. Grace Richter had come to Hollywood at nineteen and achieved instant stardom. At twenty-six, with a best actress Oscar under her belt, she went to Harvard to study business and foreign relations. A decade later, she was back in her native Europe as head of the European Central Bank. It was widely predicted that she would be the next woman chancellor of Germany. She was bright, articulate, blond, gorgeous, and only forty-seven.

A pop artist, Warhol would be easy to replicate, or so Pablo first thought, and fun. Warhol was famous for his paintings of icons, including Marilyn Monroe, Elvis Presley, Mao Tse-tung, Jackie Kennedy, and Elizabeth Taylor. He would have loved painting Grace Richter. Pablo Ingersoll would give him that chance and do him justice.

Ann was right about one thing. Taking on this commission turned Pablo's life upside down. He was busy with a heavy season of gallery commitments, and being Warhol proved harder than he expected. There was a reason the guy was a genius. Pablo worked hard to get it right. He worked nights and days in Brooklyn and weekends at the farm. He worked harder than he ever had in his life, not with the personal commitment he had to *Annabel's Eyes* but out of a desperate desire to make things right with Ann. He would not fail her again. He would validate her belief in him. He would produce a masterpiece.

Finally, it was done. The result was classic Warhol. Four identical images of the amazing woman were presented in vivid colors and accents, simply painted in four different background hues, a blue, a green, an orange, and a red. Each image was a square, and the four abutted each other to form a larger square. The contrasting presentations of the single striking image made the *Grace* painting far greater than the sum of its parts.

In the late fall of 2020, right on time, *Grace* was unveiled. The art crowd showed up, not knowing what to expect. Those who had initially intended to stay away based on the previous year's underperformance changed their minds. Some came because, against all odds, Barry had delivered on his promise to do it in a year—that was a herculean task, and it rekindled their belief in *Imagine*. Some came out of curiosity—Barry had vowed something extraordinary, and they wanted to see the rabbit that jumped out of the hat. Whatever the reasons, their skepticism turned to awe when they saw *Grace*.

"Oh my God, that's absolutely fabulous," said one.

"I loved the Picasso, and the Jawlensky for that matter, but this one is the best," said another.

"I see the hand of the original artist. They've returned to their senses," said a third.

"Project *Imagine* is back!" said a fourth.

Ann and Barry listened to the comments. They almost giggled with relief and pleasure. Barry took the mic and clinked his glass. "Ladies and gentlemen," he began, but stopped because he couldn't be heard over the roar of the crowd. He dropped his head in appreciation and smiled.

He tapped the mic and took advantage of a momentary pause to say, "I give you the extraordinary Grace Richter." She stood, laughed, and walked around waving to the crowd, every inch the Hollywood star the world adored. The crowd was on its feet, yelling its approval. She walked to the painting, looked at it admiringly and applauded it in appreciation. The crowd was with her all the way, showing its love for her and the painting. When the guests were exhausted from clapping and began to collapse into their seats, Grace walked to the center of the floor, raised a champagne glass to the painting, and quietly said, "Thank you, my friends. But all credit to the artist. Really, all credit and all thanks to the artist."

Back in Barry's office, Ann and Barry hugged each other in pure joy. He poured the Blanton's while she called Pablo.

"How quickly can you and Sally get here?"

"About forty-five seconds. We thought it was a good night to visit the Hemphill and have a look at the current exhibition. It's Rauschenberg, you know."

"Get your ass down here. In forty-five seconds, you'll be a glass behind Barry and me."

"Can't let that happen." They were at Barry's office thirty-nine seconds later. Two glasses of Blanton's awaited them.

It was a lovefest.

CHAPTER FORTY-FOUR

Angelo (May 2022)

Angelo left his office before dark. He was on his own, since Frank had a meeting at the Moose Lodge, and that was OK with him—he wanted an evening alone, even if that meant the joyless surroundings of his hotel room. He was confident that a glass, more likely two glasses, of Elijah Craig and a call home would lift his spirits.

He got into his sweats, had a sip of bourbon, and immediately felt better. Even this brief respite from the case was good for his soul. He would wait until nine thirty to call home—it was his dad's bowling night, and he wouldn't be in until shortly after nine. In the meantime, Angelo would try to make some progress on his personal to-do list. He looked around the stark room and decided finding a place to live was his top priority.

He pulled out the notes he had begun a couple of nights ago. He hadn't gotten very far because the case kept nagging at him, but his notes reflected one important decision: he didn't want an apartment. He expected to put down roots in Woodstock, and his new job paid well enough that he could make a down payment on a modest home. Frank's place was nice, but Angelo wasn't looking for a duplex. He wanted a house, a real house, with a yard he could walk around in and call his own. He wanted to be able to do yardwork. He enjoyed working with his hands, getting dirty, not thinking about work.

He knew he let his work consume him too easily. Having a house would give him a break, a sanctuary to look forward to at the end of the day.

Maybe he could find something along the river. That would be nice. He pictured himself sitting in an Adirondack chair with a dog beside him, a big dog, watching the river flow by. The river. *I wonder if the rest of the victim's remains are in the river. If so, they should show up soon. It would move the investigation along to know whether they contain a bullet or a stab wound.* He shook his head in frustration. He was trying to take a night off from the case, but he was failing.

While his laptop was booting up, Angelo poured himself another bourbon. By design, it would be his last of the evening. He googled "houses for sale, Woodstock VA, near river," wondering what people did before the Internet. He saw two or three places that satisfied his imaginings, but they were way too expensive. There was another he liked, and it was in his price range, but it wasn't on the river. It was on Hollingsworth, just off Water Street. *That's about a mile up from Ivy's house,* he thought. *I wonder where she is. I hope she's safe and hanging tough.* He looked back at his computer and made a note to call the listing agent. He really liked the idea of the river though, so he continued his search, starting suddenly when he realized it was nine thirty-five. Time to call Mom and Dad. It was a narrow window before they'd be going to bed.

His dad was in a great mood because he had scored a 187 and had three strikes in a row. "They call that a turkey, ya know," his dad said, roaring heartily. "You're a turkey," laughed Angelo in response. He and his dad had always enjoyed an easy relationship.

Angelo's mom was in a great mood, as she always was, because she enjoyed life to the fullest and managed to see the best in everything and everybody. She filled him in on what all the Giovanettis were doing—even though the government had changed their name to Jones when they came to the United States, they still viewed themselves as Giovanettis for family purposes. Sam had a new car, Mamma Rosa was having some health problems but staying strong, little Louie was making his first communion; mindless stuff but warm, loving, and distracting.

The conversation filled Angelo's soul. He thought about his family as he got into bed and turned out the light. He lay there, waiting for sleep to come, until the embrace of his family was muscled aside by worries about Ivy and visions of bodies floating in the river.

CHAPTER FORTY-FIVE

Ivy (2020)

The story of Laura shooting *Annabel's Eyes* only had a week's worth of legs with the American public. By then, the national interest had shifted to the most recent UFO sightings and the impeachment proceedings against President Trump. Next week, there would be a story about an alligator eating a baby at Hilton Head, or a grandmother fighting off a pterodactyl, or whatever.

The interest was more sustained in the art community. In that world, shooting a painting, particularly a painting that had just sold for 24 million pounds, was big news. *Art Today*, one of the leading art journals in the United States, ran an in-depth story in early 2020. It was thorough and exhaustive, bypassing the sensational perspective of *The Dirty Laundry* to talk seriously about Pablo Ingersoll, Laura Marcus, the creation of *Annabel's Eyes*, and the history of important paintings that had been intentionally damaged. The four-page spread featured photos of Laura, and Pablo, before and after photos of *Annabel's Eyes*, and, of course, the photo *The Dirty Laundry* had run on its front page.

George Johnson read the *Art Today* story with interest. He could not fathom why anyone would damage a great piece of art. It was pure vandalism, but people of the stature of Laura Marcus didn't engage in pure vandalism. Somehow, the human element was involved. Love, hate, passion, jealousy:

those emotions were capable, George knew, of driving such behavior. He wondered what the backstory was.

Ivy walked in as George was contemplating human achievement and human failure. It was the second Friday of February 2020. She entered his office, greeted him with a bright smile, and placed her backpack on his desk. George was happy to see her, as he always was. Her cheerfulness brightened his life, and he was eager to see what she had created since their last meeting.

There were twenty-six drawings in her current offering. They exhibited Ivy's consistency, quality, and strength. They seemed somewhat repetitive as a whole, at least to someone who had seen as many of her drawings as George had, but looked at individually, each was fresh and exciting. "These are terrific, Ivy," George said as he counted out $3,000 in cash.

Ivy was largely unschooled, but she was financially astute and scrupulously honest. When George handed her the money, she gave him $400 back. "You gave me too much, George," she said. "I only brought twenty-six drawings."

Refusing the money, George responded that he was giving her a bonus. He had calculated that it would reduce his profit margin to eighty-five percent, but he could live with that. He liked Ivy. Then he realized he didn't have to live with it. He could easily sell Ivy's drawings for $225. That would actually increase his profit; he would recoup the bonus money and make even more than he had before. And why wouldn't he? Any businessman would.

Ivy was not a cynical person and didn't suspect George of mental gymnastics; she took his apparent generosity at face value and was deeply appreciative. "Thanks, George. You're very kind."

"I'm always happy to help you, Ivy." As she readied to go, George said, "Say, did you follow that story a few months ago about the woman who shot the eyes out of a painting she had bought at an auction in London?"

"No, I didn't hear about it. I don't really follow the news."

"I was reading about it in *Art Today*. They have a big write-up, and it's fascinating. A famous artist in New York had made the best painting of his life. It came up at auction a few years later, and the artist's former girlfriend bought it and shot holes in it. Right at the auction house. Weird. Here, I've finished the article. Take the magazine with you. You'll enjoy the story. We can talk about it the next time you come in."

"Thanks, George. I will." Ivy put the magazine in her backpack without looking at it.

"By the way," George said as Ivy was walking out the door, "the woman in the painting looks a little like you. Younger though."

Ivy took out the magazine when she got home. She read the article. She read it again. She read it a third time. She studied the photographs at length. She had never heard of Pablo Ingersoll, but she ached for him. His life's work had been destroyed. *Why?* She looked at the photo of Laura Marcus. She looked at it searchingly. *Why? Why would you do that? You look like a nice person, and you're rich and beautiful. What could he have done to you to deserve that?*

Ivy didn't dwell on the before and after photographs of *Annabel's Eyes*. The painting was less interesting to her than the human story surrounding it.

She made two decisions that afternoon. She had always wanted to paint but considered it a luxury she couldn't afford. Now, she felt an urgent need to paint Pablo Ingersoll. His story touched her, and she wanted to tell that story in a painting, maybe several paintings. He was a handsome man, and she wanted to show that. She wanted to capture the success and recognition he had earned, and she would never be able to in a drawing, but in a painting, maybe. Mostly, she wanted to portray the empathy and sorrow she felt for the sad and anguished artist, the man who carried himself with quiet dignity as he stood in the ashes of his greatest commitment and deepest love. She needed the depth, texture, and shine that only paintings could provide. She would take the bus to an art supply store she had heard about in Harrisonburg. She would use the bonus money George gave her to buy a used easel, some paints and brushes, a palette knife, and a couple of scrapers. She knew she would figure out how to use them.

Ivy's second decision was easier. She would make a drawing. She would send a message.

CHAPTER FORTY-SIX

Laura (June 2020)

The world first learned about the Covid 19 outbreak in China in January 2020. The worst fears of the medical community, that Covid would become a pandemic, were soon realized. The lockdown in the United States began in March.

As it was for most Americans, the requirement to stay home was an adjustment for Laura. She liked going to the office. She enjoyed the interactions at the coffee station, the back-and-forth of working with colleagues to ready a case for trial, the lawyer lunches where significant court decisions were discussed, the quiet meetings with Gooey to work through management issues and discuss the future of the firm.

Laura particularly liked going to the office since her return from London. Her embarrassment and regret at having dragged the firm into her scandal had largely evaporated. She knew the firm would lose some clients because of her actions, and it did, but her disappointment was offset by the unexpected net business gain. Potential clients signed on because they liked what they saw as her toughness. She was surprised and gratified that most of her colleagues treated her as a conquering hero. By and large, the disapprovers kept their feelings to themselves out of a fondness for Laura and a commitment to the firm. Although she was privately remorseful (because, really, who would do such a thing?), she enjoyed the attention she and the firm were getting.

It was harder to savor the affection when Covid struck, and she had to work from home. Love doesn't feel the same when it comes in over the phone, or by email or text. But Laura adjusted. She had no choice. Soon she was an expert at managing her business remotely, handling meetings with colleagues and arguments before judges on Zoom calls, and being her own typist, scheduler, billing clerk, and IT department. She found she liked the peace and freedom of staying in pajamas all day.

She reveled in her Park Avenue apartment, which had a new and special addition. *Annabel's Eyes* hung beautifully over her living room sofa. She looked at it often, for long moments, and never failed to see, and appreciate, something she hadn't noticed before. It truly was a masterpiece. Her dream of having an Ingersoll had come to pass. It wasn't the one she had visualized when she and Pablo were together, when he had promised to paint her, but it was his painting, his best painting, and it bore her indelible mark. It may not have been a painting of Laura, but it was something she and Pablo had created together.

It was a lovely June day when the package arrived. Laura was enjoying a second cup of coffee between calls. She was in her favorite chair, daydreaming as she alternated her gaze between her magical city and *Annabel's Eyes*. There was a knock on the door to alert her as the day's mail came through the slot and settled on the floor. She picked up the pile and riffled through it. There were the customary bills, a card from London (that would be Jane!), a sinful number of catalogues intended to part her from her money, and a legal-sized brown envelope that had been mailed to her office and couriered from there to her home.

Laura put the other things aside and opened the brown envelope. Her address at Marcus, McGoohan was printed in block letters. Next to it was a caution, underlined, that said, "Do Not Bend." There was no return address, but the package carried a postmark from Woodstock, Virginia. Laura didn't know anyone in Woodstock, and in fact had never heard of it.

She removed a letter-sized drawing from the envelope, along with a stiff piece of cardboard that had been inserted to protect it. She looked for a note, but there was none, only the drawing. Her curiosity peaking, she flipped the drawing over, so it was face up, and gasped. It was a black-and-white drawing, very good actually, very realistic. She recognized the format immediately—it was the now-famous photo posted by *The Dirty Laundry*. But there were differences in the details. The woman looking at the painting and dangling a pistol was not Laura or anyone she could identify. And the woman in the painting was not Annabel, though she was posed as Annabel. It was Laura, very clearly Laura. There were bullet holes through each of her eyes. At the bottom of the drawing, in the same block letters used to address the envelope, were the words, "BANG! BANG!"

Laura returned to her chair, puzzled, taken aback, and mildly afraid. *Who would send such a thing,* she wondered. *And why? Is this someone's idea of a joke? Is it meant as a message? If so, what is the message? A threat? It feels like a threat. What goes around comes around. Is this the opening salvo of an extortion effort?*

She called the police to report what had occurred. She was connected to a Detective Kehoe, who listened carefully to her story, then said, "You were right to call this in, Ms. Marcus. People do strange things sometimes, and this shutdown for the pandemic has made matters even worse. People are bored, and some seek entertainment in harassing other people, usually on social media. Doing it by mail is a little weird. I'll put a call in to the Woodstock police to alert them, but I don't expect anything to come of it."

"And what should I do about this in the meantime?" asked Laura. "How should I think about this?"

"As a threat. Definitely a threat."

CHAPTER FORTY-SEVEN

Ivy (May 19-21, 2022)

It had been a week since Bart brought Ivy to the barn. He had visited her the first two days, but she hadn't seen or heard from him since. She was convinced that harm had come to him. He would have been there otherwise.

Ivy was doing well physically. She missed her daily walks, which got her out of the house and gave her the opportunity to exercise, see what was new in town, and say hello to people. Even with her drawings and her bird friends at the barn, she was bored and lonely. There was plenty to eat. The food supply would last another five days, until the following Tuesday. That would be May 24. That's when Ivy had to leave the barn, one way or the other, no matter what.

Her time at the barn had been productive. She had come to grips with her major preoccupation. She hated living as a fugitive, fearing for her safety, committed to solitude and camouflage so she wouldn't draw attention to herself and facilitate her capture by Jaime and the Browns. She knew she would be killed if Jaime found her, but he was killing her as it was by forcing her to live in the shadows. She was ready for the sunlight. She resolved to stop living in fear.

It had been fifteen years since her escape. Jaime and the Browns had been chasing her that whole time. She had been careful, and lucky, and they hadn't found her. It was time to do things differently. If she ever got out of here, she was going to start chasing them. She would go to the police—she didn't know exactly who, but Sam would tell her. She would give them names, the address of the house in Los Angeles, the name of the clothing business. She would give them descriptions of Jaime and the Browns.

Her decision gave Ivy a new confidence, a promise of freedom. She convinced herself that going on offense would actually be safer, because if the police knew her story and knew about Jaime, they would protect her. She would even be helping others like her; when the police found Jaime and the Browns and shut down their operation, the other captives would be freed.

It was a bold and courageous decision, a reversal of what had been her guiding principle for fifteen years. Ivy was clear-eyed and committed, eager to put her plan into action, but first she had to get out of this barn. *Should I go now*, she asked herself, *or should I stay the course and wait until Tuesday? There's a possibility Bart will come back if I wait a few more days. I'm OK here until then. I'd like to go now, but I'm not sure I can get down that ladder. I'd say it's fifty-fifty. Besides, if my crutch breaks when I throw it down ahead of me, I'm in real trouble; I can't hop to Woodstock on one leg. If I fall or lose my crutch and die up here, wherever here is, the police will never know about Jaime and the Browns. They will be the winners. I can't let that happen.*

Suddenly it hit her. She would wait until Tuesday and use the intervening time to prepare a message to take with her when she made her try. If the worst happened, someone would find the message when they found her body. They would give it to the police.

Ivy started to draw. She would make a drawing each day for the next three days. They would have to be the best drawings she ever made. They had to be stone cold accurate, with no frills or embellishments. They had to be perfect if they were to achieve her goal.

She recalled her earlier drawing of the evil man. She drew him again, not as a caricature this time but as a living, breathing depiction of Jaime Roxas. She showed him from the waist up, his straight black hair glistening with grease and framing his handsome Filipino face. She gave him the unsmiling look, the slight sneer she remembered so well. She put a *balisong*, the toy he was never without, in his right hand. Below the drawing, she wrote, "This is Jaime Roxas as I knew him fifteen years ago. I was his captive in Los Angeles.

He hurt me then, and he's been trying to kill me since I escaped in 2007. He is evil and very dangerous."

Ivy's recall of Mrs. Brown was less clear, but it was good enough to produce a detailed drawing of a pleasant-looking Caucasian woman of middle age. Ivy presented her in a stylish business suit, with serious eyes and an attempt at a grin. It looked like one of those professional photographs of a business executive who wants to appear content and worldly but won't risk looking frivolous by smiling broadly. Ivy's descriptor said, "This is 'Mrs. Brown' in 2007. I don't know her real name. She had a house at 27 Eucalyptus Drive in Westwood. Jaime ran a human trafficking operation for her there. She was kind to me once, but don't be fooled. She knew who Jaime was, and she ordered and funded his work anyway."

Ivy's final drawing was of Bart. It showed a trim Caucasian man in his mid-thirties. He had closely cropped hair and a nice smile. He looked alert, ready to spring. She gave him a gentle toughness. She wrote, "This is Bart. I met him in Woodstock last month. He was good to me. He protected me."

CHAPTER FORTY-EIGHT

The Investigation (May 2022)

Two black trash bags ferrying human cargo scudded along the North Fork of the Shenandoah River, bouncing and bobbing, hanging up on a tree limb here, resting on a gravelly shoal there, then breaking free to move swiftly across good water until their next impediment or diversion. By the end of the day Sunday, the day after the original recovery, both had been found and recovered.

The first bag was firmly pinned between a fallen tree and a concrete support for the bridge that carries car traffic over the North Fork between Edinburg and Fort Valley. It had started to slip below the surface when it was spotted and plucked from the river. It yielded a human torso, apparently male, that had what appeared to be a stab wound below the left pectoral muscle.

The second was recovered at Meems Bottom, down near Mt. Jackson. It was bobbing up and down among eight or ten apple crates intertwined with metal strapping that someone had evidently decided to dump in the river instead of taking another five miles to the landfill. That bag gave up the missing leg and a human head, Asian in appearance, with a bullet hole near the right temple.

The six body parts from the three trash bags were reunited in the medical examiner's office. They were laid out on a table in the same relation to each other that they had known in life. The medical examiner, Dr. Christian, had come in early to perform some tests, and he was ready to report his findings when Angelo and his team arrived Monday morning.

Dr. Christian stood at the head of the table while the others gathered in a semicircle around the reconstructed body. Julie lagged back a step and was having obvious difficulty looking at the body. The others, more experienced, had learned the investigative importance of making a thorough visual examination of a victim's remains. They held their gazes, even though they didn't like what they saw much more than Julie did.

Angelo signaled their readiness to proceed, but he was careless with his choice of words. "What's up, Doc?" he said. Beth stifled a groan. This was not the time or place for Bugs Bunny.

Dr. Christian looked at him with annoyance but decided to let the inappropriate reference pass. "This body is now intact or would be if the separate members were joined together. The parts all belong to the same original person, an Asian male whose blood type was AB negative. The separation of the body parts appears to have been accomplished by a saw of some sort. The severance of the bones was relatively clean, not hacked or jagged as we might expect to find if a machete or bolo had been used. There's a bullet wound to the head, near the right temple, that appears to have been the cause of death. The cutting of the bones came later. There's also a knife wound in the left side of the victim's chest. Death had already occurred when that wound was inflicted."

"That's helpful," said Angelo solemnly, trying to assure the others that he had recovered from his gaffe and was firmly in control. "Have you recovered the bullet?"

"Not yet, but I will. It's still in there."

"Have you measured the knife wound to the chest?"

"Yes." The medical examiner looked at his notes. "It's just over two inches wide."

Duane was energized. "That's just a little wider than the blade of the palette knife we found at the scene. The probability is that the knife blade wiggled a little when it went in, which would account for the wound being slightly wider than the blade."

Things were starting to come together. Angelo probed further. "Could you tell whether the knife in the victim's wrist sheath was used in the altercation?"

"There was no blood on it, but I suppose it could have been washed away in the river. The blade of the knife was smooth and sharp. It had no rough spots, which it might have had if it had struck anything hard recently. Most importantly, it was still snapped into the sheath. The victim couldn't have done that once he was shot. Whoever cut him up might have snapped it in, but why? I don't see that knife as having been a factor in whatever happened."

"How about fingerprints? Anything useful there?"

"I'm afraid not," said Dr. Christian. "After a week in cold river water, the fingers had blanched and there was some skin slippage. Nothing reliable in the fingerprint department."

Angelo's team took a long moment to consider the findings and determine whether they had missed anything. They returned to Angelo's office to try to put the pieces together and assess where they were.

"Alright, we've finally got something to work with," Angelo said. "I'm going to try to fast-track an update of the assumptions. Stay with me on this.

"Somehow, Jaime Roxas, who we're assuming is the victim, figured out where Ivy lived and went to her house to kill her. She wasn't there, either through luck or the help of a third party. Roxas entered the house, his knife still sheathed; he knew Ivy lived alone, and he could overcome any resistance she might offer. When he was in the living room, he was shot through the window screen. The shooter then entered the house, used a saw to cut Jaime into six manageable pieces, and put the pieces into three trash bags that he— or she—dumped into the river. What am I missing?"

Everyone talked at once. Frank's drawl carried the day. "I think the shooter was trying to kill Ivy. She was always there at night. How could the shooter have known someone else would be in her house that night?"

"The problem with that, Chief," Duane said, "is that Roxas was the only one we know of who wanted to kill Ivy, and he was in the house to do it by hand. Who else would be out there wanting to shoot Ivy?"

"You're right, that's a dead end," Frank grunted.

"The only way I can make sense of it," said Beth, "is that there was a third party, someone who had gotten word that Jaime was coming for Ivy and wanted to protect her. Whoever that was got Ivy out of her house before Roxas arrived, then returned to take him out."

Angelo didn't buy it. "That's a good theory, Beth, but it's a reach to get there. Who out there knows Ivy, cares about her, and has the skills and the balls to move her and then go back for Roxas? She's lived in Woodstock fifteen years with lots of acquaintances and well-wishers, but only a couple of real friends. Who would know about her past with Roxas? Who would know he was coming for her, and when? We shouldn't lose sight of the possibility that there was a third party, but it seems like a very long shot." He paused in concentration. "Ivy's a simple woman. I have difficulty seeing that many moving pieces. It feels more like something local, a simple grudge."

"Except that we have Jaime Roxas from Los Angeles on a table in the medical examiner's office," replied Frank. "And before that, we have him splattering blood all over Ivy's living room."

"Do we?" asked a quiet voice from the corner of the room. Julie spoke for the first time and drew everyone's attention.

"What are you saying, Julie?" Angelo was alert.

"I know we want the body to be Roxas and we think it is, but remember, Ivy is forty-three now. She was seventeen when Jaime took her captive. He had to be at least eight or ten years older, maybe even fifteen. That would make him early to mid-fifties now, possibly sixty."

"And?"

"And the guy on the table didn't look that old." Julie had been paying attention after all.

"Yeah, but he had been in the water a few days, with no blood circulating in his chopped-off head," said Duane. "His looks were distorted. Everything else points to Roxas. It has to be Roxas."

"Julie's right," Angelo said. "We're making an assumption that fits our desire. We need to slow down and follow the facts." He was on the phone and put it on speaker. "Doc," he said, "how old was that guy on the table?"

The answer was quick and sure. "Mid-thirties, maybe. No older than forty. We'll know more closely when we get the bone density test results."

"Any chance he was over fifty?"

"None."

Angelo hung up the phone. "It's not Roxas," he said.

CHAPTER FORTY-NINE

Sam (May 23, 2022)

Things had been moving slowly. Now they were happening fast.

While Angelo and his team were meeting with the medical examiner to view what they thought were the remains of Jaime Roxas, Sam Picken was having her morning coffee at the Woodstock Café. Sam started her day there every morning and always looked forward to it. The Café was the town's social center—its great food and friendly service drew people from around the county and well beyond. Sam liked the young couple who owned and ran the Café and firmly believed in supporting local businesses that were working hard to better Woodstock.

Cindy, a friendly fifty-something who worked three jobs to make ends meet, was Sam's regular server. She looked for Sam each morning and took pride in having her coffee, a medium roast with a dash of milk, on the table when Sam arrived. When Cindy delivered the coffee on this particular morning, she accompanied it with a sealed envelope. Sam put her newspaper aside to look at the envelope. It had no markings except Sam's name, which was in Cindy's handwriting.

"What's this?" Sam asked Cindy, curious and slightly alarmed.

"A man gave it to me last week as I was coming into work. He handed me fifty dollars and asked me to deliver the envelope to you with your coffee on Monday, May 23. That's today."

"Who was the man?"

"I don't know. Nice looking guy but I'd never seen him before. He said it was important."

"Isn't this your handwriting on the envelope?"

"Yes," said Cindy. "When he gave me the envelope, he asked me to write your name on it so I wouldn't lose it. He said he would have done it himself, but he didn't have a pen, and he was running late for something he needed to do."

"Just one more question, Cindy. What did the man look like?"

"Average. Nondescript. He was wearing a baseball cap with an NYY on it, you know, for the Yankees. Honestly, I was so taken aback when he came up to me that I really didn't pay much attention to what he looked like."

"OK, thanks," said Sam, turning to her coffee and the mysterious envelope as Cindy moved two booths down to take an order.

Inside the envelope was a single sheet of paper. It bore a message in Arial font that could have been typed on any computer. Sam read it, slowly and with full concentration.

Sam, we have a mutual friend. She needs help, TODAY, and if you're reading this, I'm not able to give it to her. Go to Riverview Park, turn left, then right onto a dirt road and through a cow gate to an abandoned barn. You'll know what to do. Be there by noon. TODAY. It's important.

Sam sat back, took a sip of coffee, and studied the message. *Could this be about Ivy? Could it be a ruse? Could it be a setup? Of course, I'll go because it could be about Ivy, but should I take someone with me? Should I tell anyone about this? Angelo or Frank? No, I don't want to bring the police into this, not yet. Chris maybe? He'd come along, and he'd keep his mouth shut about whatever it is, but he has an important meeting with the town council this morning.*

I'll go on my own. I'll be careful, leave the cow gate open, turn the truck around so it's facing the gate before I get out, walk in slowly, make plenty of noise. If I get spooked, I'll get the hell out of there and come for help. Then we'll go back in force. Easy-peasy. It'll be fine.

Sam didn't stay for the usual second mug of coffee. She went by her office and asked her assistant to reschedule her appointments for the day. She changed into blue jeans and a T-shirt, climbed into her Dodge Ram pickup, checked to see that it had plenty of gas, and headed to Riverview Park.

The directions were straightforward, and Sam knew the general area well. Her anxiety mounted as she went through the cow gate, which she left open for a quick exit should it become necessary. She saw the barn and parked the truck twenty feet away, facing the gate. She got out and began walking slowly and warily toward the barn. Time to make some noise.

"Hello," she yelled. "Hello. Is anybody there? Ivy?"

A sound from the barn. A woman's voice. Ivy's voice. Upper level on the right side. "Sam, is that you?"

"Ivy, thank God! Are you alone?"

"Yes, it's safe. Just me and my bird friends."

Sam was in the barn in a flash, looking up at the hay mow, seeing Ivy. "You stay right there," she said. "I'm coming up."

Seconds later, Sam was up the ladder in the loft, hugging Ivy frantically. They were both crying and laughing, the emotion and tension of the past ten days released at last.

Finally, Sam said, "My God, it's good to see you." She hugged Ivy again. They laughed and talked, stopping briefly to acknowledge the visit of a bright red cardinal who seemed curious about Ivy's visitor.

"How long have you been here?" Sam asked. "How did you get here?"

Ivy told Sam about Bart. He was new in town and befriended her. "He came to my house on a Thursday night, not last week but the week before, May 12, I think it was. He said we had to leave immediately, that I was in danger in the house. He brought me here."

"Why did you go with him? You didn't even know him."

"I trusted him. I can't say why. I just did. Was there any trouble at my house?"

"Yes, Ivy, there was. A man was killed there two nights after you left. It turns out you were right to trust Bart, whoever he is. He saved your life. There was blood all over your living room, including some of your paintings, I'm afraid."

Ivy looked down, sadness on her face. "Well, I'll try to fix those. I think I can. Anyway, they're only paintings. Who was the man in my house?"

"The police are investigating that. Apparently, he was a Filipino."

"Was it Jaime Roxas?" Ivy asked, hopefully. "It had to be."

"I don't know."

"Did they find anyone else? I'm worried about Bart. I haven't seen or heard from him in more than a week. I hope he hasn't been hurt or killed. By the way, I should have asked you this earlier. How did you find me? How did you know to come here?"

Sam explained about the anonymous note she had received at the Café. They agreed it must have come from Bart. No one else knew where Ivy was. But that didn't mean Bart was unharmed because he had given the note to Cindy a week earlier. It wasn't clear exactly when. It could have been before the killing at Ivy's house. Sam made a mental note to try to pin that down with Cindy.

"Let's get you out of here, Ivy," Sam said. "I'm sure you'd like to be back home. I've cleaned the place up as best I could, but there's more to be done, and you'll want to get it the way you like it. You can stay with Chris and me for a while if you want. It might be spooky to be in a place where a man has just been killed."

"Thanks, Sam. Thanks for everything. I want to go home. I'll be fine there now that Jaime is dead."

"There's just one more thing we need to talk about before we go. Everyone in town has been worrying about you. The sheriff's office and the police are investigating the crime at your house. The new sheriff, Angelo Jones, is leading the investigation. You haven't met him, but you'll like him. He's a good man. He'll want to talk to you."

"I'm ready. I've made some decisions about my life. I'll tell him everything."

"Good. I'll ask Angelo to set up a meeting for tomorrow morning."

CHAPTER FIFTY

Ivy (May 24, 2022)

"Pleased to meet you," Angelo said, extending his outstretched hand to Ivy. "I'm Angelo Jones, and we are extremely happy to have you back. I know it's been a rough time for you, and I want to hear all about it, but I must say you look to be in good shape."

"Nice to meet you, Sheriff. Sam says you're a good man, and that counts for a lot with me. I appreciate your concern." Ivy shook his hand, then turned to Beth, whom Angelo had asked to join them. He didn't know Ivy, but he did know she had been under severe stress, and he thought the presence of another woman, especially a caring person like Beth, might have a calming influence. Ivy and Beth exchanged a loving hug.

Angelo poured Ivy a cup of coffee, watched incredulously as she sweetened it with six lumps of sugar, and got down to business. "If you're ready to begin," he said, "let's start with the recent past. Please tell us where you've been staying, how you got there, and everything that's happened to you since you left your house a week or two ago."

Ivy told them about Bart, their friendship, and his taking her to the abandoned barn and providing for her. She told him she hadn't seen or heard from him in more than a week, and she was worried about him. She told them about the message Sam had received and her belief that it must have been sent by Bart, because he was the only one who knew where she was.

Angelo and Beth listened intently, but by prior agreement, they reserved their questions for later. They wanted to hear everything Ivy was prepared to give them and ask their questions in the larger context.

"That's helpful," Angelo said. "We've heard about Bart during our investigation, but we can't find him and don't know much about him. We'll want to talk more about him later. For now, are you comfortable telling us about Jaime Roxas and your period of captivity in Los Angeles?"

Ivy looked up, startled. "How do you know about that?"

"Sam told me about it in confidence. We haven't broken that confidence, and we don't intend to. It's important information for us to know because Jaime's the only person we can identify with a motive to harm you. Mrs. Brown, too, of course, but finding one of them will probably lead us to the other. Jaime has been the focus of our investigation."

"It's alright. I was just surprised that you knew about Jaime. Sam is the only person I've told, and I trusted her not to talk, but I guess she did, to you anyway, in order to help me. It doesn't matter that you know because I made some life-changing decisions during my stay at the barn. I don't want to live in fear from Jaime and Mrs. Brown any longer. I want to tell you everything. I want to help you find Jaime and Mrs. Brown. They are evil people who do terrible things to children. That needs to stop. They need to be put away."

Ivy spent most of the next hour talking about herself, how her mother had been duped into sponsoring her trip to Los Angeles, how she had been placed in captivity there, what she had been forced to do, her efforts to escape, and how she had finally gotten away and hitched a ride that ended in Woodstock. It was all the way across the country, but she was still afraid, living a quiet life in the shadows so she wouldn't be found. The one thing she didn't tell them was her true name, Estella de la Rosa, or Stellie. That was the name Jaime and Mrs. Brown knew her by, and she didn't want it to become public.

There was a long silence when Ivy stopped talking. Angelo and Beth were transfixed by the sad and sordid tale, exhausted at hearing about the perils Ivy had experienced at the hands of Roxas and Mrs. Brown during her long odyssey from the Philippines to the safety of the present moment. At long last, Beth spoke.

"What happened to you is unimaginable, unconscionable. To use your word, it is evil. We will work tirelessly to find them. I promise you that."

Angelo nodded his agreement. "Yes, we will. For now, I have some follow-up questions. First of all, who's the man you got a ride with from Los Angeles to Woodstock? We'd like to talk with him."

"I don't know. He never said his name and I didn't need to know it. I just needed a ride."

"Have you seen him since you've been here?"

"No. He said he had a house near the river and was getting ready to retire there. I guess he did."

"Do you think Roxas is still looking for you, even though it's been fifteen years since your escape?"

"Yes. My escape made him look bad. He will never stop looking for me."

"Do you think he would come all the way across the country to seek revenge if he found out you were here?"

"I have no doubt about it."

"Do you think it was Roxas who went to your house on May 14?"

"I don't know, but it must have been. He's the only one who's trying to kill me as far as I'm aware. Except Mrs. Brown, I suppose, but she would do it through Roxas. I hope it was Roxas at my house because if it was, he's dead now."

"Do you have any reason to think Bart knew Roxas, or knew of him?"

"No. Why? How would he?"

"I'm just thinking out loud here," Angelo said gently. "Bart got you out of the house to protect you. He wouldn't have done that unless he knew, or sensed, danger was coming. Roxas is the only danger to you that we can identify. What would have tipped Bart off to Roxas or your imminent danger?"

"I have no idea. No idea at all."

"There's something there. I feel it. We're going to find it. Meanwhile, let's work on what we know. You've given us names and addresses, and we'll follow up on those. Now let's get some descriptions. The central characters in this drama seem to be Jaime Roxas, Bart, and Mrs. Brown. With your permission, I'm going to ask our sketch artist to come in. She can draw their faces based on your descriptions."

"I've already done that," said Ivy, reaching into her backpack. "I thought it was important, and I wanted to leave a trail for you in case I didn't get back." She handed Angelo the three drawings she had made in her final days at the barn.

"Wow," said Beth, "these are detailed and precise. They'll be an enormous help to our investigation."

Angelo was studying the drawings. He was focused on the evil man. The drawing confirmed what Angelo and his team had earlier concluded: Roxas wasn't the man on Dr. Christian's table. "Ivy, I'm afraid the man killed at your house wasn't Jaime Roxas. Will you come with us to look at the body and tell us if you know who it is?"

Moments later, they were staring at the lifeless head that was previously thought to belong to Roxas. "He looks Filipino," Ivy said, "but I don't know him. He's much younger than Jaime."

As they stepped outside, Angelo took out his cell phone and called Duane. "Will you get with that restaurant manager and—"

"Already did," Duane interrupted. "The man on the table is Chico Santos. Mr. AB negative. He's the man who was killed at Ivy's house."

CHAPTER FIFTY-ONE

Pablo (April 2021)

Barry handed Pablo a photo. It was Ann Merriman. Pablo was surprised and not surprised. Surprised because he didn't see Ann at the same level as the others on the *Imagine* wall, and because he thought she would be uncomfortable being in their company in her own project. It would look contrived and presented a non-trivial risk of devaluing *Imagine*, and Ann wouldn't want that. Not surprised because Ann had done a magnificent job with *Imagine*, and he knew Barry and the selection panel adored her.

Barry put words to what Pablo was thinking. "There are good arguments for not including Ann, as I'm sure you realize, and the panel considered them at length. We ultimately came out in favor of inclusion. What she has accomplished through her vision and implementation of *Imagine* is such an advancement for women that she deserves to be on that wall. In fact, we plan to honor her at the unveiling of the tenth painting."

Pablo was confused. "I don't understand. The *Grace* painting was the seventh. Next up is number eight, which would be unveiled in the ordinary course in the fall of 2022. If Ann is slotted for number ten, why are we talking about her now?"

"Because, frankly, we haven't reached agreement on who number eight should be. We're working hard to make that selection, but we thought it prudent to give you Ann now so you can get started on it. If we don't come up with someone soon, we can plug Ann in at number eight so that we stay on schedule."

"Got it. So, I should be thinking about this now, and get started on a leisurely basis, but with an eye to picking up the pace if we end up needing it for the 2022 unveiling. What artist have you decided should paint Ann?"

"David Hockney. Ann very much admires his work and relates to his *Celia* paintings, and she'll be thrilled to be painted by a fellow Brit."

"I'm on it," Pablo said, taking his leave. He looked forward to channeling Hockney, but he wasn't at all sure including Ann on the wall was a wise decision. He genuinely hoped the panel would come up with an alternate soon. That would give them more time to think about Ann, and maybe they would reconsider their position.

Back in Brooklyn, Pablo told Sally about his meeting with Barry and asked what she thought about the panel's selection of Ann. Sally's reaction was immediate and unequivocal.

"That's the dumbest thing I've ever heard! I like Ann, and she's been nothing but good to us, but she's not an astronaut or a Supreme Court Justice or the next chancellor of Germany. Plus, I can't believe she would want this. If it happens, it's going to look like she put this whole project together to advance her own interests. It would undermine everything she's been fighting for. Has Barry talked to her about it?"

"I don't think so. We didn't have that conversation, but my sense is that the panel wants to surprise her with it."

"Well, I don't think that's fair, either to Ann or the project. Would you be willing to give Ann a heads-up?"

"No, that's not my onion. But I think your assessment is spot on, and I'd be willing to share it with Barry. I would emphasize the second point and not the first. Better to say she wouldn't want it than tell her disciples she doesn't deserve it."

"Agreed. Hey, it's after six. How would you feel about heading down to Sal's? I feel a bottle of chianti coming on, and I need something Italian to sop it up." Moments later, they were seated in a quiet corner at one of their favorite neighborhood haunts. The chianti was served, a nice riserva from

Castellare, and they had ordered. Sally opted for the veal Milano and Pablo the osso bucco. It was a nice evening. They were good together.

"Say," ventured Pablo, "since we're into the heavy stuff, I'd like your take on another questionable proposition. It's something that's been on my mind, and I'd love for you to tell me it's crazy and I shouldn't do it."

"Sure. Shoot."

"I've been thinking about calling Laura and asking if I could go by to see *Annabel's Eyes*. I haven't seen it since it was shipped off to Sussex four years ago, and never with the eyes shot out. It's such an important part of me; I think I need to see it in person to know how I feel about the whole shooting thing."

"Of course, you should go. You need closure. But there's more to it, isn't there?"

"What do you mean?"

Sally thought she understood, but still chose her words carefully. "The painting ended your relationship with Laura. Maybe she hated your commitment to the painting. Maybe she hated the woman in the painting, Annabel. You need to know why she shot it, don't you?"

"Yes," sighed Pablo. "I do."

CHAPTER FIFTY-TWO

Laura (October 2021)

Several months elapsed. Pablo wanted to call Laura, and he started to punch in her number at least five times, but he always pulled back. Sally had said it well. He needed closure. But he knew the conversation with Laura would be painful. He still had feelings for her, and hearing her tell him why she wanted to hurt him by destroying his proudest achievement would tear them both apart.

In the end, it was Laura who called. She had been having parallel thoughts. She knew what the painting meant to Pablo, and she could only imagine how her attack on it must have hurt him. She wanted to have that conversation with him. She needed him to know why she had done what she had done. It might rip apart the last thread between them, but at least it would be out there. Pablo was a good man. She owed him that.

"Pablo," she said tentatively when he answered the phone. "I'd like to invite you to my apartment to see your painting. I'm sure you want to, and I know my actions in London must have been on your mind. We should talk about it, all of it, and clear the air if we can."

"Thank you, Laura. I've been meaning to call you." They set a date for the following week, both carefully avoiding Wednesday.

Pablo had bittersweet emotions when he entered Laura's apartment. He had spent a lot of time there, and in a sense, it felt like coming home. But that ship had long since sailed, and he felt the weighty truth of Thomas Wolfe's enjoinder that you can't go home again.

Laura hadn't changed. She was still beautiful. She greeted him with a slight hesitation, then a kiss on the cheek. They would never be together again, and they both knew it, but they had given much to each other. What they had would always be a part of them, would always bind them.

Annabel's Eyes transformed the room. Pablo looked at it for a long moment. Laura saw the reverence in his eyes, and the memory. "Wow," he said. "I can't believe I did that. Thanks for letting me see it, Laura." He went to the painting and touched it lovingly, the hair, the mouth, the cheek. Annabel was beautiful; he had captured her perfectly and frozen her in time, on a canvas. She would be seen for generations in the blossom of youth, never aging. He felt pride, humility, disbelief that he, Pablo Ingersoll, had done that, awareness he would never do it again.

He tried to avoid looking at the holes in the canvas where the eyes had been, but ultimately, he couldn't. He didn't know what to think about how they changed the painting. They marred it, yes, but in a way, they humanized it. Nothing is perfect. Nothing lasts forever. Shelley's great sonnet came to mind: "My name is Ozymandias, King of Kings; / Look on my Works, ye Mighty, and despair!"

Laura gave him time to make his peace with *Annabel's Eyes* and what she had done to it. She sat quietly, watching him closely. She took in every gesture, every loving touch of the work, every smile, every grimace. She gave him his hour of reunion and closure. She said nothing. At length, he took a seat across from her. She knew it was time for the conversation neither of them wanted, the conversation they needed to have.

"I'm so sorry, Pablo. I know I've hurt you terribly."

"Why did you do it?"

"You left me for the painting. You broke my heart. I wanted to get even. I wanted you to feel my pain. I wanted to destroy what you loved and left me for."

"The painting or the woman in it?"

"I don't know. The painting, I guess, and your commitment to it. I don't know the woman, and I don't think you do either. But she was in your head and in your heart, and you were engaging with her in ways you no longer did with me."

"But why the eyes? They were the best part of the painting."

"I knew that. I knew how hard you had worked on them. You were the best of me, and you took that away. The best of you was in her eyes, and I wanted to take that away from you."

There was little more to be said. Then Laura added, "I can't tell you how much I've regretted this, almost from the day I did it. Sotheby's suggested I have it restored. I didn't want to do that. I wanted to be a continuing part of Pablo Ingersoll's life and legacy. I know now how selfish and immature that seems. I'll have it restored if you want, or I'll give it to you to restore if you prefer that."

"No," Pablo said quickly. "I don't want it restored. It's damaged, yes, but so is life, so why shouldn't art, which represents and reimagines life, be damaged? Let's let the painting be a testament to the pain, and the beauty, of what we had."

Pablo walked to the door. Laura was trailing behind. They were both raw and spent with emotion. They still cared for each other. There could have been a moment, but that door had closed, and they knew it needed to stay closed.

"Goodbye, Laura. Thanks again for letting me see the painting, and for your honesty."

"Goodbye, Pablo. Be safe and happy."

CHAPTER FIFTY-THREE

Jaime (April 2022)

Jaime Roxas was a broken man. He didn't look anything like he had when Ivy knew him. At fifty-eight years old, he was battling diabetes and not faring well. He had lost two toes and could feel his eyesight beginning to go. He had lost weight and coughed and wheezed constantly with emphysema. He had not been able to hold a job since Mrs. Brown shut down the Long Beach operation in 2018. He was on the long descent and gaining speed.

The glory days of living in a fine house in Westwood were long gone, as were the less glorious yet still comfortable days of a warehouse loft in Long Beach. He now occupied a cramped, one-bedroom apartment in Filipinotown, near the 101 freeway. It wasn't how he had envisioned spending his final days, but it was what he could afford, and he liked the access it gave him to a broad array of Filipino foods. His favorite was *balut*, a fertilized duck egg with a developing embryo that incubates for fourteen-plus days and then is served steaming hot. Jaime ate *balut* three nights a week; he liked the taste, the crunchiness, and he loved the hype, which he took as the gospel truth, that it was an aphrodisiac. His *balut* ritual was to buy two eggs from his favorite food truck, wrapped in newspaper to keep them hot, and take them home to savor on the small table in his kitchenette.

On April 16, 2022, Jaime's ritual delivered a surprise. As he spread out the newspaper and reached for an egg, something in the paper caught his eye.

It was a picture of Stellie. He couldn't believe it. He turned the paper over to see what it was and check the date. The *Los Angeles Times*, from the fall of 2019. He quickly turned back to the article, which told the story of a woman who bought a painting in London and shot it. She shot the eyes out of the woman in the painting. She shot out Stellie's eyes! Jaime had little doubt the woman was Stellie. He recognized her immediately. She bore a striking resemblance to the photo he had taken of Stellie when he was pimping for her. A smile crossed his face, his first smile in a long time.

Jaime read the article carefully. His heart was racing. There were so many questions, interesting questions. Why was Stellie in the painting, a painting that sold for 24 million pounds? He didn't know how much that was in dollars, maybe around 30 million? The artist was named Pablo Ingersoll. How did he know Stellie? Why did he paint her? And who was the woman who shot her eyes out? Why would she do that? He read the article again.

Those were interesting questions, and he was curious about the answers, but his focus was on the only pressing question: Where was Stellie? How could he use this information to find her? He realized the article was almost three years old, and Stellie might have moved from wherever she had been then, but this was a breadcrumb on her trail. It was the best lead he had had for finding her.

He studied the article line by line. It didn't say anything about the woman in the painting, though the title suggested her name was Annabel. Well, that was nuts. It was Stellie, clearly Stellie, Stellie from the old days, before the scar, before the crutch. Jaime knew that in his soul. He had her. But he didn't know where she was.

As far as he could tell, there were two main actors in this drama—the painter and the woman who shot the painting. One of them had to know Stellie; maybe they both did. He would ask them. He would start with the painter, who the article described as "a highly successful contemporary artist living in Brooklyn" who had "studied art at the prestigious Pratt Institute." That was easy enough—a moment on the computer, and Jaime had a phone number.

"Mr. Ingersoll? This is Jim Rose," Jaime said, pleased with his quick adaptation of Jaime Roxas.

"Yes?" Pablo said warily. He hadn't recognized the number on his caller ID and knew instinctively that he shouldn't have answered the phone.

"I'm sorry to bother you, but I recently saw an article about one of your paintings. *Annabel's Eyes*? Annabel looks exactly like my sister, who disappeared seven years ago. We're desperately trying to find her. Do you know where she is?"

"No, I'm afraid not. I don't know the woman in the painting, but I hope you find your sister."

"If you don't know her, how did you paint her?"

Pablo wasn't going to play this game. He hung up. "Just some crank," he said to Sally when she asked who had called.

Jaime went back to the article to read it again. The woman who shot the painting was Laura Marcus, identified as "a name partner in the boutique litigation firm Marcus, McGoohan in Manhattan." Jaime restyled his approach. If Marcus shot the woman in the painting, she had to have known her. What's more, she must have had something against her, something seriously against her. Jaime would try to exploit that.

He had a work number, and Marcus was on East Coast time. The call would have to wait until morning. He was up early. "Ms. Marcus? Pardon the interruption, but I have a question. It's very important to me. My name is Jim Rose, and it's about my wife."

Laura was annoyed but relented. "Go ahead. Quickly, please."

"I think the woman in the painting you shot is my wife. Do you know her? Why did you shoot her?"

"No, I don't know her. My reasons for shooting the painting, which probably is not of your wife, are personal, complicated, and frankly none of your business, Mr. Rose." Laura began to hang up, but Jaime pleaded.

"Wait! Please hear me out. My wife and I have an eight-year-old daughter with cancer. Sarah, that's my wife, left us and took all our money. I've been trying to care for our little girl, but I have emphysema, and it's hard." He wheezed on cue. "Sorry, it's bad sometimes. I'm sure that's Sarah in the painting. I need to find her. Anything you could tell me, anything at all, would be helpful."

"What do you plan to do if you find her?"

"Go to wherever she is. Reason with her. Try to get her to come home. Try to get the money back to help our baby."

"What if she says no? Do you plan to harm her?"

"No, I don't want that. But I'm angry, and I don't have many options. Who abandons a sick child?"

Laura could see what the caller had in mind. If Jim Rose found his wife, he was going to kill her, either by plan or in a fit of rage. Too bad for Sarah, who didn't sound like she'd be much of a loss, but that wasn't Laura's concern. She had had her own beef with Annabel, or Sarah, or whoever the woman in the painting was, and she firmly believed the woman was the source of the "BANG! BANG!" threat drawing she had received. Laura had shot the painting of the woman; the woman had retaliated by depicting Laura in the painting and shooting her back. The drawing didn't make Laura afraid, but it pissed her off.

"Mr. Rose, I don't know who the woman is, and I don't know where she is. You might look around Woodstock, Virginia though. That's just a hunch. I hope things work out for you and your little girl."

CHAPTER FIFTY-FOUR

Mrs. Brown (April 17, 2022)

The phone rang on a bright and breezy spring afternoon as Mrs. Brown was enjoying a cup of tea and tending to her rose garden. It was the seldom-used Washington, DC line. She put down her pruning shears and picked up.

"Good afternoon," said the familiar voice.

"Jaime, it's nice to hear from you. How are you getting along?"

Mrs. Brown knew generally of Jaime's medical problems and that he was struggling. That was one reason she had shut down the operation in 2018. Jaime just couldn't handle it anymore. The other reason, and the larger one, was that she had been having increased misgivings about what she was doing. It was a highly profitable business and had enabled her to enjoy a good life and the benefits of modest wealth, but in her heart, she knew it wasn't right. Her concerns were underscored by America's recent focus on human trafficking and the damage inflicted on its victims. She wanted a more respectable life. Jaime's health issues gave her a way out.

"Oh, the usual aches and pains. The emphysema seems to be getting worse. That's not why I'm calling, though. I have news I think you'll like."

"Tell me about it."

"I've found Stellie. At least I think I've found her. I'm pretty sure I have." Jaime recounted the article he had stumbled across, the photo of a painting of a woman he was sure was Stellie, and his conversation with Laura Marcus.

Mrs. Brown listened impassively. She was out of the business, and recapturing or killing Stellie wasn't the imperative it once had been. On a personal level, she had liked and admired Stellie for her toughness and determination. She had been moved by Stellie's courage when she visited her at the hospital, and she had no desire to see Stellie hurt again, or maybe even killed.

"Where is she?" Mrs. Brown asked at last.

"In Virginia," Jaime said. "The Shenandoah Valley. A town called Woodstock."

"What do you plan to do?" Mrs. Brown had viewed Stellie's escape as a business problem, and it had gone away when the business was closed. She knew Jaime didn't see it that way. It had been business for him, too, but also personal. She would have to manage the conversation carefully. Jaime was no longer her employee, but he had been loyal to her, and she appreciated that. She was sorry for what he was going through. When she shuttered the operation, she continued to send him money, just to help out. And she kept her phone line active, the one reserved for his use, and encouraged him to call if he needed anything.

"I don't think there's much choice," Jaime said. "We no longer have a business to bring her back to. She needs to be taken out, Mrs. Brown. It's as simple as that. She was my biggest failure, and I can't let that stand."

"I know where you're coming from, but Jaime, it doesn't sound like you're in any condition to travel across the country and carry out your plan."

"I'm not, and that's a monumental disappointment. I'd like to slit her throat myself. But I have a good man that I plan to send. Chico Santos. Young. Strong. Good with a *balisong*, takes pride in his knife work. He was a protégé of mine. He's the guy I told you should take over the business when I got sick."

"Yes, I remember his name, and our conversation. You had a high regard for him, and I probably would have gone with him if I hadn't decided to dissolve the operation. It had become more of a risk than I was willing to take."

"Yes, well, all that's in the past now. You've been kind to me since our business together ended. I'll always be grateful for that. As they say in Manila, *salamat po*."

"What's your timetable for Stellie?"

"It's going to take longer than I want it to, but we need to do it right," Jaime said. "I'd guess maybe three weeks. I need to get Chico on board and see what his schedule is. He'll have to go to Woodstock and spend a little time there, finding Stellie and confirming that it's her. We don't want to be carving up the wrong person. He'll have to assess the situation and come up with a plan. I want his encounter with Stellie to be up close and personal. I want her to know it's coming from me. I want payback. I can be patient to be sure it's done right. I estimate that Chico will dispatch Stellie sometime between May 12 and May 17."

Mrs. Brown pondered his response. She voiced a concern she knew Jaime would appreciate. "I'm sure Chico is a good man, but he's not you. What if he screws up? What if he's captured or killed? Wouldn't there be a trail leading back to you?"

"I have confidence in Chico, and I don't think it's a serious risk, but I'll have insurance in place just in case. If things go wrong, I guarantee you Chico will not be taken alive, and his body will never be found. There will be no trail."

"I don't even want to know what that means," said Mrs. Brown, sickened. "Goodbye, Jaime."

Mrs. Brown rang off. She sat quietly, deep in thought, for almost an hour. She couldn't do this anymore. She was no longer the person who ran Jaime's operation and had trouble believing she ever had been. She couldn't be a party to Jaime's premeditated slaughter of a young woman who did nothing worse than escape a life of subjugation, indignity, and abuse. On a practical level, she couldn't risk being seen as an accessory to that slaughter. She liked Jaime, but this was too much. She was done with him.

She had two calls to make. The first was quickly handled. She called the phone company and deactivated her Washington, DC line.

The second was more sensitive. She thought for a long moment and made the call.

CHAPTER FIFTY-FIVE

Laura (April-May 2022)

Laura found herself fretting about two issues, and neither had to do with work. They weren't major preoccupations, more the kinds of things that ate at her in the middle of the night when she couldn't sleep, during that awful period some historians and psychologists refer to as "the watch." Both had to do with *Annabel's Eyes*, the beautiful painting that was becoming the curse of her life.

The first was the bigger issue, but it felt more remote, less urgent. She had taken comfort in her meeting with Pablo the previous fall. She believed they had achieved something resembling closure. But the sense of peace she gained from that meeting was temporary; she could feel it slipping away. *Annabel's Eyes* was a dominant presence in her apartment. She couldn't escape it, and the burden of what it was, what it had done to her, and what she had done to it, and to Pablo, weighed more heavily with each passing month. She didn't know if she could live with it much longer.

Moreover, Laura wasn't sure she should live with it. Like all great art, *Annabel's Eyes* was meant to be seen, not tucked away in the sanctuary of a rich person's living room. She had little doubt that Pablo would want it seen. She had taken enough from him without denying him the public acclaim his magnificent painting deserved. She knew the time was fast approaching when she would have to make a decision.

The more immediate issue involved her recent phone call with Jim Rose. *What was that all about anyway?* she wondered. *Who is this guy? He had a sad story, but there was something about it that was too convenient. Was he playing me? What if Sarah isn't the awful bitch he says she is? What if he's some nutcase looking to get even with someone who may or may not have done anything to him? I don't know him from Adam, and yet I did nothing to check him out or verify his story before giving him information about the woman's possible whereabouts. That was stupid. I may have put an innocent person in jeopardy.*

The more Laura thought about it, the worse she felt. By the end of the first week of May, she had convinced herself that she needed to remedy the dangerous situation she might have created. She had to try to find the woman in the painting, Sarah or whoever she was, and warn her about Jim Rose. She decided to go to Woodstock the following weekend. She had always wanted to visit the Shenandoah Valley anyway. People said it was lovely in the spring. She would make it a long weekend.

Laura got an early start from New York on the morning of Thursday, May 12, and drove the inland route through Allentown, Harrisburg, Carlisle, Hagerstown, and Martinsburg. She had fooled around on the internet the night before to see what Woodstock had to offer. She decided to go to the Woodstock Café for dinner; the ratings said the food was outstanding and the place was popular, and that combination promised a pleasant meal and maybe some conversations that would help her find Sarah. She would have time between her check-in at the Hampton Inn and her six o'clock dinner reservation to walk around town and visit the local art gallery.

After browsing in an antique store and a shop that specialized in local handcrafts, pottery, carved wooden decoys, and such, Laura went to the gallery. She spent fifteen minutes looking at the current exhibition. It featured charming, well-painted images of the Valley—babbling brooks, forested mountains, abandoned barns—that were serene and pleasing but not her thing. She wandered over to the station that every gallery has for unframed prints and works on paper that customers can flip through to find something inexpensive. She stopped cold about halfway through the stack when she encountered four drawings of faces, three men and a woman, that were different from everything else. They were distinctive, bold, fresh—and drawn by the same hand as the "BANG! BANG!" picture. Her heart stopped momentarily. This was the break she needed.

"Are you the gallery owner?" Laura asked of the man at the desk.

"Yes, ma'am, I'm George Johnson. How can I help you?"

"I'm quite taken with these four drawings. What can you tell me about the artist?"

"She's a local woman," said George. "She's been around for quite a while, and she loves to draw. She's very good at it, too, as you can see. Totally self-taught. I sell a lot of her work, some of it at art fairs in New York."

"Is her name Sarah, by any chance?"

"No. It's Ivy. Ivy Villanueva."

Jim Rose lied to me, Laura thought. *I knew it. I don't know what his business is with this woman, but I need to let her know he's coming for her for some reason. Maybe she'll know who he is and what this is all about. Anyway, it'll be her problem at that point.*

"I'll take all four of these drawings. Do you have any contact information for Ivy, by the way? I'd like to get in touch with her to see if she has any other work I could see."

"She doesn't have a phone, so you can't call her, but she lives down on Water Street across from the dairy farm. It's a small cinder-block house. Yellow. You can't miss it. Ivy lives alone, so you won't want to startle her by showing up tonight. Best to go tomorrow morning before eleven. That's when she leaves for her daily walk around town."

"Thank you, George. You've been very helpful."

Laura left with her purchases. *Screw that,* she thought. *I'm not waiting until tomorrow. It's almost six now. I'll have a nice dinner and be done by seven. I'll head to Ivy's house after that and give her a heads-up about Rose. This is all turning out to be easier than I expected. Then I can relax for the weekend, see what there is to see, and maybe head back to New York a little early.*

She went to the Café and had the pasta special, tortellini with bacon and spring peas. The chef was known for his handmade pasta, and it was divine. The spring peas, picked that morning at Adam's Apples and Herbs, were full, sweet, and delicious. The accompanying cabernet from Paso Robles that her server recommended featured notes of black currant and grilled toast that were a perfect complement. Laura was beyond satisfied; she could easily have taken a nap, but she had work to do.

Water Street was a few blocks over from the Café, and Ivy's house was easy to find. Laura spotted activity there when she was still a block away. She pulled over and parked so she could try to figure out what was going on. A man and a woman were leaving the house. The woman had a crutch. She looked like she was trying to move as quickly as she could. The man was helping her get into a vehicle.

Is that Jim Rose? Laura wondered. *Is he taking Ivy, or Sarah, or whatever her name is, somewhere to hurt her? Did I get here too late? If so, I need to try to stop this.*

Laura watched some more. She was thinking fast. She had never seen Jim Rose, but she had heard him wheeze. He said he had emphysema. This man wasn't laboring at all. He was quick, catlike in his movements. Ivy didn't seem at all afraid of him, and presumably she would have been if it were Jim Rose and he was out to harm her. This guy, whoever he was, seemed solicitous, caring. He hoisted a duffel bag into the vehicle, then took Ivy's crutch, put it in the back seat, and helped her into the passenger seat.

That can't be Jim Rose. He's protecting Ivy. He's moving her out of her house. He must know there's trouble coming. He's getting her out of harm's way, like I was intending to do, only he's making a better job of it. Should I follow them? No, she'll be OK. He's on her side. I think I'll nose around here a bit.

Whoever the man is, he has a sense of urgency about the situation. He must know there's trouble coming and coming soon. If Ivy is the Sarah that Rose is looking for, Rose knows she's physically challenged. He knows he doesn't have to hurt her from a long distance; he can do it face-to-face, and quietly, and painfully. She seems to be safe, but maybe I'll stick around to be sure. After all, it was my stupidity that put her in danger. If Rose shows up and breaks into her house, I may have to take him on. I can't let him hurt her. Besides, he played me. I wonder who that is who's helping Ivy.

Laura got out of her car and walked toward Ivy's house. She scouted out the small yard, carefully noting patches of light and open areas—danger zones. She looked for locations that provided cover and would be good spots for surveillance. She identified a small patch of woods about twenty yards from the rear of the house. It offered a view of the living room through a back window. She went to the double-hung window and raised the bottom half. She would have a better view through the screen. *What have I gotten myself into?* Laura said to herself, smiling. *I'm getting that old Iraq feeling.*

She had a fleeting thought that she should step away, notify the police, and leave everything to them. *Nah, too hard for me to explain and too difficult for them to believe.* She'd keep an eye on things herself. She'd call the police if things went south and she needed them.

Then she walked around to the front of the house and knocked on the door. She knew no one would answer, but if anyone was observing her, approaching the door openly and knocking would give her cover for looking into the living room through the larger front window.

What she saw took her breath away. There were several paintings of Pablo.

CHAPTER FIFTY-SIX

The Crime (May 14, 2022)

Laura hadn't come to Woodstock looking for trouble, and she didn't want trouble, but as things were developing, she decided to make an unantici-pated purchase. She was going to be doing surveillance and didn't want to be unprepared if things unexpectedly got hot. Fortunately, arming herself was easy in the Valley—there were gun stores everywhere. Automatic weapons were all the rage, but this situation didn't require that—few situations did. She picked out a rifle she knew well and had used many times before. It had good weight and balance, and a trigger that was easy to squeeze. She added a scope and a suppressor and was out the door in fifteen minutes.

Nothing happened the first night or the second. It was the Saturday of her long weekend. She would give Rose one more night to show up. If he didn't, or even if he did, she would head back to New York the next day.

As she had done the previous two nights, Laura headed for the small patch of woods at the rear of the house at ten o'clock. By then, most people were at home, readying for bed, and she could slip in unnoticed. She was confident the assailant, if one was coming, would wait until ten or later for the same reason she did. She took a position in a small swale under two dense bushes. It was a good hiding place; if she didn't do anything foolish to call attention to herself, no one would see her. She placed her small pack beside her, assembled her gear, took out a water bottle and two candy bars, made herself comfortable, and began to watch.

There was movement near the house at 11:23 p.m. Laura stiffened and inched into position to get a better look. Someone—it appeared to be a man—moved around the rear of the house, stopped to look through the back window into the living room, and then disappeared around the far corner, presumably to a side window or the front door. She couldn't see him, but a moment later, she picked him up again. He was inside the house, in the living room. He had broken and entered, but too quietly for Laura to hear.

She watched intently. The intruder's movements were furtive at first, then became more open, brazen, as he realized no one was home. Suddenly his movements became rapid and angry. Laura heard thuds. *He's throwing furniture around,* she thought. *Jim Rose came for Sarah, and she isn't here. He's pissed.* The intruder had been moving in and out of her vision, but now he was standing squarely in front of the back window, facing the far wall. She had him in her scope. Head shot. Right temple. Her finger was on the trigger. *So easy,* she thought. *So easy.*

Pfft. The shot was muffled by a silencer. Most people wouldn't have heard it or wouldn't have recognized it if they did. Laura's training kicked in. She remained motionless, her eye looking through the scope. The intruder in the living room was down. Head shot. Right temple.

Laura didn't move but was on high alert. Fifteen minutes went by, then twenty. She waited to be sure the target was neutralized. She waited to be sure no one in the neighborhood had heard anything, no one was coming to the scene, all was quiet.

At the thirty-minute mark, just after midnight, Laura picked up movement out of her peripheral vision. A shadow to her right. Quick. Around the far corner of the house. Moments later, she saw a figure in the living room. He—Laura was pretty sure it was a man—was dressed in black and wore a mask that covered his head. He was kneeling over the fallen body. Something was in his right hand, an odd-looking knife of some kind. He jabbed it into the dead man's chest, then let it fall to the floor. Jim Rose was no longer a threat to Sarah, or Ivy, or anyone else. Laura waited ten more minutes but saw no more of the black-clad figure who stabbed Rose. The show seemed to be over. It was time to get back to New York for some peace and quiet.

Laura was deep in thought and the next day's drive passed quickly. She was relieved that an apparently innocent woman had not been harmed because of her blunder in giving Jim Rose her whereabouts. She felt certain she had stumbled into something bigger than a domestic drama about a man who was angry over his wife leaving him and their sick child. She wondered what it was, and realized she might never know. Beyond that, there were the questions that wouldn't go away.

Jim Rose said he had emphysema, but Ivy's intruder wasn't wheezing and didn't seem to be physically compromised. Did Rose lie about the emphysema? Or was the intruder someone other than Rose?

Who was the man who moved Ivy? Why was he helping her?

Who was the man who went into Ivy's house after the intruder was shot? Was he the same guy who moved Ivy out of the house? Did he come back for Rose after getting Ivy out of harm's way?

Why was Ivy painting Pablo?

CHAPTER FIFTY-SEVEN

Laura (June 2022)

Barry and his panel were still unresolved about the selection of number eight for the *Imagine* wall, and they could not risk missing their October schedule. Pablo had been working on the *Ann* painting slowly, consistent with the plan to unveil it in 2026 as number ten, but he kicked it into high gear when Barry told him it would be needed in 2022. He was distressed by Barry's message, not because he couldn't get the painting done—that wouldn't be a problem—but because it meant there would be no reversal of the decision to include Ann on the wall.

Laura unknowingly came to the rescue and gave the *Ann* painting more time. She had continued to anguish over *Annabel's Eyes* and had reached a decision. She would give the painting to the Hemphill Museum for inclusion in the *Imagine* project. That would provide a worldwide viewing audience, promote Pablo as a great artist worthy of inclusion with the likes of van Gogh, Picasso, and Vermeer, and get the damn thing off her back. She was tired of having Annabel's lifeless eyes looking over her shoulder, haunting her.

Laura was comfortable with her decision but anxious because she knew it wasn't a done deal. Barry and the panel still needed to accept the painting. She knew from Pablo and from following the project in the news that inclusion on the *Imagine* wall required two things: a woman of importance, and a world-renowned artist to paint her.

She thought she could make the case for Pablo—maybe. She reviewed the list of the artists to whom the first seven paintings were attributed: Jawlensky, van Gogh, Waring, Picasso, Kahlo, Vermeer, and Warhol. A stellar lineup, but Laura saw Waring and maybe Kahlo as enough of a stretch to justify adding Ingersoll to the list. Besides, Pablo's role in creating six of the seven paintings—unknown to the public but well known to Barry and the panel—might be an emotional lever that would carry the day. Demonstrating Annabel's importance would be a steeper climb. Laura didn't begin to know how to frame that argument.

"Mr. Thomas," she said when Barry answered the phone, "my name is Laura Marcus. We haven't met, but I have been following Project *Imagine* for some years with great admiration."

This is interesting, thought Barry. Of course, he knew who Laura Marcus was. Everyone in the art world did. She was the woman who bought *Annabel's Eyes* for a record price and then shot it. She was also the woman, he knew from Ann, with whom Pablo had had a long-term affair.

"I wonder if we could meet," Laura continued. "I have a proposition that I believe you'll find of considerable interest."

A date was set, and the venue established. Barry hosted Laura at a private lunch in one of the several elegant dining rooms the Hemphill reserved for donors and other important guests who had business with the museum. After pleasantries and a sip of the lovely sauternes that accompanied the foie gras, Laura got to the point of her visit.

"As I'm sure you know, I acquired a wonderful painting by Pablo Ingersoll several years ago. It's called *Annabel's Eyes,* and it currently graces my living room."

"Yes, of course I do," Barry responded. His gentle smile let Laura know he also knew the rest of the story and was willing to discuss it if Laura wanted to.

"I'm sure you also know the painting suffered some damage."

"Yes," Barry said. He smiled but was noncommittal. He offered no judgment.

"I would like to donate *Annabel's Eyes* to Project *Imagine*, on the condition that it will be the painting that is unveiled this fall, in October, I believe."

Barry took a moment to consider his response. He had given some thought to what Laura might want to discuss, but he had not expected this. A world-class painting that had sold less than four years ago for 24 million pounds? Museums all over the world would compete mightily for it, and here it was being offered to the Hemphill and Project *Imagine*, apparently exclusively. He had to play it cool, reel it in slowly, not look too eager. He had to control his pounding heart.

"I must say, that's very generous, Laura. There's a lot to unpack about your offer. First, why would you want to part with such a magnificent painting?"

"It truly is magnificent, but Pablo and I have some history. The damage I did to the painting is part of that history. I have come to regret what I did, and the painting is an unwanted reminder. On a more altruistic level, it should be broadly seen and admired, not hidden away in my living room. Its inclusion in *Imagine* will help promote Pablo. I would like to do that for him after ruining his masterpiece."

"Do you think your shooting *Annabel's Eyes* ruined it?"

"Absolutely. The eyes were the best part of the painting. I told Pablo I would gladly have the work restored, but he wants to leave it the way it is, and I must respect that. How big a negative does the damage present for your decision about accepting my offer?"

Barry laughed and said, "It's not a negative at all." Laura looked puzzled.

"Let me tell you a story you apparently don't know," Barry went on. "It's quite remarkable. In 1964, Andy Warhol painted five silkscreens of Marilyn Monroe, each with a different background color. He had four of them stacked against a wall in his studio when he was visited by a good friend. The friend was accompanied by a performance artist Warhol didn't know. She saw the stack and asked Warhol if she could shoot the paintings. Warhol said yes, thinking she was going to photograph them, but instead, she pulled out a pistol and put a bullet through the stack. Those four paintings became known as *The Shot Marilyns*.

"That's interesting in itself, but the most fascinating part of the story is what happened after the shooting. One of the paintings, *Shot Sage Blue Marilyn*, sold at auction at Christie's last month for 195 million dollars. That's the most ever paid at auction for a work by an American artist. It shattered the previous record of 110 million dollars, held by Basquiat. As a footnote, the one Marilyn silkscreen that was not in the stack, while still very expensive, has not fared nearly as well.

"I tell you this to reassure you that the damage you caused to *Annabel's Eyes* has not hurt its market value, and it won't be a factor in our decision. But there are other issues we must consider. If you have followed Project *Imagine*, you know the standards that must be met for the paintings to be included on our wall."

"Yes," Laura interjected. "The women in the paintings must have achieved importance through their qualities and achievements, and the artists who paint them must be among the world's best."

Barry nodded. "Exactly."

"Let me try to make the case for Pablo," Laura said.

"That's not a problem. We know Pablo's work very well. He has been Jawlensky, van Gogh, Waring, Picasso, and Warhol for us, and his work has been so good that many art critics have mistaken it for the real thing."

Laura noticed Barry's omission of Kahlo and smiled. *Farah* had been another casualty of Pablo's commitment to *Annabel's Eyes*.

Barry continued. "He has also sold a painting at auction for 24 million pounds. It's undoubtedly worth considerably more now. That alone moves him into the pantheon of the great artists we require for our wall. It would be good to give him the recognition he deserves, and I'm confident our panel will agree."

Laura sighed, happy that one of the challenges had apparently been met. But the tougher one remained.

"How do you make the case for Annabel's worthiness?" Barry asked.

"I honestly have no idea. I don't even know who she is." Laura had a suspicion that Annabel might be the woman she saw in Woodstock, the one with the crutch who had drawn the "BANG! BANG!" picture in apparent retaliation for Laura's having shot her eyes out, the one who was painting Pablo in her living room, but she wasn't going to tell Barry that; it would kill any chance *Annabel's Eyes* still had for being included in the project. Besides, in her heart of hearts, Laura didn't believe it was the same woman. The middle-aged woman she had seen shambling along with a crutch couldn't possibly be the seductive beauty in Pablo's iconic painting. "I was hoping you could help me, selfishly hoping you would want the painting enough to work it out."

"Hmm," Barry said, looking perplexed. He desperately wanted the painting but knew he could not trample on the standards that were responsible for *Imagine*'s success. "Let me give this some thought. I'll get back to you next week if that works for you. I've very much enjoyed our lunch and, whatever we decide, I'm enormously appreciative of your generous offer."

Barry returned to his office, his mind churning. He knew exactly who Annabel was. She was Christina. Pablo painted her as Picasso would have, in the Dora Maar style. It was a triumph, but Pablo's enchantment with Christina was so great that it wasn't enough, so he painted her again, in his own style, and named her Annabel.

That answered one question and created others. Who was Christina? She hadn't been present for her unveiling, and Ann had been vague about who she was, suggesting that she worked undercover and that her greatness lay in private acts of courage unseen by the public. At one level, that made things easy. Annabel had already been accepted, as Christina. The proof of her worth was hanging on the wall in the Picasso painting.

OK, thought Barry. *But are we really going to have two paintings of the same woman, a shadowy woman at that? The Picasso and the Ingersoll are so different that no one will see them as the same woman. I may need to smooth over some rough edges in selling this to the panel, but I think I can get it done. I want that painting. It will take our little project to new heights!*

Barry called Laura early the following week. "The panel and I have prayed over the issues you and I discussed last week. We are unanimous in our gratitude to you, and we are delighted to accept your offer. *Annabel's Eyes,* which we will simply call *Annabel* consistent with our tradition of using first names for our paintings, will be unveiled at our October dinner. It will be a very special occasion, no doubt the biggest night of the year in the art world. Please put it on your calendar and plan to join us at the head table."

CHAPTER FIFTY-EIGHT

The Investigation (May 2022)

Angelo and his team had nothing. Well, that wasn't entirely true. They had a body. Chico Santos, whoever the hell he was. They had a body with a gunshot wound to the head and a knife wound to the chest. They knew there had been a murder, but that was it. They didn't know Chico's relationship to Ivy, or why he had entered her house armed with a butterfly knife. What motive did he have for hurting her? Was Roxas involved somehow? If so, why wasn't he there himself? From everything Ivy had said, this wasn't a job Roxas would have delegated. And who took out Santos? How did he know Santos, or anyone else, was coming? Maybe Ivy was the real target, and Santos got shot by mistake because he happened to be in her house. They just didn't know.

Angelo felt his frustration rising to a danger point once again. He knew that wasn't helpful, but he couldn't control it. Ivy had told him everything she knew, but it hadn't gotten them anywhere. 27 Eucalyptus Drive in Westwood had changed hands twice since Mrs. Brown had sold it for cash in 2012. There was nothing about Mrs. Brown in the records. The house was now occupied by a UCLA professor and his wife. The trail ended there. The updated search for a Jaime Roxas in greater Los Angeles came up empty. Roxas and Mrs. Brown were in the wind.

The urgency to solve the crime was lessened since Ivy's safe return, but she was still at risk; whoever was behind the crime might try again. Besides, no one investigating a homicide easily accepts having it become a cold case. Angelo got the team together so they could try to refocus. He put Ivy's three drawings on his wall. "These are the three people we can tie to this thing, other than Santos, and he's not going to tell us anything. We can't find Roxas or Mrs. Brown. Duane, did you run the drawing of Bart by the people at the dairy farm?"

"Yes, they say it looks just like him, but no one's seen him since he stopped working there the day before the murder."

"We have to find him." Everyone agreed. No one knew how.

"There is one other person," Frank offered. "The artist, Pablo Ingersoll. Ivy was painting him. When you talked to her, Angelo, did she say why?"

"Yes, we went all through that. She doesn't know Ingersoll and had never heard of him until George Johnson gave her an art magazine that had a story about him. Apparently, he made a painting that sold at auction in England for more than 25 million dollars. Can you believe that? Who pays that kind of money for a painting? Who even has that kind of money? Anyway, the woman who bought the painting did, and then she shot the eyes out of the painting right there at the auction. Crazy stuff.

"Ivy said she read the story, and her heart went out to Ingersoll because the best painting he had ever made had been ruined, and he carried himself with dignity despite his crushing loss. She thought that showed real character, and she wanted to paint him. She doesn't know anything about him except what was in the article."

"What did she say about the palette knife?" Frank pressed.

"Just that she used it in the paintings she was making of Ingersoll. She has no idea why there would be fingerprints on it other than hers, or whose they might have been."

"Did she talk about her relationship with Bart?"

"She had met him in her neighborhood not long before he moved her out of harm's way. He told her he had recently gotten out of the army and was in Woodstock looking for a job. He was kind to her, and she trusted him, and she readily went with him when he came to her house on May 12 to move her. He told her she wasn't safe there, and she believed him. He set her up in an abandoned barn near Riverview Park and left her plenty of food and personal items. He said he'd visit every day, but he stopped after the first two. She worried about him and feared the worst. She hasn't seen or heard from him since, but she assumes, and I think we need to also, that he's the person who told Sam where to find her. He seems to be one of the good guys, but he's apparently not in Woodstock anymore. Another dead end."

Now everyone spoke at once. "How would he have known about Ivy?" asked Beth. "How would he know Santos or anyone else was coming and that Ivy was in danger? Even if he knew, why would he care? Why would he want to protect her?"

"From what Ivy said, she and Bart had never crossed paths before they met in Woodstock," Angelo answered. "That suggests he didn't know her and had no reason to care about her or want to protect her. Maybe someone else knew her, someone from her past who also knew about Santos, or Roxas, and sent Bart to get her out of harm's way."

"So Bart was a guardian angel, looking after Ivy at someone else's direction?"

"Maybe," Angelo said. "Makes sense since Bart didn't know her himself. But who?"

"Let's break it down and look at the possibilities," Frank said. Always the cool head, the one who understood the importance of getting back to basics, establishing what was known and building from there. "Couldn't have been Roxas—he wouldn't have hired Bart to protect Ivy from himself."

Julie disputed that. "He might have if he knew about Santos. He could have hired Bart to keep Ivy safe until he could do the job himself."

"That's possible, but it seems unlikely," said Angelo. "I'm with Frank. I say we rule out Roxas as a person who might have sent Bart to protect Ivy."

"That brings us to Mrs. Brown, or possibly Pablo Ingersoll," resumed Frank.

"Why Ingersoll?" shot Angelo.

"He knew Ivy was painting him. Maybe he had a soft spot for her?"

"But how would he know anything about Roxas? Or Santos? More importantly, he didn't know Ivy was painting him until I told him, and Bart had already moved Ivy out of her house by then. Couldn't have been Ingersoll."

"Right," said Frank. "Mrs. Brown, then?"

"Who knows?" said Angelo. "She's the most elusive character in this whole thing. Ivy doesn't seem to figure it for Mrs. Brown though. She wrote on her drawing not to be fooled by Mrs. Brown because she ordered and paid for the nasty work Roxas did. That doesn't sound like someone who would be trying to protect Ivy."

"Maybe she got religion," offered Frank. "People change, you know."

"Yes, they do. But there's nothing we know about Mrs. Brown's background or character to suggest she was one of those people."

"Maybe it was someone who didn't know Ivy," Duane said thoughtfully, "but did know Roxas, or Santos, and heard they were planning to go to Woodstock to kill a former captive. Maybe it was someone who was a captive with Ivy in the LA operation, someone who got out one way or another and was committed to helping former captives."

That was as good a guess as any other. "Can't rule it out," said Angelo. "Good thought, Duane."

"Since I'm on a roll here," said Duane, "can we talk about who killed Santos? Does anyone think it was Bart? After getting Ivy to safety, he might have gone back to stake out her house and eliminate the danger."

"What does the physical evidence at the house tell us?"

"No help inside the house," Duane replied. "There are the fingerprints on the palette knife that belong to someone other than Ivy. They could be Bart's, but we don't know since we don't have his fingerprints to compare them to.

"There's also very little help outside the house. The shot was fired through the back window of the living room. It clearly came from the grove of trees at the rear of the house. We didn't find any footprints back there, but there's a slight depression under some bushes that seems a likely spot. It had been brushed, like with a tree branch or something, you know, to hide any sign someone had been lying there. Because of that, we couldn't tell much from the depression—no idea of body size, weight, or anything else. No shell casings, needless to say. One shot to the head, no trail of evidence left behind. Whoever it was, it wasn't his first rodeo."

"Military training?"

"Possibly. Some kind of training, definitely."

People looked at each other, stumped. "What next?" Frank asked.

Angelo didn't like it but voiced the only conclusion he could reach. "I'd say we're at a point where we need to be patient and let the answer come to us. We've done everything we can proactively, everything I can think of anyway."

"No argument here, but what does that mean?"

"We sit, we watch, and we wait. We can't watch Roxas, Mrs. Brown, or Bart because we don't know where they are. We watch Ivy. She says she's told us everything she knows, and I believe her. But this is all about her, for whatever reason, and sooner or later that reason will make itself known. Someone will make another move on her, and we'll be there. Or maybe she knows something she doesn't realize she knows or doesn't recognize its importance. One day she will, and she'll act on it. We'll be there."

"Sounds like a lot of manpower, boss," said Duane.

"Yes, but not as much as you think because she has no phone or computer, so there's nothing to monitor. She never goes anywhere, so keeping an eye on her won't be hard. If something's up, we'll spot it. Sam and George will also be eyes and ears for us. If anything unusual happens, she'll tell one of them, probably Sam."

"We'll track Pablo Ingersoll through Beth's computer trace. I don't see him in this, except inadvertently, but if there's anything happening in his life, we'll want to know about it."

"It's getting to be late afternoon, and I know you want to take us all to the Brewhouse for a beer, Angelo," Beth said with a wry smile. "Can we meet the others there in an hour? I want to swing by and see George Johnson first, and I think you should come with me. We should ask him why he gave Ivy that magazine article and if he knows more about the underlying story."

Moments later, George was answering their questions. "I had read the article and thought it was interesting. I mean really, it's a hell of a story. I thought Ivy would enjoy it. That's all there was to it. Or so I thought at the time."

"Meaning what?" Angelo was alert.

"I'm not sure, and I probably should have mentioned this earlier, but about three weeks ago, a woman who was visiting in town came into the shop to browse. She found some of Ivy's drawings in the bin and bought four of them. She asked how she could contact Ivy because she wanted to see more of her work. I told her Ivy didn't have a phone, but she could go to her house the following morning before Ivy left for her daily walk."

"Did you tell her where Ivy lived?"

"Yes."

Shit, thought Angelo. *This is important information that we should have had before. Better late than never, I guess.*

Beth beat Angelo to the punch. "George, we need to know the exact date she was here. Can you check that?"

"Sure." George took a moment to consult his records. "It was Thursday, May 12." Then the realization hit him. "Damn, that's the day before Ivy missed our regular monthly meeting. Do you think the woman had anything to do with it?"

"I don't believe in coincidences. Not this big, anyway. Did you get the woman's name, or did she pay in cash?"

"She paid by credit card." He looked it up. "Her name was Laura Marcus."

Beth was on her phone, googling Laura Marcus. "Angelo," she said excitedly. "That's the woman who bought the Ingersoll painting in London and shot its eyes out. That would connect her to Ingersoll, but how would it connect her to Ivy?"

"I don't know, but she was in town when Ivy disappeared, and she knew where Ivy lived. There's a new player in the mix. We're a giant step closer to figuring this out."

Beth was still looking at her phone. "There's something else about Laura Marcus, something important. She was a sniper in Iraq."

CHAPTER FIFTY-NINE

The Investigation (June 2022)

Angelo met with Laura at her New York office the following afternoon. She was gracious and gave every appearance of being forthcoming.

Yes, she had bought *Annabel's Eyes* at auction in London, and yes, she had shot the painting. Her reasons were personal and involved a prior relationship with Pablo Ingersoll that wasn't relevant to Angelo's investigation, and she wasn't going to talk about it. No, she didn't know the woman in the painting and no, she didn't know Ivy Villanueva.

Yes, she had been in Woodstock from May 12 through May 15. She had always wanted to visit the Shenandoah Valley and drove down for a long weekend. Yes, she had visited the art gallery and bought four drawings made by Ivy Villanueva. Yes, she had gone to Ivy's house on the night of Thursday, May 12, right after an excellent pasta dinner at the Woodstock Café. She had gone because she wanted to see more of Ivy's work, but no, she and Ivy never actually met. As she was nearing the house, she saw someone she assumed was Ivy leaving with a man; she was apparently going away because she had a duffel bag. No, she didn't know who the man was and couldn't describe him, other than that he was average looking. Yes, she went to the house once or twice more that weekend, but Ivy was never there. No, she didn't see anything unusual at the house.

She said nothing about the "BANG! BANG!" drawing, the Woodstock postmark, the call from Jim Rose, the paintings of Pablo in Ivy's living room, her surveillance activities at the house, the intruder, or the man who went into the house after the intruder was shot. She was a good lawyer and knew any of those disclosures would be the thread that, when pulled, would draw her into this thing, deeper and deeper, to a place she didn't want to go. She had merely enjoyed a long spring weekend in the Shenandoah Valley and stumbled onto some artwork that she quite liked.

Yes, she was surprised to learn that a man had been shot in Ivy's house that weekend. Who? Why? Yes, she had been a sniper in the army many years ago, and yes, she was familiar with many different kinds of weapons, but no, she hadn't fired a rifle in years. Yes, she would be happy to provide her fingerprints and help in any other way she could. Yes, she would be pleased to talk again if Angelo had more questions.

Laura's story checked out. It was the truth—not the whole truth, but there was no one around to say there was more. Her fingerprints did not match the prints on the palette knife. The lead to Laura had been promising, but like everything else about this case, it went nowhere. Angelo and his team were back to watching and waiting. Their only hope was that one way or another, Ivy's life would again intersect with Roxas, Mrs. Brown, or Bart. They would be there when it did.

CHAPTER SIXTY

Christina and Annabel (June 2022)

Barry met with Pablo shortly after accepting Laura's offer. "Sorry to whip-saw you around like this, old man," he said, "but you can stand down on the *Ann* painting. We won't need it for the 2022 function after all."

"Oh?" replied Pablo. He was pleased there was a chance that Barry and the panel would come to their senses and reverse their decision to include Ann in the project. He was also concerned by the implications of what Barry had said. "If you've made another selection, I'm afraid there isn't enough time between now and October for me to paint it."

"Not to worry. You've already painted it. It's ready to go." Pablo looked confused. Barry was enjoying this.

"I believe you know Laura Marcus?" Barry asked. Pablo nodded, warily. "She has generously donated *Annabel's Eyes* to Project *Imagine*. Her only condition is that it be unveiled at this year's function, in October. That means you're off the hook for the *Ann* painting until at least 2024, and maybe even 2026. More importantly, it means your masterpiece—and it truly is a master-piece—will be available for the world to see, and you will have a place on the wall with the likes of Picasso and van Gogh. Congratulations, Pablo! This is a tremendous honor and one you richly deserve."

Pablo was speechless. He looked down, shaking his head slightly and grinning. "I don't know what to say. That's very kind of Laura. I'll have to call her and thank her."

"We hope you and Sally will join us at the head table for the event. As the first living artist represented on the wall, you should be there. This next part is a little delicate. As the donor of the painting, Laura should also be there. Given your history, will it be a problem for you and Sally to be seated at the same head table with Laura?"

"No, I shouldn't think so, especially considering her generosity in donating the painting and promoting my work and me in the process." Pablo looked like he had more to say, but Barry stepped in.

"Good, then it's settled. Unless I misread you, there's something else on your mind."

"Yes. I'm honored and humbled by this turn of events, and the last thing I want is to risk undoing it, but I'm committed to the integrity of Project *Imagine*, as we all are. The paintings on the wall are to be of women of stature and character. I never knew who Christina was, and I still don't. When I painted her as Picasso, I took her greatness for granted because Ann vouched for it. I do know Annabel and Christina are the same woman, because I painted her in the Picasso version and in my own version from the same photograph. Who is she, and how do you intend to present her at the unveiling?"

"I'm still working on that. It's a bit of a problem, frankly, and I hope we can keep it between us. Quite honestly, the painting is so extraordinary that I'm willing to take some risk to have it on our wall. My belief is that the quality of the work will earn some leeway for the woman in it. And I'm going to enlist Ann's help with the presentation. She somehow made the case for Christina, and I'm certain she will for Annabel as well."

Barry was elated with the way things were working out. He had filled five of the six seats at the head table. He and Ann would be there, as the originator and successor curator of *Imagine*. The painter of *Annabel's Eyes*, Pablo Ingersoll, would be there with his wife, Sally Sullivan. And the donor of the painting, Laura Marcus, would be there. The sixth seat was reserved for the guest of honor, the woman in the *Christina* and *Annabel* paintings. Barry's problem returned like a pounding migraine: *Who the hell are we going to produce?*

Pablo had raised the issue, and now it was eating at him. He had painted

Christina, then Annabel, from a photo Ann had given him. Ann didn't tell him who the woman in the photo was. Pablo was pretty sure Ann knew—she wouldn't have chosen a stranger for the *Imagine* wall. What was the mystery? Ann had said Christina worked undercover; maybe Ann didn't know where she was, or how to contact her.

He had a flash of memory: the crank caller said he had seen *Annabel's Eyes* in a magazine article, and the woman in the painting looked exactly like his sister. What if it was his sister? Pablo didn't remember the caller's name and had no way of bringing it back. He had hung up on the guy. No help there. Then another flash: the visit from a sheriff who was investigating a murder that had happened at the home of an artist somewhere in Virginia. They had found several paintings of Pablo at the murder scene. The sheriff had shown him photographs of the paintings. They were good. Very good. He had never heard of the artist and didn't know why she would have been painting him. Maybe she had seen an article about him and liked the way he looked. Who knew? Maybe she had seen the same article as the crank caller, the one about *Annabel's Eyes*. What was the name of that town in Virginia? Woodstock! He remembered telling the sheriff he had been to Woodstock, New York, but didn't know there was one in Virginia. What was the name of the artist? He had no idea, but Sally would know. She knew these things.

Pablo was on the phone. "Just a minute," Sally said after hearing his question. "I wrote it down. Here it is. Her name is Ivy. Ivy Villanueva. The sheriff's name is Angelo Jones."

"You're amazing," Pablo said, hanging up.

He called Barry. "I think I know where Christina is." He was excited but paused to check himself and consider whether he was jumping blindly to reach the conclusion he desired. Ann had said Christina engaged in private acts of courage and was no stranger to pain. Pablo recalled Sheriff Jones saying Ivy had a scar under her eye and walked with a crutch. That certainly fit. She had to be Christina. Barry was enthusiastic about the information Pablo put forward and suggested they invite Ivy to the event but vet her before introducing her as Christina. If she was Christina, Ann would know her; if she wasn't, her seat would remain empty, and Ann would need to do her magic with the audience once again.

CHAPTER SIXTY-ONE

Ivy (July 2022)

"Sheriff Jones, this is Pablo Ingersoll. You visited me in Brooklyn in May." Angelo sat up straight and signaled to Beth to trace the call. "I was thinking about your investigation. Did you solve the case?"

"No, we're working on it. We found the body of the man who was killed, and we're trying to find out how he knew Ivy and what he was doing in her house. No luck so far. Ivy's back home safe and sound, I'm happy to say. She had been moved out ahead of time for her own protection."

"I'm very glad to hear that," Pablo said, "and she's the main reason for my call. I keep wondering why she was painting me."

"I can help you with that now that we've been able to debrief her," Angelo interrupted. "She saw an article about you in a magazine. It was about a painting you made that a woman bought and then shot. Ivy was touched by the grace you showed in handling the matter; she admired you for it and wanted to capture your character and dignity in a painting."

Bingo, thought Pablo. *The same article the crank caller had seen.* "That was kind of her. I'd like to talk to Ivy about her paintings and see if she'd be willing to show them to me. I might like to buy one. Could you possibly give me her address? I'd like to send her a letter and include a small drawing to thank her for her kindness."

Angelo gave Pablo Ivy's address and looked at Beth. "He was calling from Brooklyn," she said. "His home phone."

"This all seems innocent enough. A guilty person wouldn't be likely to call the police for fear of calling attention to himself. Still, it's an interesting point of contact. It gives us something specific to watch. Might be something, might be nothing. We'll see how Ivy reacts when she gets his letter. I think she'll tell us about it, but if she doesn't, we'll have to follow up."

Ivy went to Sam's office five days later. She was very excited. "I got a letter from Pablo Ingersoll. He's the big-time artist I've been painting. I'd like to show it to you and Angelo." Sam called Angelo, and he was there in ten minutes. Ivy was all smiles as she opened the letter before them.

Dear Ivy,

My name is Pablo Ingersoll. I'm an artist in New York. Sheriff Jones contacted me when he was investigating your disappearance because he found paintings of me in your house. The paintings are very good. I'd like to see them and maybe buy one.

I have another reason for writing. My wife and I would like you to join us at a dinner at the Hemphill Museum in New York on Friday, October 7. The museum has acquired one of my paintings and will be unveiling it that night. It's called *Annabel's Eyes*, and it's my best one. I think it's the one you saw in the magazine, and I'd like you to see it in person. If you can come, I'll have a car pick you up at your house and bring you to New York. I'll get you a room for the night at a nearby hotel, and the next day we can tour the museum together. The car will take you back home when we're done.

I'm enclosing a drawing of the woman in my painting. I think maybe it looks a little like you? It's my way of thanking you for painting me.

The letter was signed Pablo and had his Brooklyn address and phone number. Ivy looked at Sam and Angelo earnestly. "What do you think? I'd like to go—this would be the biggest thing in my life!"

Sam and Angelo looked at each other. Sam spoke first. "I think you should go, Ivy, unless Angelo says it's dangerous. If you want company, Chris and I could ride up with you. We'll disappear and have a nice dinner in New York while you're at the museum event; then we'll ride back to Woodstock with you the next day."

"That would be wonderful," Ivy replied. "You're a real friend, Sam. What do you think, Angelo?"

"You're a grown woman, and you've been through more than most of us. You deserve a trip like this and a chance to spend time with an artist you admire. I feel good about Sam and Chris riding up and back with you. I think you should do it. I'll have someone at the museum to keep an eye on you while you're there. I don't see much risk, and we might learn something."

"Yes!" exclaimed Ivy triumphantly. "Thank you both so much. I'll write back to Mr. Ingersoll and get things set up."

"That's a nice drawing he sent you," added Angelo. "I wonder why he thinks it looks like you. I don't see the resemblance, personally."

Sam frowned at Angelo and looked at the drawing. "The hair is different. Ivy's older than the woman in the drawing, and she's been through some rough times with Roxas. Could be. What I'm wondering is why Ingersoll would think there's a resemblance. He's never met Ivy. How could he possibly know what she looks like?" Then she turned to Ivy. "The October event will be fun. I'll help you get ready. We'll go shopping and find something nice for you to wear."

CHAPTER SIXTY-TWO

The Investigation (July-September 2022)

T hings had quieted considerably. Ivy had resurfaced and was unharmed, the body of Chico Santos had been found and identified, and all leads had vanished. The investigation had become a slow and distant stakeout of Ivy and Pablo, and both were leading unremarkable lives. Pablo's letter didn't sound like anything to get excited about, but it presented an occasion for the team to do some brainstorming.

Angelo briefed the group on Pablo's invitation to Ivy to attend the event at the Hemphill Museum, where one of his paintings was apparently going to be showcased. "Beth, have you figured out what the event is?"

"Yes, it's posted on the museum's website. It's a dinner that's held every two years by an organization called Project *Imagine*. Quite a big deal in the art world. The project's mission is to promote significant women leaders by presenting paintings of them that appear to have been made by well-known artists, people like Warhol and Picasso. The dinner is a lavish event, and the highlight is the unveiling of a new painting. Although the subject of the painting and the name of the artist aren't made public until the dinner, evidently this year's artist is Pablo Ingersoll."

"Why would a big-time artist like that invite Ivy?" Duane asked. "I mean, she's great, but that doesn't sound like her crowd. Or her thing, really."

"She's been painting him at her house, as you know," Angelo replied. "I showed him photographs of her paintings when I interviewed him in May. He's flattered, and he likes the paintings. He wants to thank her. I think that's nice. And this is a very big deal to Ivy."

Frank nodded but observed, "This doesn't sound like an event Roxas will be attending. Or Mrs. Brown or Bart for that matter, and those are the people we're looking for, aren't they? What's your thought about how we handle this, Angelo?"

"Those are the people we think we're looking for, but you never know. Ingersoll seems like a straight arrow to me. Our plan has been to watch Ivy, on the theory that she'll lead us to whomever we're really looking for. She'll find them, or they'll find her. I'm not expecting much from this, but we need to be there and take in whatever's happening."

"All of us?" Frank was incredulous.

"No, of course not. Just Beth and me. You can have the night off, Frank. Go home and enjoy a nice glass of bourbon."

"You and Beth, like on a date?" Duane teased.

"Duane, you are such a dork," Beth said. "Angelo's not my type. Too young. Too Italian. I prefer Swedes. But I can certainly see how a man and a woman at a social event like this one would be less conspicuous than two beady-eyed men playing detective. Can't you?"

"Except we won't be just a man and a woman, Beth," said Angelo. "You'll be an art critic for some obscure periodical no one's ever heard of. Since it won't be mainstream, no one will be surprised if your art knowledge isn't comprehensive. I'll be your tag-along husband for the evening. Find a way to get us in and put us at a table near the back with a good view of the room."

"On it, Angelo. Is Shenandoah County willing to buy me a new dress for the occasion?"

"In your dreams. Just wear something black. That's what artists and people who live in New York do. It will have the added advantage of not calling attention to us. We're just there to have a good time, ooh and aah about the art, and watch."

"Incidentally," Angelo added, "Chris and Sam will ride up to New York with Ivy and ride back with her the next day. We'll have to keep an eye on her at the event, at her hotel after the event, and while she tours the museum with Ingersoll the next day. I'm going to call my friend Gus Fortini—we grew up together in Roanoke, and he's now with the NYPD—and give him a heads-up so he can get us local support if we need it."

CHAPTER SIXTY-THREE

The Unveiling of *Annabel* (October 7, 2022)

Angelo and Beth arrived early at the Hemphill Museum. They wanted to get the lay of the land before things started to happen. Their seats were at a table at the back center of the large rectangular room that was the museum's *Imagine* wing. They had a clear view of the head table. Beth had done her job well.

Eight paintings hung on the long wall facing them. From the left side to the center were paintings one through four: *Lydia* by Jawlensky, *Claire* by van Gogh, *Lucy* by Waring, and *Christina* by Picasso. From the right side to the center were paintings five through eight: *Farah* by Kahlo, *Helen* by Vermeer, *Grace* by Warhol, and *Annabel* by Ingersoll. The design had a symmetry rationale, but it subtly achieved three more important objectives. It got the two weakest paintings, *Helen* and *Farah*, off to the side. It brought the star of the 2022 event, *Annabel*, to the center. And it also brought *Christina* to the center so that the two paintings of the same woman, *Christina* and *Annabel*, were side by side in prime position. They were a stunning pairing.

The head table was set on a one-foot-tall platform below the paintings, facing the dinner guests. It held six places, and a nameplate in front of each indicated the occupant's identity. At the left side, as the guests faced the head table, would be Sally Sullivan, and next to her would be her husband, the artist of the moment, Pablo Ingersoll. Then came Ann Merriman, the visionary who had created *Imagine*. Barry Thomas, the curator of the project and to-night's host, would occupy the fourth seat from the left. Christina Cruz, the apparent guest of honor, would be next, and Laura Marcus, the donor of *Annabel*, would take the final seat.

Sam called Angelo to say they were running late. There had been heavy construction traffic in the stretch of Pennsylvania between Lenhartsville and Allentown and a slow bumper-to-bumper crawl across the George Washington Bridge; and the crosstown trek through Manhattan, always bad, had been nightmarish. Ivy was making a quick stop to change at the hotel. She would miss the cocktail hour but would make the dinner, likely arriving as the guests were being seated. Angelo was relieved; Ivy's absence as the art crowd milled around, sipping drinks and admiring *Annabel*, had him worried.

Sam was true to her word. Angelo saw Ivy being ushered in from the left side of the room as people were moving to their assigned tables. She was flushed with excitement and all smiles as she hobbled toward the head table, where Sally, Pablo, Ann, Barry, and Laura had gathered but had not yet taken their seats.

"Showtime," Angelo whispered to Beth, who had her camera out and at the ready. "Record everything you can. Focus on Ivy. When this is over, we want to be able to review every interaction she has with others."

"On it, Angelo."

He turned back and watched intently as Ivy approached the head table. She shook hands warmly but somewhat formally with Sally and Pablo, as people do when they meet for the first time and exchange pleasantries. *Nothing sinister there,* Angelo thought. *She and Pablo seem to be making a good connection and are probably anticipating tonight's dinner and tomorrow's museum tour.*

She moved on to the next guest with her hand outstretched but dropped it as she looked into the eyes of Ann Merriman. Angelo saw recognition on Ivy's face but also something else. Fear maybe? Revulsion? *What's that all about?* Whatever it was, he didn't have time to analyze it because Ivy's interaction with the next guest was even more surprising. She moved quickly past Ann, and when she saw Barry Thomas, she disregarded his proffered hand and gave him a hug. Angelo thought he saw tears on her cheeks, but he was too far away to be sure. Ivy shook hands with the final guest, Laura Marcus;

it looked like a first meeting, but Angelo read recognition on Ivy's face, and alertness.

What the hell is going on here? Angelo thought. *This is turning out to be a lot more interesting than I expected. Ivy seems to know all these people except Pablo and Sally.*

"You getting all this?" he whispered to Beth.

"Every facial expression, every twitch." Beth was calm and focused.

We come to an art show in New York where we shouldn't know anybody, yet we know four of the six people at the head table. I've interviewed three of them in connection with the murder of Chico Santos. Maybe I let Pablo and Laura off the hook too easily. Maybe these art people aren't as innocent as I thought. But how would they know Roxas? Or Santos? Maybe they don't, maybe they're independent actors with independent motives for wanting to harm Ivy, and we've been looking in the wrong places. If that's so, Ivy could be in a kill zone tonight.

He was on his phone, speaking urgently. "Gus, I need two police officers at the Hemphill ASAP. The mission is to protect Ivy, to be on watch for anyone who might make a move against her."

"Roger that. They're already there, standing by. I'll move them quietly into the room. They'll be watching."

Angelo turned back to the head table and studied the faces of Ann Merriman and Barry Thomas. Ivy had greeted them both with recognition, fear in Ann's case and friendship in Barry's. Angelo didn't know them, but they looked familiar. He reached into his briefcase for Ivy's drawings as Barry took the mic and walked to the front of the head table.

"Ladies and gentlemen, thank you for coming tonight. We have a blockbuster evening, and I won't try your patience by indulging in preliminaries. We are honored to present an extraordinary painting that is well-known throughout the art world, *Annabel* by Pablo Ingersoll." The crowd rose as one, roaring their approval of one of their own, a Brooklyn guy. Pablo had come a long way from Dubuque. "This painting was generously donated to the Hemphill, and specifically to *Imagine*, by Laura Marcus." Laura stood, smiled, and nodded to the appreciative crowd. The applause continued for two minutes.

Beth was capturing it all on camera. No movement, however subtle, escaped her. Suddenly she took her eye from the camera to look directly at

Barry. She couldn't believe her eyes. She jabbed Angelo with her elbow and said, "Are you seeing what I'm seeing?"

"This is too easy," Angelo said with a smile. Barry was standing in front of his nameplate, his head obscuring the last two letters of his first name. To the left of his head, Angelo read the letters "Bar" and to the right of his head was the capital "T" of his last name. *Bart! No wonder Ivy hugged him. She had been worried about him when he didn't come back to the barn, and she was relieved to see him tonight. Her protector, her guardian, is safe and well.*

Angelo pulled out Ivy's drawings of Bart and Mrs. Brown. They were unmistakably Barry Thomas and Ann Merriman. Ivy had nailed them. Angelo showed the drawings to Beth. They looked at each other and smiled.

"Gus," Angelo said into his phone. "There's been a change in the mission. Ivy is not at risk tonight. We have some people to apprehend instead. Let's let the evening play out, and when the dinner wraps and the guests start to leave, I need your men to move quietly to the head table and detain the six people seated there. We'll want to talk to them. Strictly low-key. No spectacle."

"You got it, brother."

Having acknowledged Pablo and Laura, Barry moved on to the evening's guest of honor. "We have an extraordinary woman for you to meet tonight, and there is no one better to introduce her than her friend Ann Merriman."

Ann took the mic from Barry and smiled at the adoring crowd. No one could know it would be her last hurrah. "Friends," she said, "we are all so grateful, and I personally am so very grateful, for your wonderful support all these years. The woman in tonight's painting, Annabel, could not be with us because she is on duty, working for our government on a top-secret assignment at an undisclosed location. We will introduce you to her when she is safely back home and able to join us.

"You will recall that we had a similar experience with the fourth woman we honored, the woman I called my courage. Christina Cruz wasn't able to join us when we unveiled the wonderful painting of her by Picasso. She is here tonight, however, and I am humbled to present her as a woman who stood up to evil without flinching and paid a terrible price for it. My friends, please welcome Christina, a woman of unparalleled fortitude and resilience."

Ann raised her arm in the direction of Ivy and beckoned her forward. She had totally misjudged the moment and her former captive. She had thought the kindness of a hospital visit, the passage of years, and the honor of tonight's event would have softened Ivy, and occasioned forgiveness. She had believed her own press clippings, which portrayed her as a champion of the underprivileged. Ivy cared nothing about that. She only knew the hell that this woman, Mrs. Brown, and her henchman, Jaime Roxas, had put her through for ten years in captivity and fifteen years in hiding after that.

The art crowd was applauding, full-throated in its adulation. Who doesn't love and respect a courageous woman who stood tall and endured the suffering she had? Ivy sat for a long moment and glared at Ann Merriman, her eyes filled with loathing. Finally, she reached for the nameplate in front of her and turned it face down. She bent over to collect her crutch, rose slowly, and made her way to the front of the head table.

It was Ivy's moment. She faced the enthusiastic crowd unapologetically. The jagged scar beneath her left eye was in full view, as was the crutch that was an essential part of her being. She turned around and looked for what seemed an eternity at the *Christina* and *Annabel* paintings, one with the classic Picasso double face so reminiscent of the *Portrait of Dora Maar,* the other the simple raw beauty that Ivy had been at eighteen, when she was still Estella de la Rosa. She was filled with emotion.

At length, she turned back to face the crowd. She took the mic and slowly said, "Thank you, but I am not Christina Cruz. Whoever she is, she was painted by Picasso. That speaks to her importance. I do not know her. I am not her."

The art crowd quieted. They were confused. What was going on here? How would this sort out? They strained to hear Ivy's next words. They waited while she turned again to gaze at *Annabel's Eyes*. She was smiling, proudly. A tear dampened her cheek. They waited, hushed, as she faced Ann Merriman squarely.

"You know who I am," she said. "I was beautiful once, and you took that from me. I am a simple woman. I am that woman." She gestured toward the painting. "I am Annabel."

EPILOGUE

Angelo released Pablo and Sally and sent them home. They were nice people who clearly had nothing to do with the criminal aspects of the case. Pablo and Ivy bonded during their museum tour the following day. Pablo praised her work and told her that maybe, just maybe, he could get a gallery in New York to include one or two of her paintings in an upcoming group show. He had the Stockbridge Gallery in mind. He owed Jennifer Stockbridge a favor.

Angelo took a sworn statement from Ivy. She affirmed that Ann Merriman was Mrs. Brown. She detailed her life in captivity under Mrs. Brown and Jaime Roxas, who ran a human trafficking operation in Los Angeles at least from 1997 to 2007. She stated that Roxas had shattered her leg with a baseball bat, leaving it useless, after she tried to escape. She alleged that Roxas, and she believed Mrs. Brown, had been searching for her, with the intention of killing her, since she finally did escape in 2007. Angelo turned Merriman over to the FBI's human trafficking division for further investigation and prosecution. She would get credit for having sent Barry Thomas to protect Ivy in May 2022, but she would spend most of her remaining life in prison.

Project *Imagine* collapsed under the weight of the scandal. The Hemphill Museum considered suing Ann Merriman but contented itself with adding the eight paintings from the project, including the magnificent *Annabel*, to its permanent collection.

Ann sang like the Mormon Tabernacle Choir. She gave up Jaime Roxas in a heartbeat, stated that he had debilitating health issues, and confirmed that he had sent Chico Santos to Woodstock to kill Ivy. The FBI arrested Roxas, a wheezing wretch of a man, at his tiny apartment in Filipinotown. He was held without bail pending his trial for human trafficking and assorted other crimes. Still thinking he was a big shot, he talked trash to another prisoner who took umbrage and put a shiv in his heart. Jaime knew what he was facing; his life was miserable and was only going to get worse. His death was ruled suicide by prisoner.

Angelo and his team had reason to be elated. They had solved the plot to kill Ivy; she no longer had anything to fear. They had uncovered a human trafficking operation and, with the FBI's help, had scored rare victories against those engaged in that loathsome enterprise. Two creeps, Roxas and Santos, had been eliminated and a third creep, Merriman, was off the street. The questions the people of Woodstock and Shenandoah County cared about had all been answered. But for Angelo and his team, there was unfinished business. Someone had shot Santos. Who? Someone had sawed him into pieces and dumped him in the river. Who?

The focus was on Bart and Laura. "It has to be one of them," Angelo said at what would otherwise have been a wrap-up meeting for the team. "They were both in the military, one in Iraq and one in Afghanistan, with serious marksmanship skills. They were both in Woodstock the night Santos was killed."

Laura was back in the mix because Angelo followed up with Ivy after she appeared to recognize Laura when they met at the dinner. When he asked her how she knew Laura, Ivy said, "She was the woman in the magazine article who shot the eyes in the painting of me. I knew how that must have hurt Pablo, who seemed like a good man, so I made a drawing that showed her in the painting and me shooting her eyes, and I sent it to her."

Angelo got back with Laura immediately. He had let her off too easily the first time, and he wouldn't make that mistake again. He confronted her with what Ivy had told him about the drawing she had sent Laura. "Why didn't you tell us that?"

"It just didn't come up." A weak parry.

"Did you come to know who sent you the drawing?"

"The postmark was from Woodstock, Virginia. I didn't know Ivy or anything about her, but sometime later I had a strange call from a man named Jim Rose." Laura went on to tell Angelo about the man with emphysema who was looking for his wife because she had abandoned him and their sick child. His wife looked just like the woman in the *Annabel* painting, he had said. Laura made the connection to the woman who sent her the drawing and stupidly told the caller he would probably find his wife in Woodstock.

There were too many points of contact to ignore. Jim Rose? A man with emphysema? Looking for a woman who looked like Annabel? "Jaime Roxas," Angelo murmured. "Jim Rose was Jaime Roxas." He shook his head in disgust. "What was the real reason you were in Woodstock that weekend, Ms. Marcus?"

"I kept fretting about the call, because I came to realize I might unintentionally have put a woman in danger by disclosing her whereabouts to a stranger who was angry with her and wanted to find her. My conscience bothered me. I felt I had to find her first and warn her. That's why I went to Woodstock. But I never met Ivy. As I told you before, she was leaving her house as I was arriving."

"Did you shop at a store called Dixie Firearms when you were in Woodstock?"

Laura looked startled. She apparently hadn't thought Angelo would uncover her arms purchase. "Yes. I bought a rifle there."

"And a scope and a suppressor?"

"Yes."

"Were you back at Ivy's house, with the rifle, at any time that weekend? Please take your time in answering and remember that you are under oath."

"Yes. I staked the place out a couple of nights. I was curious to see who might show up. As I lay there watching, I convinced myself that the woman I had come to warn was no longer in danger, and anything else that was going to happen was a job for the local police. I left without firing the rifle."

"Did you see any unusual activity at the house before you left?"

"I saw an intruder in the house. I saw him get hit by a silenced gunshot.

I saw someone else, a man I believe, in the house shortly thereafter. He was masked, and I don't know who he was. I saw him stab the dead body. I didn't see him again after that. I returned to New York the next day."

"Do you still have the rifle, and will you give it to us so we can have it tested?"

"Yes, certainly."

Bart was in the mix because Ivy identified him as the man who had protected her. He had done that at someone else's bidding, and it wasn't clear how broad his mandate was. Ivy didn't know anything about Bart that she hadn't already told Angelo.

"You did our community a service by saving Ivy's life, Mr. Thomas. Let's start with my thanking you for that." Angelo quickly moved on. "There's still an open question about who killed the man in her house, Chico Santos, and that's what we're here to investigate. First off, why did you tell Ivy your name was Balthasar?"

"It is my name. It's also a conversation piece. I used it to try to get Ivy talking. I needed her trust if I was going to protect her."

"Who sent you to protect her?"

"Ann Merriman."

"You now know of Merriman's past as Mrs. Brown, who ran a human trafficking operation. When did you first learn about that?"

"After you had us detained the night of the *Annabel* unveiling. I was stunned. Ann was always good to me, and we talked about art. I had no idea she had another life, and a disgusting one at that."

"When she sent you to protect Ivy, what were her instructions to you, as precisely as you can recall them?"

"She told me she had a friend—she called her Stellie—from a time when she had lived in Los Angeles. Stellie had escaped from an abusive relationship in which she had been held captive and treated badly. Ann received information that Stellie's former captor had located her in Woodstock and was sending someone there to kill her. Ann knew of my special ops background in the British army and asked me to protect Stellie, who turned out to be Ivy, from whoever was coming for her."

"Did she instruct you to kill the person who was coming for Ivy?"

"No. I had the impression she wouldn't mind if I did, but my only instruction was to protect her."

"You befriended Ivy and took her to an abandoned barn, which was effectively a safe house?"

"Yes, and I became very fond of her. She was vulnerable and didn't deserve the life she had been forced to live."

"Would you have killed to protect her if her would-be assailant had returned?"

"I might have, but that wasn't my instruction, and I didn't."

"Were you at Ivy's house the night Chico Santos was killed?"

"Yes."

"Why?"

"Two reasons. One was curiosity. The other was a continuation of my protection mission. I wanted to be sure the house wasn't booby-trapped when Sam brought Ivy back home from the barn."

"Just to clarify, you sent the note to Sam?"

"Yes. I was back in New York then. I knew an investigation would be underway soon after Santos was killed and, as a new guy in town who was friendly with Ivy, I would be a logical suspect. Once I had arranged for Ivy's safe return from the barn, my job in Woodstock was done."

Angelo made a note and thought for a moment. "Back to the night of the murder. Did you have a rifle with you at Ivy's house?"

"No. I can handle a rifle, but I'm basically a hand-to-hand, close-combat kind of guy. Those were my skills, though I don't use them anymore."

"Did you see anything unusual when you went back to Ivy's house the night of the murder?"

"I saw the intruder, who I now know was Santos, in the house. I heard a weapon with a suppressor, and I saw Santos go down. I waited almost half an hour. All was quiet, and I entered the house. I wanted to be sure he was dead. He was."

"What else did you do when you were in the house?"

"Once I determined he was dead, I grabbed a palette knife that was near the easel and stabbed him with it. I remember saying it was for Ivy. Then I left."

That accounts for the prints on the palette knife. "Did you remove the body from the house?"

"No. Until just now, I didn't know it had been removed. Once I confirmed that Santos was dead, I didn't care where his body was. I wouldn't have wanted Ivy to come home and find the body, but I knew someone would remove it well before then."

"Did you have a bone saw with you at the house?"

"A bone saw? If I didn't have a weapon, why would I have had a bone saw? As I said, I wasn't there to kill Santos. That wasn't my assignment. I was at the house to watch, to be sure he didn't leave some deadly surprise for Ivy on her return. Once I was satisfied that wasn't going to happen because he was dead, I left."

"OK, we're good for now. Thanks for your time, Mr. Thomas. We'll be in touch if we need anything further."

A week later, Angelo, Frank, Duane, and Beth got together for a final meeting. They wanted to review what they knew and didn't know about the killing, dismembering, and removal of Chico Santos. They wanted to decide whether they had enough to recommend prosecution.

They began with Laura Marcus. "I think we got the truth out of her this time," ventured Angelo. "Does anyone have reason to believe she's lying?"

"The serial number on the rifle she gave us matches the receipt from Dixie Firearms," said Duane. "The lab checked out that rifle and said it hasn't been fired in years."

"Sounds like game, set, and match to me," Frank offered. "She didn't kill Santos, and even if she did, we couldn't prove it."

"When we're done here, I'll call and let her know she's off the hook." Angelo switched the discussion to Barry Thomas. "Do we have any evidence of gun ownership, a recent bone saw purchase, or anything else that might tie him to Santos?" Silence all around.

"He admits to sticking the dead body with a palette knife. I'm sure there are laws around somewhere prohibiting the mutilation or desecration of dead bodies, but I don't see trying to hang one of those around the neck of a war hero who saved Ivy's life and did nothing worse than help her kiss an already dead lowlife goodbye."

"No argument here," said Beth, "and we can't prove he had a gun, let alone fired the shot that killed Santos. But what about cutting up and removing the body? That's more serious than the stab with the palette knife. And he was the last one in Ivy's house."

"That may not be," cautioned Duane. "He's the last one we know of, that's all."

Frank weighed in, thoughtful as ever. "Duane has a point. What is it the Navy Seals say? Leave no man behind? The mafia has the same mentality, and so do gangs in this country and elsewhere. Unlike the Seals, though, their reasons for leaving no man behind are to eliminate evidence so there won't be trails. You guys don't watch enough crime and mob shows. The guys who come in later to remove bodies or shell casings or whatever are called cleanup crews, or simply cleaners.

"From all we've heard, Jaime Roxas was a smart guy. He probably sent along someone he trusted to keep an eye on Santos to be sure he got the job done, and to clean up the evidence if he didn't. In this case, as it turned out, the removal of Santos's body and its disposal in pieces that would likely never be found was a protection Roxas set up for himself. That's my theory anyway, particularly since Laura and Bart both deny cutting up the body, and their denials are credible because neither would have any apparent reason to do so."

Angelo was on the phone, asking to be patched through to Ann Merriman at the prison that was her new home. He put it on speaker so the team could listen. When Ann picked up, Angelo said, "You told us Roxas sent Chico Santos to kill Ivy. Did he tell you he was sending anyone else?"

Ann answered readily. "Not specifically, no, but he did say he was arranging for insurance, as he called it. He promised me, he guaranteed—that was the word he used—that if things went wrong, there would be no trail because whatever was left of Santos would never be found."

Angelo rang off. "That's good enough for me," he said to the team. "I guess we'd all be better investigators if we watched as much TV as Frank does." Beth, Duane, and Frank snickered. They were feeling good, sensing that this nightmare of a case was about to be over.

"I'm prepared to accept the fact that Santos was cut up by a cleaner sent by Roxas," Angelo went on. "Is cutting up a dead body a crime? Maybe.

Probably. But they cut up unidentified corpses in medical school every day, and no one seems to care. Even if cutting up the dead body of Chico Santos was a crime, our limited resources aren't sufficient to pursue it. Besides, I'm too tired to try to chase another rat down another rathole. I say we close this investigation and declare victory. Ivy is safe, the bad guys are dead or in prison, and the good guys—who may or may not have sinned in trying to protect Ivy—are free. I call that a win. Thanks for your help, everybody. See you at the Brewhouse. I'm buying."

With that, the death of Chico Santos became just another unsolved case on a list a mile long.

A slightly hungover Angelo called Laura Marcus the following afternoon. "We have the lab results," he said. "They show that the rifle wasn't fired the night of the murder, as you said. We won't be charging you for killing Chico Santos."

"Thank you, Sheriff," Laura replied. She rose from her sofa and walked to the trophy case that held her two Olympic medals and the pistol she had used to win them. She picked up the pistol and held it lovingly. *They always look for a rifle,* she thought, a grin lighting up her face. Her little diversion had worked. *So easy.*

She put the pistol down and moved to the "BANG! BANG!" drawing Ivy had sent her. It had been nicely framed and now occupied an intimate space on one side of the fireplace. She admired it and spoke silently to Ivy. *Even though I didn't know you then, I was wrong to shoot you in the painting. Thanks for calling me out and putting me in touch with myself. I hope I've atoned for my mistake. Now we're both free and clear. Cheers, Annabel!*

AUTHOR'S REQUEST

Thanks for reading Annabel's Eyes. I hope it surprised and rewarded you. We learn and grow from feedback. If you liked this book, or even if you didn't, I'd be most grateful if you'd take a few minutes to review it on Amazon.

ABOUT THE AUTHOR

John Macleod practiced law in Washington, D.C. for forty-seven years. He was a founding partner and chairman of Crowell & Moring, a major Washington-based firm. This is the fourth book he has written since retiring in 2015.

John and his wife, Ann Klee, live on a farm in the Shenandoah Valley with an assortment of dogs, thousands of books, a nice collection of modern and contemporary art, and plenty of wine.

Made in the USA
Las Vegas, NV
31 August 2024

94605170R00166